MIDNIGHT ENCHANTMENT

Nancy Gideon

For Mary —
Enjoy
Romance with
a "bite"!

Nancy
Gideon
10/00

ImaJinn
Books

MIDNIGHT ENCHANTMENT
Published by ImaJinn Books, a division of ImaJinn

ISBN: 1-893896-04-8

10 9 8 7 6 5 4 3 2

Cover design by Patricia Lazarus

ImaJinn Books, a division of ImaJinn
P.O. Box 162, Hickory Corners, MI 49060-0162
Toll Free: 1-877-625-3592
http://www.imajinnbooks.com

DEDICATION

For the readers who insisted that Gerard's story see "the light of day!"

Note from ImaJinn Books

Dear Readers,

Thank you for buying this book. The author has worked hard to bring you a captivating tale of love and adventure.

In the months ahead, watch for our fast-paced, action-packed stories involving ghosts, psychics and psychic phenomena, witches, vampires, werewolves, angels, reincarnation, futuristic in space or on other planets, futuristic on earth, time travel to the past, time travel to the present, and any other story line that will fall into the "New-Age" category.

The best way for us to give you the types of books you want to read is to hear from you. Let us know your favorite types of "New-Age" romance. You may write to us or any of our authors at: ImaJinn Books, P.O. Box 162, Hickory Corners, MI 49060-0162. You may also e-mail us at imajinn@worldnet.att.net.

Be sure to visit our web site at: http://www.imajinnbooks.com

ONE

Fog.

It rolled off the river to muffle empty streets. Thick curtains of it hung in the air, draining drooping live oaks to a frail transparent gray. Wrought iron fencing made disembodied boundaries against that devouring mist, then disappeared into wisps of cool oblivion. In the last hour before dawn, the natural world became a distant dream and time hung suspended in concealing layers of the night.

Footsteps.

One solitary set, brisk with determination, echoing forever. A single figure cut through the cloak of approaching day. His passage collected a film of heavy moisture upon the fine wool of his greatcoat. It glistened there, a match to the cold sweat upon his brow. In the depthless silence, his heartbeats seemed unnaturally loud, their tempo urgent, fueled by the purpose that drew him out in this time of unearthly shadow where he was the only living thing stirring along that lonely street.

Iron fence gave way to somber stone as he reached the next property. A solid wall over six feet in height protected what lay beyond from the casual eye. He followed that forbidding line, sure it must end at an opening somewhere. Finally, he came to a break in the stone where sturdy iron gates barred entrance. Thick greenery laced through the filigree, obscuring the view with a rooted permanence undisturbed by years. Perhaps there was another way in, but he lacked the time to discover it. Here would have to do. He gave the satchel he carried an awkward toss. It spiraled and disappeared over the gate, landing with a muted thud somewhere on the other side.

After glancing in either direction to make sure he was unobserved, he took hold of the vine-wrapped metal and began to climb. He was no athlete, so the task was long and arduous. By the time he dropped down to the interior drive, his breath shot out in foggy plumes. Beneath his heavy coat, his skin was clammy from exertion. Now, closer to his goal, doubts concerning his sanity held him momentarily paralyzed. Then, he caught sight of his leather case upon the broken ground. Renewed fervor fortified him. Lifting the attache, he started determinedly down the drive.

It was impossible to see anything of the house beyond a huge gray shape until he nearly bumped into the front steps. Then, details appeared out of the mist—stone walls of a ghostly white accented by four pairs of French doors framed in shutters on either side of the huge main entry. The upper gallery was engulfed by a tangle of myrtle tree branches. Delicate cast iron supports were shrouded with mimosas. Their sweet scent couldn't quite disguise the underlying odor of dampness and decay. It was hard to believe that anyone actually dwelt within the crumbling mansion. There was no sign that the vine-covered door had opened in welcome for years. And the uninvited visitor knew there would be no warm welcome for him now.

He stepped up onto the porch, shivering at the sudden enveloping chill. Imagination perhaps. Perhaps not. He hesitated, then dragged up a deep breath before knocking. The sound pealed through the interior like booming thunder. Even before it settled to silence in the far corners of the house, he tried the knob, surprised when it turned in his hand.

The stench of mustiness and disuse overpowered his senses. Still, he stepped inside. The foyer was dark as a tomb, *his tomb*, he thought uneasily, gripping his case before him. From out of it, he withdrew a candle, brought for just this purpose. A flame flickered briefly then took to the wick, illuminating the entrance hall in wild, distorted shadow. The foyer floor boards were coated with at least a half inch of dust, undisturbed except by his own footprints, which followed him in a damning trail of intrusion as he advanced.

It was quiet. His heart thrummed a nervous rhythm, filling his ears with the cadence of alarm, filling his throat with the thickness of fear. Through that clog of fright, he forced a single, "Hello?" The word hovered on the stale air, loud as a cannon shot.

He waited, breathing in anxious chugs, beginning to shake with tension and a cold seeping terror. Silence. No one was home. He didn't know whether to feel disappointment or a wild relief. But a sober truth settled; he would just have to wait, because he wasn't sure he could ever again muster the courage it had taken to bring him to this point. The opportunity was prime, and he wasn't one to ever miss an opportunity, no matter what the risk.

Even when the risk was to his life.

He never heard anything. A slow hair-raising awareness of being watched brought him around to face one of the shadowed rooms. Beyond the reach of his meager candle, the darkness was complete, revealing nothing to his wide, fretful gaze. Not at first. Then gradually the outline of a man separated from that deep blackness. The figure's stillness sent a shudder to his very bones, for it was a preternatural lack of movement, that sudden, inexplicable appearance.

As he stared in horrified dismay, the man's eyes began to glow within the darkness, so pale and blue, as opaque as the mists winding through the streets of the French Quarter. That unwavering gaze sucked at his soul like stagnant waters reflecting clear over the bayou swamps, almost pulling him under before he had a chance to struggle.

"Mr. Pasquale?" His words quavered, echoing through the empty rooms like frantic bird's wings.

"Are we acquainted?" His tone slid, a rasp of silk, low, sleek, mellifluously accented. And though he spoke with the same degree of volume, no resonance followed. It was as if a stone were thrown into a pond to sink without a ripple.

The intruder began to tremble.

"N-no. Not exactly. I am Percy Cristobel. I recently bought out the legal firm of Whitney and Devrou."

No shift in movement, just that dazzling gleam of blue eyes, pulsing now with a hypnotic brilliance. "So? What does that mean?"

Percy shook his head to scatter the effect of the drugging gaze, then stated, "They were handling your affairs, Mr. Pasquale. Now, I do."

"Ahhhh. And do you always meet with your clients at such an odd hour?"

"Only when they keep hours such as yours, sir."

A low chuckle rolled from the silhouetted figure. "Forgive me. I am being a bad host. Please come in where it's comfortable. You have business to discuss with me, no?"

"No. I mean yes. T-thank you."

His case hugged to his thin chest, candlelight wavering in his other hand, Percy followed the elegant wave toward the parlor at his host's back. When he neared Pasquale, a sense of dread tightened about his frantically beating heart, for with one look, all the fantastic truths he'd learned were confirmed. From Pasquale's unnatural stillness and the icy blue fire of his gaze to the chalk-white pallor of skin clinging in hollows and ridges to the dramatic structure of his face, there was nothing normal about him. Even if Percy didn't have a name for what he was, he would have known right then that Gerard Pasquale wasn't quite human. Percy hesitated when the time came to cross before him. Pasquale smiled, a slow, sinister curl of his lips, as if he knew every panicked thought within the lawyer's mind.

"After you, *Signor* Cristobel," he drawled like a genial host, giving Percy no option but to precede him into the room. Percy did so with proper fear and trembling. The skin at his nape crawled with the knowledge of what followed behind him. Though not actively religious, he touched the piece of silver beneath his dampened shirtfront, comforted by the cross's outline.

Not until his host lit a branch of candles did the little lawyer have a full scope of his impressive surroundings. The double parlor was cavernous and exquisitely detailed, from the medallions, friezes and fretwork adorning the fifteen foot ceilings to the Cararra marble of the mantles and Baccarat crystal dripping like glistening tears from the great chandeliers overhead. All was white, from painted floor boards to the pillared triple arches separating the two rooms. And all was empty. Not a chair, not a table anywhere within those grand areas.

"Now then, what was so urgent that you were compelled to break into my home to see me?"

Percy swallowed, for that was what he had done. He feared no retribution from the authorities. Men like Pasquale didn't go to the law. They settled their grievances personally. "Please forgive my intrusion. I wasn't sure you would see me, and what I have to discuss isn't fare for my offices."

Pasquale crossed his arms over the gaudy waistcoat he wore beneath the sober black of his coat. He leaned with a practiced negligence against one of the pillars, his air one of bored amusement. One could almost believe him to be an idle aristocrat. Almost.

"I am intrigued. Do go on."

Forced to stand awkwardly in the center of the room, Percy began his prepared speech, his confidence returning when matters turned to business.

"When I began with the firm of Whitney and Devrou, the gentlemen were on the verge of retirement and had let things go to seed. It was my job to make sense of their cases and properly document them. The old gentlemen kept deplorable records, so many of the files had to be completely reconstructed. A tedious job, but one that was most rewarding."

"I applaud your diligence, *signor.* Are you here to inform me that I am not paying you enough?"

"Oh, no, sir. In fact, your fee is quite generous considering what little upkeep your case requires. It was your case, itself, that interested me."

"Really?"

Percy didn't imagine the sudden sinister overtone that crept into that single word, but he'd already gone too far to turn cowardly now. He plunged onward, speaking more rapidly in his excited agitation. "You see, I began my legal internship at Whitney and Devrou with the intention of buying them out. I wanted to learn everything I could about the clients who yet retained them, though the number was discouragingly few. There was a hint of mystery to your financial matters that I couldn't resist. I was unbearably curious about a fortune such as yours, accumulating over the centuries and left to the care of strangers without a single withdrawal or inquiry in over three years. I confess I did some unauthorized digging."

"And what did you find?" There was no mistaking the edge of menace now.

At Pasquale's mounting wariness, Percy's posture reflected an attitude of boastfulness as he confided, "It was quite exhaustive, really, sifting through centuries and across continents, but I discovered the most amazing thing. After following a trail of documentation listing births, deaths, inheritances and transfers of property all the way back to the fifteen hundreds, I found that all were channeled through the same benefactor, one Gerardo Pasquale, of Florence, Italy. I have copies of that information right here if you would like to examine them." He patted his case and waited, but the other man never moved. It was as though he'd become a pale marble statue to compliment the white rooms. Only the luminescence of his gaze betrayed any animation as Percy came to his bold conclusion. "That would make you over four hundred years old, sir. Might I compliment you on your resilience. I wouldn't have thought you a day over five-and-twenty."

Pasquale was no longer lounging in contemptuous indifference. He still rested with one shoulder against the pillar, but his manner was one of tense attention. He smiled, deceptively. "Of course, what you are suggesting is utter nonsense. Who would believe such a thing?"

"I believe it, Mr. Pasquale. And it would be nonsense...if you were human."

Percy had no warning. One second, he was gloating over his own cleverness, and in the next he was strangling within the crush of Pasquale's fingers. He'd never seen Pasquale move, but suddenly his client loomed over him, pale and deadly. Long fingers tightened, until Percy felt sure his windpipe would crumple as Pasquale lifted him effortlessly off the floor to dangle in that crushing grip. The candle dropped from his nerveless fingers to gutter out on the floor.

"Do you have any idea with whom you are dealing?" The words were hissed out inches from his face. The rush of breath against his skin was cold, cold as death.

Percy clawed at the powerful hand without effect. He wheezed and managed to choke out frantically, "I not only know who you are, I know what you are. And if you want to continue as you have been, you will release me."

He was dropped so suddenly his legs buckled, sending him to his knees before his angry attacker. He massaged his bruised throat, forcing air through the abused passage in noisy rasps. Finally the pain eased and black dots stopped whirling before his watering eyes.

Pasquale began to pace, his movements full of majestic fury and yet so graceful even the fierce strides seemed like a ballet— a danse macabre. "So, what is it you intend to do with what you know...provided I let you live long enough to do anything?"

"Nothing so blatant as blackmail, believe me," Percy gasped hoarsely. "And you will not harm me, Mr. Pasquale. I've seen to that."

Pasquale regarded him narrowly. "How so?"

"I'm an ambitious man, sir, but not a foolish one," he claimed, stumbling, wobbly, to his feet. He kept a wary eye on his host, alert to any further aggression. "I wouldn't have come here if I didn't have the means to protect myself. In the past, you have been very trusting with your fortune by leaving it in the hands of your legal representatives. I've taken the liberty of placing those funds into an account which only I can access. You were good enough to sign over a power of attorney when you brought your account to us. I've also made careful documentation of all that we've discussed. Now, I may not be able to convince anyone that you are a...a vampire, sir, but I can make your life a living hell, if it's not one already."

Percy thought he would feel ridiculous when the time came to make that claim, but he didn't, for now he believed right to the marrow of his bones such things existed. And for the first time, he realized the precariousness of his position. He hadn't expected such speed and strength in a man undead for centuries. Pasquale could kill him in an instant, if Percy couldn't convince him to let him live. He sped on with his explanation.

"No one truly needs to believe such a fantastic story, but all will want to hear it. I'll give this information to the newspapers. They will hound you unmercifully, and without access to your monies, you'll have no means to flee the city."

Silence as the dark night creature pondered this. He seemed unperturbed, and that alarmed Percy. As did the words that followed.

"And if I were to just tear out your throat before you could give that information to anyone?"

The casual way he presented Percy's death made the lawyer's blood run icy. It was no idle threat, he knew. He was dealing with a cold, dangerous being who'd survived centuries by preying upon human lives. Such an individual would snatch his soul without a moment's remorse. But Percy was prepared for that, too.

"As I've said, I am not a fool. The original papers aren't with me. They are in a safe place with instructions to turn them over to the authorities should anything happen to me. They might not believe what you are, sir, but be assured they take murder very seriously."

Gerardo Pasquale stood staring at him. A frustration of rage pulsed from him in palpable waves. Suddenly, Percy knew an instant of true terror as the solidity of Pasquale's figure seemed to flicker before his eyes, becoming so faint as to be transparent, edges shifting, transforming into something else, something horrible, alien and monstrous, but exactly what was not quite clear. Standing frozen, Percy feared he'd made an irrevocable error in believing himself safe.

Then, to his relief, Pasquale assumed his human shape once again and with a deadly quiet, asked, "What do you want?"

"I want you to marry my sister."

Pasquale was silent for a moment, then he threw back his dark head to send a gigantic laugh heavenward. The sound was huge, forcing Percy to clap hands over his ears until it had run its course. Still chuckling with vestiges of his own vile amusement, the vampire said, "You must not care for this poor relation to wish such a thing upon her. I am not what you would call a...marrying man."

"Oh, you sell yourself short, sir. You are infinitely eligible," Percy argued, as if to flatter his way into the man's good graces. "You have a tremendous fortune any woman would be happy to share. I seek financial security for myself and my family. In exchange for our keeping your secret, you will take my sister for your bride and deed one quarter of all your assets over to me as a dowry. And, of course, she will receive a comfortable allowance."

"My bride?" His laughter was now low and vicious. His stare fixed upon Percy with chill promise. "I will rip your dear sister to shreds and dine upon her blood before I would share anything with such grubbing parasites. You will not manipulate me, *signor*. I am a nightmare from which there is no escaping. You have no protection, you puny mortal fool. You do not truly understand all that I am, or you would not be here trying to force this ludicrous bargain upon me. Be gone before my amusement fails me, and I let you see of what I am capable when irritated. Oh, and of course, you are fired."

"Don't be too hasty, Mr. Pasquale. You're also a creature who enjoys his comfort and is quite vulnerable to the truth. I am not asking for everything. All I require is what you'll never miss. You can go on as before, considering us as a...family of convenience. An occupational hazard, if you will." And judging the degree of Pasquale's troubled frown, he felt secure enough in the trap he'd made to smile.

"You ask too much."

Pasquale turned away and, for a desperate moment, Percy feared he'd lost his leverage. Then the sleek creature began to pace again, this time with the power of an animal duly caught and caged. "What kind of man wishes his kin to wed a monster?" he demanded in a sullen snarl.

"One who holds to high ambitions, sir. Ambitions are expensive. I would insist that my dear Laure be untouched by you, of course, or you'd be exposed for what you are. With me in control of your finances, you wouldn't be able to escape your destruction should you consider harming her. Come now," he cajoled reasonably. "What can a few years married to a mortal mean to a man who holds eternity? We'll both be gone from your life before we become a bother. What do you care? Why should it matter to you if we live well off your generosity for the short lengths of our human lives?"

"I do not like to be told when to be generous."

Percy continued to smile as he watched the vampire mull over his non-existent alternatives. He'd been very thorough in his plotting and knew,sooner or later, the creature would have to capitulate. He let his avid gaze roam the spacious rooms, dreaming of how they would appear when he was the master of the house and hosting his first successful reception within them. He imagined liveried servants bearing silver trays and champagne, the sound of laughter, the strains of tasteful orchestration. Words of praise for him upon all lips. What he hadn't counted on was Pasquale's sudden, silky smile as he named a condition of his own.

"If this woman is to be my bride, I would demand one small thing of her. If she's to share my name, she will also share my home. She will live here with me of her own free will, but if she should decline my hospitality for any reason and leave me, the terms of this arrangement will be voided, and the marriage annulled. And you will, at that time, forget all that you ever knew of me."

Percy was momentarily flustered. "But why? She's a stranger to you. Why would you want her here?" he stammered.

Pasquale's grin widened, lending his lean face a certain wickedly cunning charm. "Let us just say I long for a little companionship. After all, I will be paying quite dearly for the privilege. If your sister's greed rivals your own, it should not be too big a price to pay."

Now it was Percy who twisted in the trap. Exposing Laure directly to this monster had never been his plan. Depending upon her courage to secure his comfort was too tenuous for his liking. She'd be placed in daily—or rather nightly—peril. All would hinge upon Laure's ability to endure and survive a fiend, and Percy was uneasy with the idea of his financial future in tender female hands.

But, like Pasquale, what choice did he have?

"I see you are considering this carefully, *Signor* Cristobel," the vampire smirked. "As well you should. Remember what I am. I am not always in complete control of my basic nature. Your poor sister could fall victim to my appetite in a regretful lapse of composure. If I were in your position, I would consider asking for a single amount—a modest sum, mind you, for me to forget the impertinence of your demands. Then you will go away and trouble me no more."

Percy's mind turned frantically, seeking a way around the vampire's suggestion. He'd slaved for years to get this chance. He'd breathed in dust and bowed to those two doddering old fools to charm them into trusting him with their accounts. They'd never even known that he'd bought out their firm with monies 'borrowed' from their own clients. He'd risked much to gain control of that decrepit firm. It wouldn't have been worth the effort if not for Pasquale's potential. The mere thought of how much lay dormant in the creature's accounts made him salivate with a hunger for what that fortune could bring him...power, influence, respect to a man now ignored as insignificant within better circles of society. With the proper financial backing, he could mingle with the elite, gain their business and rob them blind.

All hinged on Pasquale and his outrageous demand.

And then there was the matter of convincing Laure to do her part.

"I stand by my original terms, Mr. Pasquale, and will accept yours. You will acquire a bride and companion, and I will take very good care of our money."

If he expected further argument, he didn't get it.

"Then where shall we ask God to bless this unholy union?" the vampire growled in obvious displeasure.

"Saint Michael's Cathedral...providing you can enter a church."

"After the sun sets, I can go anywhere I choose." A slight smile flickered, full of dire consequence, but Percy was undaunted.

"Then we shall see you at the altar tomorrow night to say vows and sign the proper papers." Business concluded, Percy turned his thoughts to escape. "Will you see me out? Your front gate is locked."

Pasquale glared through him. "You may leave the same way you came in. And you had better hurry before I change my mind and decide to make an early breakfast out of you."

Percy bowed his head nervously, taking the warning with all due seriousness as he started quickly for the door. Once outside, even the heavy air smelled sweet to one who'd cornered a devil and was yet breathing. A slow, smug smile flirted about his lips. It had gone well, better than he'd expected. Now to see to Pasquale's annoying condition to his success. He would talk to Laure. If played just right, she wouldn't stand in his way.

And soon he'd have all that he'd worked for, all that he deserved!

He'd just started down the broken drive, his step cocky and self-satisfied, when a horrific sound burst from the silent house behind him. Half howl, half unnaturally pitched shriek, it brought the hairs to anxious attention along his arms and nape. He risked a glance over his shoulder and gasped at the sight of a phosphorescent light darting wildly through the house like heat lightning gone mad. And that sound, that nerve-grating screech escalating to the point of shivering glass, had his insides in a similar quake. Abandoning his sense of victory, Percy raced down the drive, expecting at any moment to find the blazing eyed demon on his heels lunging to devour him for his bold folly.

Within the house, all unnatural sound and light ceased. Stillness fell over its musty rooms, even as the brightening of dawn began tugging up the veil of shadows.

Breathing hard, Gerard pushed himself up off the floor onto hands and knees, exhausted by his self-indulgent display of temper. His solid form reassumed, he tottered to his feet, a growl of rage rumbling up through him as he thought of how one frail mortal had managed to overturn his world.

In the old days, such a thing would never have happened. Fear of his legend alone would have prevented such a presumptuous confrontation. But these were not the old days, and he knew a shiver of fear that one man, a human, had successfully breached his safe haven. He had grown careless in his indifference, and laxness led to death.

His tantrum conquered by a deeper, darker and more deadly calm, he moved with a fluid glide toward one of the French doors, crossing the dusty floor which contained one set of tracks, those of his uninvited guest. He ignored the effects of his temper, the streaks along walls and ceiling where paint had been peeled away as if by some great scorching heat. He was in control now, and he was angry. And afraid.

Through carefully parted curtains, he watched the cunning little solicitor's scrambling climb over his front gate, and it was with supreme command of will that he didn't swoop down with all the supernatural power of his kind to end the pompous presence of one sly mortal who dared—DARED!—impose conditions upon him. But caution and the strong will of self-preservation held him helpless for the moment.

He, with all his abilities, was not without weakness, and the nasty little lawyer had thrust cleanly through that Achilles heel without being aware of it.

Ordinarily, he would have laughed in the face of the man's ploy to extort his fortune and would have gleefully drained him to the death for his impertinence. But to act now in a fit of rash retribution would expose him to unnecessary dangers, forcing him out of the hiding place he'd made for himself in the gloomy mansion. He didn't know whom Cristobel had entrusted with the evidence against him or how to stop it from gaining public attention. That was the real hazard he sought to avoid.

He heaved a sigh of reluctant resignation, a weariness centuries deep. True, he could leave the city without a trace come nightfall and foil Cristobel's clever plot, but in doing so, would sacrifice much. Despite his dramatic show to scare the meddling human, he was weak, his powers at an ebb. He'd crept into New Orleans to recoup what he could and to shield himself from outside jeopardy while yet in a vulnerable state. And here in his moldy isolation, he'd wallowed in remorse, suffering for the foolhardy arrogance that had led him to this low.   His only wish was to be left alone, to become inconspicuous among those who provided what he needed to survive as he grew stronger. His recovery was slow because his will to go on had been crippled almost as badly as his human form. He merely existed now, mourning his losses, chastening himself for his follies, separating himself from those who would care for him because he didn't deserve their love and refused to endanger them. As long as he laid low and kept to himself, he was safe. To have his presence announced, even in some tawdry tribune, would let those who believed him dead know they'd been deceived. That he could not afford. Not now.

Feeling the discomfort of approaching dawn, Gerard let the curtain fall. There was nothing he could do except seek his rest away from the reach of his relentless enemy, the sun. Come dusk, he would rise up, full of vengeful purpose. He would meet with Cristobel and his scheming sister, and he would bow to their demands to keep his secrets secure. For the moment. But he would be watching, waiting, for them to make their first mistake, which would also be their last. Then he would make them suffer for their arrogant greed.

And he would enjoy the feast.

TWO

"How could you? Percy, how could you even suggest such a thing to me?"

Percy watched his step-sister pace the room in agitation as he kept a careful rein on his impatience. He made his tone gently persuasive, the fount of reasonability.

"Laure, I do not ask this of you for myself alone. I am thinking of you and your future."

"Me?" She stopped to stare at him in amazement. "How on earth could you believe such an...an arrangement could be of benefit to me?"

He pitched his voice into a firmer calm. "You have only to consider your situation to understand my motives."

"My situation or yours? If it was your wish to rid yourself of your obligation to me, it was not necessary to go to this extreme. I can be gone from your life in moments and will trouble you no more."

Fighting the urge to shake her for making things so difficult, Percy merely sighed in fond exasperation. "Laure, dear sister, when have I ever made you to feel a burden to me? Have I complained? Have I made you feel unwelcome in my home?" A touch of wounded grievance crept in. "Have I ever treated you as less than family?"

Laure sank down upon the well-worn chaise, her features taut with just the right degree of chastened upset for him to see victory.

"No, Percy. You have been generous to a fault. Please forgive me if you thought I was implying otherwise. It's just that this whole matter has taken me by surprise. I don't understand the reason for haste. I've never met this gentleman with whom you seek to link me in matrimony." Her slender hand rose to massage her brow. "I know you have my best interests at heart, but why rush me toward such a permanent solution?"

Here's where he would make his carefully rehearsed case. She'd gone from horrified denial to weary confusion. He'd worn her down, playing upon all her weaknesses. And she was listening. Trusting soul. Trusting fool. He adopted a facade of reluctance to win her full attention.

"I had not wanted to distress you with the facts of it."

"What facts?"

He played out a little more line, letting her nudge and taste the baited hook. "You know it was your mother's wish that I see you securely settled."

"Yes..."

"And that it is her legacy that makes that very task so...challenging."

Laure had gone still, her features as bleached to whiteness as the tatted linen scarf on the cushions behind her. She said nothing aloud, but her posture betrayed volumes. Caution. Fear. And a liberal dab of anger. She waited to hear more.

"I've heard whispers."

That was all he need say to press his point home like a dagger thrust.

"These are not the old days," she said at last. Conviction trembled in her tone upon a deep seated alarm. "Surely you don't think anything will come of it." Her wide eyes begged him to tell her she had no reason for panic. Instead, he turned from her needy look to hide a cunning smile.

"Few would admit to holding to old beliefs, but this city is steeped in superstition. Especially when rumors stem from a solid source."

"Who? Who is spreading lies about me?"

"Alain Javier."

Her heard her sharp inhalation and waited for the consequence to sink deep and dire before he looked back at her woebegone figure. She rubbed her forearms as if still feeling the bruises there. When she spoke at last, her voice was thready with anxiety.

"But why would he circulate such vile gossip about me? To what purpose?"

"A man scorned, Laure. I warned you, didn't I?"

A snap of fire came into her eyes. "You think I should have stayed with him until more of my bones were broken?"

"Laure—"

"The man was a monster, Percy! The things he did...the things he suggested..." She shuddered meaningfully, unwilling or unable to pursue her argument.

"You were right to sever the relationship, dear heart. He was a beast. Not at all the gentleman I believed him to be. We were both betrayed."

"So what makes you think this—this stranger will be any better? What do you know of him? Only that he's rich?"

Percy forced a smile upon his thinned lips. Patience, he reminded himself. "Rich and influential. Even Alain Javier would think twice before casting slurs in his direction. Or upon his wife. He can protect you."

"You thought that about Alain as well."

He flinched at the cut of her observation. "I was misled." He didn't need to pretend annoyance there. He'd been wrong about Javier. After all the time he'd spent cultivating the wealthy gentleman, pushing his sister into the man's way in hopes of making that all important connection that would turn burden into profitable blessing. If only Javier had kept his heavy hands to himself until after they were wed. If only the maddeningly proper Laure had had the good sense to accept the man's alternate suggestion. After all he'd done, the girl had the temerity to resist his latest and greatest scheme by casting doubt upon his wisdom. By thinking only of herself.

"And I was mistreated. I do not wish to be in that position again."

How haughtily superior she sounded. As if beholding young women could make their own demands. As if she should have any choice at all! Her mother's doings, letting her believe she should hold out for the fantasy of love in marriage. This was not a time for romantic fancies. It was a time for hard realities. He would have said so in so many words, but he caught the hint of vulnerability behind his step-sister's staunch assertion, the fear she tried desperately to hide beneath a guise of boldness. Again, he gentled his approach, comforting her with his concern while still pressing his wishes upon her.

"Laure, this man is not like Javier."

Her gaze slitted, demanding that he prove it. Frustrating creature. His teeth ground in irritation. She was forcing him to make things more unpleasant than they needed to be. Perhaps a good scare was necessary to rattle her sensibilities.

"Laure, if Javier persists and the rumors catch hold, I can't keep you safe. You know what can happen when fear runs away with a crowd. They become a mob, which knows no control. I hold no station of power to impress my word upon the people of New Orleans. Who would take my side against him? If you think Alain hurt you before, just think of what could happen." He let that question bob upon the still and stagnant waters of tradition while fear brightened her eyes and made tender lips tremble. He should have felt ashamed inspiring her to such a state of worry. But the ends would justify any anxiousness she suffered now. He twitched the lure enticingly.

"Laure, I cannot keep you from harm. What help can I give when I could not even confront Javier with his despicable behavior? I let him get away with what he did to you. I failed you there. How do you think that made me feel? Do you think he fears any protest I might make now? I am useless to you. A useless coward."

"Don't say that, Percy." How quick she jumped to his defense. Especially after he'd pushed her into the arms of an abuser.

Remarkably, she didn't blame him. After all, he'd been the one to ice the marks imprinted in her flesh to keep the swelling down. He'd taken her to the physician at his own expense. He'd nursed her back to health with the concern of true family. And he'd allowed her to talk him out of taking any heroic, and futile, action. She restated that same argument again.

"What could you do against a man like Alain? Who would take my word over his? There was nothing you could do, and I think no less of you, dear brother. You have given me a roof over my head—more than that, a home. You have seen to my wants, my needs, and I know it is out of care for me that you now make this suggestion."

"It is, Laure. Out of care and caution. You have been harmed enough. That's why I've done what I must to keep you safe. Surely you see why an alliance with Pasquale is for the best. Javier would not dare provoke him. If we do nothing, he could see you destroyed. He could see us both ruined just for spite."

Laure considered the hands clasped tightly upon her knees. Her knuckles paled with tension, but her features were composed and thoughtful. "It would be unfair for you to suffer for my folly. That's not how I wish to repay your kindness to me and my mother."

"Then do this thing, Laure. Relieve my heart and mind of its greatest burden. The burden of my concern for you."

She glanced up, remorse coloring her sad smile. "I want to do the right thing."

Yes! He fought to keep his elation contained. "Then you will marry Pasquale."

Still she wavered just shy of complete commitment. Softly, she asked, "What is he like, this man I would marry?"

"Handsome, polite, old-worldy, wealthy."

"Why is he interested in me, someone he has never met or seen?"

Damn her shrewd mind! Percy recovered with an indulgent laugh. "You underestimate yourself, my dear. What man would not want you?"

Her steady stare called for a better answer.

"He is—eccentric."

Her brows soared. "How so?"

How to describe Pasquale in acceptable terms? "He's a bit of a recluse, sticking to his house and to his own company. He knows no one in the city and is...lonely."

He felt her nibble the bait and was careful not to set the hook too soon. Her mouth pursed in empathy. She understood isolation, and that would make her mysterious suitor all the more appealing. He hurried on to take advantage of it.

"I told him about you, bragging really." He mustered up a proud blush. "After all, what man would not boast of a relation who is all that is kind, intelligent and beautiful. He was quite taken by my descriptions."

Uncomfortable with the praise, she murmured, "I guess I can understand that, but why would he agree to make a hurried marriage?"

"He is ill." Concern darkened her gaze, and Percy congratulated himself on that flash of brilliance. Not really a lie. Everything about Pasquale was decidedly unhealthy. "He fears he may not have long to live and wishes to share all that he has with someone—worthy. I could think of no one more deserving than you, dear Laure." *Than us*, he added silently. "He has been afraid that some unscrupulous creature will deceive him by playing false upon his emotions just to have his fortune. That's why my direct petition intrigued him. No pretense. No expectations. An arrangement of mutual benefit. You will be his companion, and he will be your protector. What could be wrong in that? Most marriages are made on much less."

Laure's mood grew somber. "What if I'm with child?"

Percy gave a slight start but was quick to catch his balance. "What better reason to hurry the vows?"

"But that would be dishonest. Percy—"

He held up his hand to silence the rest of her noble sentiments. "Laure, did you ask to be in such dire circumstance?"

Her gaze dropped. A meek, "No," answered him.

"A cruel thing was done to you, and this will go far to make it right."

"But he will know the child is not his. I would not...hurt him so, even if he is a stranger to me and in a position to do me a great favor."

"What he does not know cannot hurt him." Percy drew a deep breath to quiet the aggravation that threatened. God save him from this stupid, self-righteous girl! Why did her common sense have to be cluttered by conscience? "What is a slight deception when you think of all that's at stake?"

"Percy, I cannot—"

"Does my happiness and success mean so little to you?"

His reproach had the desired effect. She was immediately all contrition.

"No, Percy. That's not at all what I meant. I owe you more than I could ever repay."

"Yet you fight against my wishes, against my chance to make a difference amongst those who are unfortunate. Those like your mother's people."

"W-what do you mean?"

"With the dowry Pasquale will settle upon me, I can build the business. I can help those who would otherwise be victims. The good people of New Orleans would listen when I spoke up of injustices. I'm not thinking of me, Laure, or even just of you, but of the deserving, of the helpless, like the child you might be carrying. Would it be fair for it to suffer because of its conception? Or for you to suffer because of what you could not escape? Think of all those children who have no one to come to their defense against the Alain Javiers of this world. Your selfless act could give them the opportunity to live with dignity. That is how you can repay me, for their sake."

As tears glistened on her cheeks, Percy fancied that he heard a thunderous applause, an ovation for his grand theatrics. Who said only trial lawyers had a flare for dramatics? He reveled in his performance, embellishing as he went along.

"Think of the good we could do, Laure. Think of the peace of mind you'll give me knowing that you'll be well cared for. Don't I deserve that?"

A soft sob from where she sat, head downcast, had him grinning to himself. But again, she snatched away his final victory.

"I would rather be truthful before vows are said."

He wanted to scream! Instead, he crossed to kneel down before her, placing comforting hands upon her cold ones. "Laure, what good would it do? You would distress him for nothing and endanger your security. You don't know that you're with child, so why take the risk of offending him? He is a worldly man but a man, none the less. Truth may not be the best policy."

"And deception would?"

"It would be deception if you were sure and you're not, are you? You don't know that you've conceived from that one— unfortunate union."

"No, I do not," she murmured wretchedly.

"Then say nothing. Don't let Javier ruin your chance for happiness. Hasn't he done enough already?"

Her hands turned, clasping his with renewed strength as her fiery spirit returned. "Yes, he has. It would aggrieve me to think our ruin would be his reward."

"Then say you'll wed Pasquale and spit upon Javier by placing yourself out of his reach."

"But if I find I am with child?"

Percy clenched his teeth and muttered through them, "You have only to convince the man that it is his. He will die happy, believing his lineage secure, and you and the babe will be safe. Tell me where the harm is in that?"

"He'll not believe it immaculate conception, Percy," she chided gently.

"Then convince him it is not."

"How?"

"I can think of only one way, my dear."

She flushed a crimson of embarrassment and deeper anxiety. "But we are strangers to one another."

He lifted her chin in his hand, his smile encouraging. "Laure, dear girl, surely you cannot be so unaware of your own charms. He won't be able to resist you for long. What man could?"

And that was exactly what he was counting upon as his sister's only heir. That Pasquale could not resist his natural instincts. Or rather his unnatural ones.

"All right, Percy. You are an excellent lawyer. You have made an irrefutable argument."

He leaned forward to kiss her cheek in genuine relief. "Good girl. You've always had an exceptional head on your shoulders. It will be a good match, you'll see. I promise, you'll have no regrets."

If things went as planned, she'd have no time for them.

Laure Cristobel stood before her cheval glass, her wedding gown held up to her shoulders. Of course, it was not meant to be for her marriage. Percy had bought it to impress Alain Javier, and for that reason alone, she was tempted to discard it in distaste. But what else did she own that would serve for such an occasion? The marriage of two strangers, a pauper to an aristocrat. She couldn't bear for her appearance to shame him or Percy.

It was a beautiful gown with its high collar of pearls, a heavily embroidered and beaded bodice that fit snugly to her form, and flirty, swagged sleeves of lace that caressed down to her elbows. The sleek skirt was of off-white silk and heavy lace, spilling in a graceful pool about her feet. Off-white seemed appropriate. Alain had said it made her look like an angel. She pursed her lips. Now a fallen angel.

She set the dress aside. It would have to do for there was no time to replace it and no real need. The gown could not be faulted for its association. She fingered the elaborate swirls of lace. Would it please him, this stranger who would take her to his home in less than five hours' time? Would she please him?

Who was this man?

In her mind, she'd created a romantic substance for the reclusive Gerard Pasquale. Handsome, brooding, with a sad, tragic mien that would immediately touch her heart. Over the years, she'd learned so much about loneliness. It was a slight surprise to find herself almost eager to belong to another, even if that other was unknown to her. If there was kindness, love would follow. She would do her best to make it so.

They were kindred souls already, tied together by their separation from all else. She'd grown up on the fringe of society, never accepted within its embrace. There'd been few willing to ignore her heritage to befriend her, but those few had been treasured like rare, precious stones. Her mother forbade her the joys of her extended family. It had been just the two of them until her mother had wed Percy's father. But even that union had been brief and marred by suspicion. Some believed her mother had killed him, only to forfeit her own life out of guilt scant months later. That had been a time of relentless terror, a whisper of which was haunting her now. Only Percy's staunch refusal to listen to what he called nonsense returned stability to her world. He'd been so good to her, and here was her chance to repay him.

She would not think of it as a sacrifice.

In a moment of clarity, she realized she'd forgotten to ask for more particulars about her husband-to-be. She had no idea about his age, but from what Percy had said, she surmised he was an older gentleman of precarious health. That was all right. She had no aversion to tending a good man in his failing years. She'd fallen prey to the dazzle of youthful charm only to know complete disillusionment. If he was too infirm to go out and about, she would sit at his side and provide him with the companionship they both desired. She was well learned and eager to share her thoughts and beliefs with another of similar or dissimilar opinion. Percy's work kept him too busy to be much company. Instead of grand passion, there'd be respect and conversation. Not a bad exchange. Not bad at all, considering what she knew of things desire bred. She shivered. Not a bad exchange.

The more she thought on it, the more she felt convinced that Percy had been right to encourage this match. She would know the fulfilling warmth of home and compassionate care, and Percy would be repaid for his generosity. She who had known only the charity of others, would have the chance to do good for many.

Was it the right thing? Was he the right man for her?

Glancing about as if those beyond the grave might see her actions and object to her use of her forbidden skills, Laure dismissed her fears then closed her eyes to summon an inner quiet. And from that serenity, she asked the question.

Is he the one?

There was no answer in words. There rarely was. Instead, the response came as an overall feeling of certainty, a feeling that settled upon her with the comfort of an old pair of shoes. A sense that the fit was right and good.

Relieved, she looked toward the events the evening would hold as an acceptance of her fate.

As she dressed during those dwindling hours of daylight, her anticipation increased. Percy had explained away the oddness of the nuptial hour by saying her betrothed had a sensitivity to light. The poor old dear. Her heart filled with sympathy for him. She considered the quiet, unpretentious ceremony as a symptom of his flagging health. It was probably best to hurry the moment with an impromptu affair and spare him the excitement of grander doings. That was all right with Laure. She'd experienced enough excitement to appreciate the stabilizing lure of the serene.

She met Percy with an accepting smile, gratified by the pleasure in his gaze. She was doing the right thing. For all of them.

"Take one last look around, Laure. You'll never live in poverty again." His arm squeezed tight about her shoulders. "Tonight you'll enter a new world, a world of plenty."

That knowledge shocked through her. She'd had no time to absorb the fact that she'd not be returning here to these shabbily genteel rooms that had so comfortably been home to her. She'd be going, instead, to live under a stranger's roof. A new wave of anxiousness spiked through her.

"But what of my things?" A feeble protest that Percy waved off with a negligent hand.

"What few things of value I can have sent to you. I'm sure your new husband will want to remake you as befits your new station."

That made her even more agitated. "I don't want to go to him with nothing." The truth was, she feared she'd be bringing him more than he'd counted on. Her palm touched to her flat belly. Again, Percy was quick to console her.

"Dear Laure, this is your chance to begin anew. Let go of what came before and move ahead without looking back."

She smiled at him gratefully. "I won't forget you and what you've done for me, Percy. Never that."

His answering smile was a bit grim. No, he was sure he would not be forgotten for what he was about to arrange this night.

Emptied of its parade of wealthy worshipers who were there to confess and be seen, Saint Michael's nave echoed eerily where faint candlelight reached out in vain to conquer soaring shadow. Row after row of vacant pews witnessed Laure's march up the aisle toward the altar on Percy's arm. There, two figures stood silhouetted against a muted pallette of stained glass. A gauntlet of saints bowed over them, seeming to weep where the dimness cast them in mournful relief. Silence steeped and thickened in an almost apprehensive hush. Or at least, that's how it appeared to Laure as she waited to get her first good look at the man she would marry.

Though the plush aisle runner muffled all sound of their approach, Gerard Pasquale turned to greet them. Laure's step faltered as she was struck by a startling fact.

The man she was on her way to meet was neither aged or infirm.

He was young and...beautiful.

All in elegant black, the stark attire accentuated his height and lean strength. Uneven candlelight played an intriguing game over the structure of his face, creating dramatic angles and mysterious hollows set upon a complexion as fine and translucent as statuary marble. He could have been one of the tragic saints, so still he stood at the front of the church, expression immobile as he watched her draw near. Inanimate, until she met his gaze. His eyes dazzled, a quicksilver of pale blue beneath the haughty arch of his black brows. It might have been the shadow dance that made them gleam with fierce and furious brilliance. Almost as if the sight of her filled him with a palpable hatred. The force of it had her reeling as Percy's determined step dragged her forward to meet her future.

Then he smiled, a gesture both serene and sinister. And Laure knew a sudden shock of alarm.

What kind of man was Percy wedding her to?

It was too late for doubt or debate as his hand stretched out to her with a graceful flourish.

"Ahhhh, here she is, my lovely bride. *Buona sera.*"

His voice slid over her senses like an intimate caress—soft, smooth and silkily accented, stirring goose flesh in its wake. Before she could react, Percy placed her hand within her future husband's. His palm was cool. His fingers curled possessively about hers to press with surprising strength as he lifted her whitened knuckles to receive his courtly kiss. That contact, too, held a distinct chill as he continued to smile with a secret amusement down upon her. A smile that held no warmth or welcome.

"Shall we get on with this little drama now that we are all here?"

And there was no mistaking the displeasure edging beneath his languid words.

Confused, both by the situation and his mood, Laure tried to draw back from his intense stare, from his intimidating presence, but his grip grew commanding, anchoring her hand in the crook of his arm as he turned to face the priest.

"Father, you may begin."

The ceremony was in Latin. In a daze, Laure managed to nod when the ancient priest looked to her for confirmation. The feeling of unreality continued to swell until it all but engulfed her. The intonation of vows she couldn't comprehend bound her to the man beside her, a man she didn't know and didn't love. Was she making a good match or a huge mistake?

The suspicion that she was a mere pawn in some bigger scheme brought a dryness to her mouth and a tremor of panic to her rapidly beating heart. Her hand shook as a signet ring was pushed upon her finger to weigh as heavily as this stranger's claim upon her.

And then the droning words ended as the priest made the sign of the cross. Her new husband faced her, and she shrank from the sudden anger controlling his expression. Then it was gone, just as all emotion was gone, leaving the flawless facade that was somehow frightening in its perfection. His hand veed beneath her chin, angling her head up. It wasn't a gentle gesture. Her breath caught as he bent to demand his first marital right with a kiss so cold and quick it brought tears to her eyes. She stumbled back as soon as he released her from the passionless display.

Why had he wed her if he found the whole of the arrangement so intolerable?

What manipulative sleight of hand had forced them together before this shadowed altar?

Percy, what have you done?

Even as she wondered, her step-brother turned her for a demonstrative kiss on the cheek and a hearty, "Well, done, Laure." Then he smiled at his new relation and gestured toward the papal office. "Shall we conclude our business, Mr. Pasquale?"

"By all means, let's conclude this charade. I find that I am most anxious to spend some time with my new bride."

The hard meaning in his glare became dark speculation when it touched upon Laure. And he added a single edict that shivered to her bones with consequence.

"Alone."

THREE

The streets outside the ancient church were empty. A misty rain gleamed slickly upon the cobbles. Percy had disappeared as soon as the formal papers had been signed, contractually binding her husband to his financial future. In his haste, he'd forgotten to say good-bye.

Staring down those vacant, water-swept avenues, Laure shivered. It would seem the road to her own destiny was desolate, indeed.

"What is it, *mia moglie?* Were you expecting, perhaps, some grand carriage to convey us to your new home, so that you might enjoy your new-found prosperity in bartered style?"

Something in the darker timbre of her husband's tone told her that was not going to happen.

Instead of voicing her concerns, Laure glanced up at him from beneath the modest sweep of her lashes. "I was awaiting your direction, sir."

"And you would follow them, regardless of where they might lead?" One black brow adopted a haughty tilt of doubt.

"Yes, of course. Whatever your pleasure."

A slow smile spread, remarkable in its lack of warmth or humor. "Be careful what you offer, *signora*, lest I take your suggestion literally."

He looked away from her then, as if she were a mere annoyance. For a long moment, he stared into the darkness, features taut and stiff, yet unquestionably glorious in silhouette. She felt his dissatisfaction, whether with her or his own lot, she didn't know, but she determined to give him no cause for further irritation.

This was not at all how she'd expected her married life to begin.

"Shall we walk then, sir?" she put forth cheerfully, as if the oddness of the idea was perfectly acceptable to her. As if the oddness of the entire arrangement was to her satisfaction. "If so, we should be on our way. The air holds a decided chill that bids us hurry."

His gaze slid to her with a cold glitter. "Complaints, my dear, already?"

"Not a complaint on my behalf, sir. I was thinking only of your health."

At his blank stare, she wondered if she'd misspoken herself. Perhaps he didn't wish his condition discussed so openly while they were still very much strangers to one another. Distressed by the idea of his discomfort, she was about to apologize when he threw back his head to laugh with shortlived amusement.

"My health? You play the *bellezza ingenuo* to rare perfection. I applaud you, but now I weary of such theatrics. No more games on this night. There is no reason to pretend with one another."

Her confusion was no pretense. "I-I don't understand."

"What don't you understand, my clever wife?"

"I don't understand why you are so angry with me."

"Anger does not touch upon what I feel, so it is best that we walk, and walk fast in hopes that this dismal night can cool my mood."

And walk he did, away from her with a quick, aggressive stride, untempered by concern for her ability to keep up. So she hurried, nearly running to come to heel at his elbow, all the while frantic questions swirled within her mind. What had she done to provoke him so?

What had she gotten herself into with the murmur of the two words, "I do."

An odd pair they must have made traversing the wet byways afoot, Gerard in the billowing greatcoat, a stalking night bird of prey; Laure trotting breathlessly at his side, a fragile dove in her wedding finery as minutes stretched closer to an hour. Though aching of foot and heart, Laure kept to the relentless pace, determined not to slow him by petition. She'd no evidence that a play upon his sympathy would have any success, for never once did he glance about to gage her stamina. If this was a test, she refused to fail it or him. Until an uneven cobble threw off her stride and had her hopping about to find one of her dainty slippers while clutching at a stitch in her side.

Her husband came about to face her with a disdainful glare.

"So much for your declaration that you would follow."

"I've lost my shoe, is all."

"And I'm to wait while you fumble about to find it?" *Clumsy girl,* claimed his sweeping stare as he assessed her from muddied and torn stockinged foot to the flush of her features. "If you cannot keep up, I've no use for you."

She spotted her soiled slipper in the dirty run-off water of the gutter. As she bent to retrieve it, the fine lace of her skirts soaked up a similar stain as they pooled upon the damp stones. She slid her foot into the slipper, trying not to grimace at the sodden feel of it.

"Where do we go in such a hurry, sir?" she asked, hoping to delay long enough to catch her breath.

"Should it matter to you? I would think you'd be grateful enough for my company as not to question our destination. Or was I wrong?"

"Of course not, sir." She glanced about then and, to her alarm, noted the seediness of their surroundings. The streets had grown narrow and sinister in their bleakness. And she feared dangerous to a well-dressed couple on foot. But her husband seemed unconcerned, for he turned and continued to stroll through murky shadow as she hobbled in his wake.

"Insensitive lout," she muttered to herself as she hoisted her now heavy hem out of the mud.

He glanced back without a pause in stride. "Did you speak?"

"No, sir."

If he was waiting for her to plead for mercy, he would have to wait a while longer. For one who'd sworn off games, he was playing a cruel one with her patience. If he thought he could break her spirit, he was mistaken. If he planned to discourage her hopes, he was right on the mark.

What kind of man dragged his new bride about the dark, dreary streets of New Orleans in sections one was wise to avoid during daylight hours?

Enough.

She stopped. After he'd gone half a block farther, he halted as well, aware that she no longer followed.

"If you've a point to make, sir, speak it plainly."

He turned to confront her, not with anger or impatience but rather with a cold gaze of challenge.

"Had you thought it would be easy to invade my life? Did you think I would change what I am for your convenience?" He made an expansive gesture. "This is my world. These uncaring streets make up the whole of my existence. Had you expected a cozy fireside and tender conversation?"

Yes. Yes, she had. Had expected it, had longed for it. Chilled to the bone by her disappointment, she managed to hoist her chin in meager defiance.

"I should like to go home now."

His generous lips twisted in a wry sort of smile. "I'm sure your brother will welcome your empty-handed return with arms wide open."

"To *our* home."

His bitter laugh clipped short. His posture straightened. His attention focused on something or someone she could neither see nor hear.

"Ahhhh." The sound sighed from him. "We have company."

Having a very good idea about what kind of company they'd find on these soiled streets, Laure gripped her skirts, preparing to run, but Gerard displayed no undo alarm.

"Do not distress yourself, my dear. It is only my dinner engagement."

She looked about, confused and no less uncertain of their safety. Then from out of the darkness a single figure emerged, a large, roughly garbed man. And quite obviously, not an acquaintance of her husband. There was no recognition in the flinty eyes, no welcome in the curl of thick lips. He held his pistol with the confidence of one who wouldn't hesitate to use it.

"Hand over your valuables, *m'sieur*."

Just the coarse growl of his voice had Laure trembling. But Gerard only smiled.

"Do you expect me to just give them to you?"

"You can give them to me, or I can take them...after I kill you."

"How very inhospitable."

"What did you expect, coming to a place like this all decked out in your fancies?"

Gerard smiled again, white teeth flashing. "I expected no less than I've received." Then his gaze narrowed into a look of unmistakable challenge. "If you want what I have, *porco,* try to take it."

He was still smiling as the man's bullet took him squarely in the chest, knocking him back against the crumbling stuccoed wall of the shuttered dwelling behind him. Laure's scream mingled with the echoing roar of the discharge. Above the hands she lifted to catch-back that cry, Laure watched in wide-eyed horror as her husband of several hours slid to the broken pavement, a bright splash of crimson widening upon his snowy shirtfront. Her stunned mind recognized it as a fatal wound even as his eyes closed and his form crumpled.

Their remorseless assailant advanced upon him, bending to reach inside his greatcoat pockets. That's when Laure ran, as hard and as fast as her already weakened legs could carry her. Away from the horror of her husband's blood upon the dark cobbles. Away from the prospect of a second fateful bullet ending her future with equal indifference. Gasping, sobbing, she fled up one street and down the next, hopelessly confusing her direction, until at last, she burst upon a well lit thoroughfare and the welcome sight of a patrolman on his rounds.

"Please! Please, you must come! My husband's been shot, killed in a robbery..."

Her knees gave way then, and she swooned into the capable arms of the officer. He steered her to a curbside bench, where she collapsed in a crumple of ruined lace. Not knowing what else to do, he began to chafe her hands between his. When her sensibilities returned and she was able to answer his terse questions enough to instruct him as to where the heinous deed had occurred, she was bundled into his fast-moving hack. Not how she'd envisioned her wedding night, heading back toward the scene of murder.

Except there was no carnage. No lifeless form on the narrow banquette.

"Are you sure this is the place, ma'am?"

"Y-yes. Y-yes, of course. He fell right over there, next to that wall."

"There's no one here, ma'am." Doubt began to build in his expression, as if he suspected some kind of prank was being played at his expense. "You must be mistaken."

"I can't be." She climbed from the carriage on near strengthless legs, forcing herself to move toward the spot where she'd seen Gerard mortally wounded. But the officer was right. There was no victim, no blood, no sign of a vile event.

She wasn't wrong. She couldn't be. She began to shake her head.

"Ahhh, there you are, my darling. I was so worried."

Strong fingers closed upon her upper arm. The power in that grip was all that kept her from dropping to the street, so great was her shock. There was no mistaking the mellifluously accented voice, but just to be sure, she looked to the man at her side, to the sharply handsome features that mocked her, and the now familiar pale, jeweled eyes.

"No..." Her protest escaped as a fretful moan. "I saw him murder you."

"Are you this lady's husband, sir?" asked the patrolman, eager to make some sense of this odd business.

"Of course. There's been some misunderstanding, Officer. No foul play has occurred. No murder. As you can see, I am fit and fine."

Laure could see he was. In fact, his earlier pallor was gone, replaced by a warm glow of health that made his looks even more heart-stopping in their appeal.

But she'd seen him fall. There was no mistake.

Without loosening his compelling grip on her arm, Gerard smiled at the perplexed policeman. "She's confused, poor thing. Too many toasts at our wedding this very night. I fear we wandered quite foolishly where we should not have, and some unfortunate creature approached us for spare coins. My lovely bride grew frightened by his appearance and, before I could stop her, she'd run off in a panic. I am sorry if her fancies have inconvenienced you. A bit too high-strung in her fears of the wedding night to come, don't you know."

He grinned with a wolfishly male indulgence that had the officer relaxing into a smile of his own.

"No harm done, sir. Might I suggest milder spirits in the future."

"Wise advice, I'm sure. Good night, Officer."

And as the policeman started across the street to where his hack waited, Gerard turned his attention back to his trembling bride. She was staring up at him, dazed and incomprehensive, pulling against his grasp.

"I'm ready to go home now, my love. How about you?"

Slowly, her hand quivering fearfully, Laure reached out to catch the closed overlap of his coat. He made no move to resist as she pulled it aside to reveal the bloody ruin of his shirt...and the charred hole the bullet had made as it tore through the crisp white linen.

Her breath faltered. Her hand dropped away.

"My God...what manner of man are you?"

"The man you married...no man at all."

She lunged away from him, and this time he let her go, merely watching as she dashed across the slick cobbles in pursuit of the uniformed man.

"Officer! Officer, please—"

She clutched the man's sleeve, knowing how things must look to him: an hysterical woman, possibly a lovers' first quarrel. She could see in his expression his reluctance to interfere.

"Yes, ma'am?"

What could she say to him that wouldn't sound like insanity? It felt like insanity, even to her. She had to think. She had to get away. To do that, she needed some degree of control. She drew a ragged breath.

"Might I beg a ride from you? I must get to my brother's house. It—it is an emergency."

"Now, ma'am, it's not my place—"

"Please!" Panic rattled through her voice.

Uncomfortable with her request, the man looked to Gerard, who was still standing across the way watching the goings on through impassive eyes. His coat was buttoned. He looked every inch the respectable gentleman. And in her dirty disarray, her eyes round and nearly black with what would be seen as irrational fear, she appeared as reliable as an asylum escapee. The patrolman sought a neutral ground.

"Only if it's all right with your husband."

Laure looked back in alarm. One word from him, the madman she'd married, and her rescuer would walk away, leaving her at his mercy.

"I would be much obliged if you would take her wherever it is she wishes to go. It's seems best under the circumstances. If it is no trouble."

Surprised and relieved by his calm dismissal, Laure didn't hesitate. Without giving the officer the chance to reply or refuse, she hurried toward the hack, dragging herself up inside it without waiting for assistance. There, she huddled, quaking in the cold grasp of shock and disbelief. She gave a nervous start as the springs gave on the driver's side.

"Where to, *madame*?"

In frail tones, she gave him Percy's address.

Would he be there to welcome her with open arms knowing she'd left her husband behind?

Would he believe her?

Once the conveyance swayed into motion, Laure dared to shut her eyes and reexamine what she'd seen. It was madness, like some nightmare gone awry. She didn't doubt her vision. She was certain of what she'd seen.

What she couldn't comprehend was how, after being shot in the chest at a range close enough to leave powder burns on shirt fabric, Gerard Pasquale could be there standing unconcerned—alive!—as if he'd suffered not a scratch.

What was he? She wasn't a stranger to unnatural occurrences, to seeing things from another, invisible world. But nothing had prepared her for the shock she'd received. What had she really seen on that rain-washed street that could make sense of it all? At the moment, she didn't care. She didn't want to know. She only wanted to get away, far away, where the madness couldn't follow.

She never looked back, but she could imagine his sly smile as he watched her go.

His bride of just a few hours, fleeing him in the night.

FOUR

"A trick, a joke, that's all it was."

In the bright flood of daylight, Percy's explanations held more substance than when Laure had arrived at his door in the middle of the night, filled with frantic claims of unnatural origin. After a few hours of brandy-induced sleep, she was in a more lucid frame of mind for listening but no less convinced of what she'd seen.

"He was shot point blank in the chest, Percy. I saw it happen. I saw the blood and bullet hole."

The soul of comfort, Percy handed her a cup of hot tea with a placating, "You saw only what he wished you to see. What else would explain it?"

"Why? Answer me that. If it was all an elaborate ruse just to frighten me half to death, what was the purpose?"

"Perhaps to see if you would run."

Laure stared at her brother for a long moment, speechless and amazed. Then one word escaped her.

Again, "Why?"

Percy settled beside her on the sofa, taking up one cold hand, the one that bore the heavy signet ring of the husband she'd abandoned in terror. "I warned you that he was a bit eccentric."

"But you said nothing about dangerous lunacy!"

"You must understand, Laure, a man of his wealth, of his position is suspicious by nature. You are a beautiful young girl wedded to a stranger. Perhaps he was testing you to discover his own answer to why."

"So I am to be subject to these tests, these games to see if my motives are worthy?" Anger touched her tone. The cleansing emotion felt good, strong, after hours of humbling panic. "I am in no mood to play for his amusement."

She sipped her tea, the cup rattling noisily in its saucer until Percy claimed it with his hand and set it aside. He was calm and practical and just what she needed to conquer her raging fright.

"Perhaps if you go there to his home, your home, and establish yourself as his wife without questions or fear, that will be all the answer he needs."

The thought of another confrontation held no charm. Yet the idea of his cruel jest at her expense fueled her courage. She could picture him standing there on the puddled street, grinning at the thought of her terror. The bastard. It was now a matter of more than the ring she wore. It was a point of principle, of will. "Do you think so, Percy?"

"I know so. He admires boldness above all things. Go. Take control of what is yours." Then his tone tempered with a warning. "Do not forget what is at stake here. Can you afford to let one poor joke turn you away from the future you deserve? This is a test of mettle, Laure. I had never believed you lacking in that area."

"I am not one to give up easily," she agreed, winning his grin of approval.

"There you go, my dear. Refuse to be shocked or dismayed by whatever trials he may put you through. Prove yourself capable of enduring all he can conceive of."

"I've endured much worse than a midnight scare," she confessed with mounting determination.

Who, indeed, was this man who would meet her willingly at the altar then go to such extravagant lengths to discourage her from the vows she'd spoken? Percy's rationality made more sense than anything she could name. Either her husband was overly cautious and desperate to protect himself from misuse, or he was utterly mad.

Or he was something not quite human.

She laughed to herself at that absurdity and sipped the tea, her hands now steady, letting the hot liquid calm her body as her practical thoughts quieted her mind. Whether manipulator, madman or monster, she would not allow a humorless trick to chase her from her only security. Percy was right. There was too much at stake.

Gerard Pasquale would soon discover that he had married no weak-livered miss. He would find her a match for his quirks of temper and mean-spirited games.

As long as he didn't play them in a physical arena.

"Shall I take you home, Mrs. Pasquale?"

She set down the cup and saucer. "Yes. It's time I was mistress of my new home. And of my destiny."

The front gate was open.

Laure hadn't prepared herself for the opulence...or the disrepair...of her new residence. Awash in the mid-morning sun, the columned mansion looked not so much majestic as it did neglected, with its over-grown greenery and peeling facade. An air of emptiness haunted the vacant windows and debris-littered porch, a sense of melancholy she would do her best to sweep away along with the cobwebs, the dirt and the chips of ancient white paint. She considered that her first objective until Percy held open the door, and she stepped into the cavernous hollow.

"It looks as though no one lives here."

"Pasquale has been traveling abroad for some time. I believe that is where he contracted his illness. Perhaps he hired incompetent caretakers and now finds himself unequal to the task."

Laure had no comment on her husband's supposed infirmity, unless it was in the mental realm. Gazing about her, that assumption didn't seem too far-fetched.

"Is the whole house like this?" she asked in disbelief, taking in the absence of all but floor, ceiling and walls.

"I truly don't know. I've only visited the lower rooms." Percy glanced about, avarice brightening his gaze. "Would you like me to escort you on a tour of the premise...I don't think your husband would mind or interfere. I doubt that we shall even see him. I seem to recall him saying business was calling him away."

On his first day of marriage.

Disheartened by her groom's indifference, Laure nodded, anxious to take stock of what she did, or did not own.

It took them the better part of an hour to explore the twenty-two rooms. Most were as empty as the first had been. Filled with puzzlement and an unexpected sadness, Laure said, "How could he exist here in this house, all alone? No food, no comfort, no companionship."

It wasn't a wonder if he were truly mad.

"Where does he sleep with no bed?" She spoke her curiosity aloud without considering the delicate topic, then blushed as her brother glanced her way.

Percy offered no solution. Instead, he advised, "You are the wife of an influential member of New Orleans society now. You owe it to your husband's name to turn this shell into a showplace from top to bottom."

That's what a good and proper wife would do.

"I shall begin with the top, I think, for I've no desire to rest upon bare floorboards."

"It would be my pleasure to help you shop for the necessities. After all, I manage your husband's purse strings. We should begin with a fitting ensemble for you, so the merchants will take you seriously."

A good place to start, convincing area shopkeepers of her new standing. Then, perhaps, she could convince herself, and her new husband, that she belonged.

She was on her hands and knees, scouring a film of neglect from the checkerboard of black and white marble in the front hall, when a bristle of awareness warned she was no longer alone.

Instead of giving way to the alarm spiking through her, Laure continued with her task, refusing to look up until she had the rush of anxiety under control. As she finished polishing the final square, she could feel the intensity of his stare as viscerally as a physical touch. Though a beading of nervousness broke out along exertion-flushed skin, she betrayed none of her alarm, calmly restoring her brush to its grime darkened water before lifting her gaze.

He stood beyond the reach of the candlelight, back by the rising curve of the stairs, as motionless as a shadow himself as he watched her work. How he'd gotten past her without her knowing it gave some cause for uneasy concern, but she displayed none of it.

"So you're here."

His flat statement held no warmth or welcome.

"Good evening, sir. I trust you've recovered well from the stresses of last night."

He didn't reply immediately, perhaps annoyed by the tartness lacing through her words. Then he spoke casually as he advanced into the light.

"Did you think I would not?"

She wondered, when first she saw him. His pallor had returned, a gleaming whiteness that cast his features into stark relief. Still, she didn't mistake his lack of healthy color for lack of health in general. The sense of latent power he exuded with even the most meager move belied that belief. If Gerard Pasquale suffered from any malady, it was most likely arrogance and disdain for the female he'd married.

His chill, blue-eyed gaze lingered over her in a contemptuous sweep. For the first time, she realized how she must look to him. Her fine new gown was blotched and crumpled, and her hair clung to her brow and neck in damp tendrils. Instead of an elegant new bride, she looked more akin to a wage-earning scullery. As a slow burn of embarrassment climbed her cheeks, an underlying dignity came to her rescue. Why should she feel ashamed for taking pride in the management of her home? Obviously her husband had no interest there, or it wouldn't have fallen to ruin about his ears. She met his unblinking stare with a haughtiness to equal his own. When she didn't back down, he was first to glance away.

"I see you've been busy drawing off my accounts." He made note of the sparse furnishings in the double parlor that encroached upon its echoing emptiness.

"Only in the receiving, dining and...master bedrooms. Nothing extravagant or beyond necessity. I didn't think you would mind. Do you?"

"I suppose not," he allowed grudgingly. "Such things are of no importance to me, since I'm rarely here to indulge in their comforts."

Laure ducked her head so he wouldn't see her blank confusion. If not here in his home, where did he spend his time? To her chagrin, another of Percy's assumptions was cast aside with the wave of one graceful hand. Her husband was not homebound and hungry for her companionship. She should have learned as much last night. If he did not sleep under this roof, apparently he'd found his companionship in more agreeable quarters. Only a wife for a day, and still the humiliation of it burned hot.

Having a mistress was nothing out of the ordinary in New Orleans society. Hadn't she recently been offered such a position herself? She should have been relieved to be spared that element of their marriage. She didn't know this man, so why should she feel betrayed by the knowledge that he preferred to spend his time with another?

She didn't know why it should, but it did.

"So it is your plan to take up residency." He made it sound as if it wasn't a given.

"My home is here." *With you.* She didn't add that, for she was beginning to suspect it would not be true.

He made an impatient gesture. "Very well. Settle in. Buy fancy trimmings, and set yourself up like a grand dame. But do not expect me to make you feel welcome."

His words were a stab to her hopes.

"There is no danger of that, sir." It took a moment for her to suppress the ravages of hurt and rejection enough to add more sedately, "Shall I prepare something for dinner?"

"You are not here to serve me, *madame.* My comings and goings are my own business and need not concern you, so make your schedule to suit yourself. I'm dining out. I should think you'd be grateful for that fact." Then the final slap. "You needn't wait up for me."

Her gaze lowered as she tried her best to salvage the situation she now feared was beyond repair. "I had hoped we might have some time to get to know one another."

He made an uncharitable sound. "I know all I need to know already. Good evening. Were I you, I wouldn't rest too easily in the bed you've made."

By the time she glanced up, angered by his thinly veiled threat, he was gone, absent from the room without sound or apparent movement.

To find his entertainments elsewhere since he'd already decided hers were so lacking.

She swallowed down the taste of her disappointment and bent to finish the floor. If she were being honest with herself, she'd have to admit that it wasn't so much his dismissal of her as it was the destruction of her dream that cut to the quick of her emotions. But she would survive it, just as she had all life's other disparages. There would be no going back to Percy in tears. It was, after all, her bed to sleep in, uneasily or no.

She would make the most of what she'd been given, with good grace and equanimity. Disappointment and embarrassment weren't fatal conditions, just bruising ones. She could bear them, would bear them, alone, as she'd done with all else these last few years.

As she scrubbed with a new ferocity, she purposefully placed those dreams aside and got on with the business of the here and now.

Despite his warning, she had waited up for him. He saw the soft glow in the window from the street. It made the big house look somehow welcoming. And that made him all the more annoyed.

Who had asked her to be there waiting? He didn't need her uninvited presence to make him feel at home.

But when had the empty mansion ever felt like a home?
Never.
Never, until tonight with that glowing of expectant light.

Bah!

He breezed into the front hall like a harsh wind, but she wasn't there to frighten. Where then was his timid little bride?

Come out, come out! His dark mood growled in vile humor.

Ahhh! He felt her now, just in the next room. One good fright, and she would go running back to her money-grubbing brother, squealing all the way. He let his anger sweep over him, swelling his shoulders, forcing his palms to the floor as his shape shimmered and shifted until no man stood in the foyer. It was a black wolf there in his place, stalking toward the scent of human in the parlor. A hungry wolf.

She was seated on a low chaise, tiny reading glasses resting near the end of her nose, a book braced open upon her knees. With a snarl, he lunged toward her, jowls opened wide, fangs exposed and gleaming - only to change back into human form in mid-leap, landing lightly on the floor beside the couch.

She was asleep.

He made a disgruntled sound. How uncooperative of her to spoil his dramatic scare. And just how could he bully her while she wore those silly little glasses that made her look both bookish and touchingly youthful at the same time. He reached out to remove them.

A growling hound from hell had not awakened her, but the slightest touch brought her up from a sound sleep with a fretful cry. Her arm shot up, her forearm catching his hand, sending her spectacles flying. The sound of tinkling glass made him feel suddenly churlish as she gazed up at him in alarm.

"Forgive me for startling you." How inane! Hadn't that been his plan, and here he was apologizing for his success?

She blinked, appearing disarmingly confused and attractively tousled. "You touched me." She made it sound like she was accusing him of a crime. Against his own lawful wife.

"You'd fallen asleep. I was going to carry you up to bed." A chivalrous lie that would have delighted most maidens. So why did she draw her knees up tight against her chest, as if his plan had been to ravish her? Her gaze shone like twin nuggets of coal freshly broken.

"I'd prefer you not to touch me without my consent," came her unexpectedly fierce command. It made his hackles rise, as if he were yet that proud wolf. Then, she followed her tart decree with another equally insulting observation. "You've not earned the right to handle me in such an intimate fashion."

"Earned?" he echoed, leaning close enough to send her pressing back against the curved back of the chaise. He had about enough of his haughty mortal bride. Flushed with an unwise arrogance, he told her, "I do not need to touch you to be intimate."

To prove his point, to impress his superiority upon her, he trapped her gaze within the silvery depths of his own, and layered on his vampire magic.

Caught in its thick, sensual haze, Laure's back warped away from the sofa. A wanton moan of surprise and pleasure tumbled from her parted lips. Sensation scalded along her body. Her trembling hands followed that trail, running over her jutting breasts, grazing the stiff peaks that ached for attention, across the bow of her heaving ribcage, down into the valley of her thighs where desire throbbed in hot, needy pulses and from there, along her legs where they shifted restlessly beneath her gown. Every inch of her begged to be stroked, kissed, adored, but there was only the whisper of inner heat whipping through her body, coiling low and tight, until she could suppress her ecstatic cries no longer.

As he evoked his charm upon her, Gerard was equally seduced, not by the tantalizing woman undulating in the throes of unnatural rapture, but by the thrum of her excitement, the way it caught up her pulse beats and made them pound out an irresistible rhythm. It was heat flamed by her arousal. The sound of it surging through her veins. Inviting him closer. Closer.

Her hands reached up of their own accord to tear open the top buttons of her staid white blouse to bare the tops of her breasts and the bend of her pale throat. In her haste, she yanked something free, some piece of jewelry that slid toward the floor with a metallic twinkle. Before he could stop the impulse, Gerard reached out to catch it. He knew what it was even as the thin chain pooled in his hand.

Silver.

His shriek of agony woke Laure from her trance. She blinked away her daze to see him on his knees, bent double, clutching his hand. That he was having some sort of attack shocked her into action. She dropped down onto her knees before him, demanding to know what she could do.

"Remove it!" he wailed.

She didn't understand until he extended his hand. Her silver chain, a gift from her mother upon the day of her own wedding, had embedded itself into his smoking flesh and was actually burning into his palm!

"My God!" She'd never seen anything like it. It was as if the metal was eating though him. Quickly, she grasped one of the dangling ends and pulled the links out of the smoldering wound. The clasp came loose with a vicious sizzling sound, and Gerard immediately closed his fingers over the oozing injury. Laure rocked back on her heels, alarmed and perplexed by the intensity of his pain.

"Are you all right?" She placed her hands lightly, gingerly upon his shoulders, but he violently shrugged away. "What is it?" she cried in dismay.

"The silver," he groaned. "I have an intolerance to it."

Was this part of the illness Percy described? How horribly she felt for having doubted it was true.

"What can I do? Shall I get a doctor—"

"No!" he howled. "Nothing. Do nothing."

"But you're in terrible pain."

She reached out, catching him by the wrists, the gesture hiking up his coat and shirt sleeves to exposure twin bands of scarring about his wrists. Even as she watched in horror, those scars seemed to shift and liquify, becoming dreadful sores that closed up almost before her gasp was complete.

"What is this?" Certainly, no natural affliction. She reared back, and the last thing she saw was his hand fanning across her eyes.

"Remember nothing," he gritted out between clenched teeth. He panted for breath as she sat there on her heels, expression blank, eyes unseeing. The pain was hard enough to endure without suffering for her sympathy and recoil.

He'd allowed her to get too close and himself to get too distracted.

She was quite beautiful in repose.

From where he stood beside her bed, Gerard admitted that much to himself. He hadn't dared come so close to her before tending to his appetite. Just her presence beneath the same roof, let alone the temptation of her in the same room, had been almost too much for him earlier. And then he'd let his vanity carry him away. But now, even as the wound in his hand itched and healed, he felt more in control and able to consider her dispassionately while she slept.

Yes, quite lovely, in that fragile, transitory way of humankind, with her softly pinked skin and gently parted lips. A fair bloom so easily bent, so quickly crushed.

Even now, as warmed as he was by the vitality of another, he was intoxicated by her, by the rhythmic brush of her breath in the quiet night, by the scent of her, the scent of living, breathing human. Drawn by the steady, hypnotic pulse of that life within her, nearly as entranced as he had been downstairs. By the strong beat of her heart, by the sluice of the blood within her veins. By the tender hollow at the base of her bared throat where he could almost taste...

He tore his gaze away from the lure of creamy skin, damning the vile bargain he'd made.

He'd been mad to allow her into his home, into his life. The situation was ripe for tragic consequence. He'd been so smugly certain that her threat was gone when she'd fled from him the night before in unrestrained horror.

Obviously, his mistake, for there she lay a short reach away in trusting repose.

Here she was, back again, her poise an affront to his plan to drive her from him. Buying furniture as if they'd be setting up house together. Hah! There was only one piece of furniture he required, and it wasn't meant to be the centerpiece in her parlor ensemble.

Stupid girl. Brave, stupid, greedy girl. To rob from him and run was one thing, but to boldly confront him with her misdeeds was quite another. What did she think to gain through her bravado? His admiration? His respect? Only one mortal female had proven herself worthy of that. He frowned as dissatisfaction for his circumstance growled through him.

On the pristine sheets of the bed he didn't share with her, his young bride shifted restlessly.

His bride.

What a gruesomely comic union. What benefit could he draw from this creature who possessed his name and his fortune without allowing him the meagerest concession? She deserved no kindness, no quarter from him, and yet her empathy—the pain he'd brought so briefly to flicker in her gaze—had wounded him in ways he'd not thought possible.

Conscience? Bah! Compassion? Hardly. Not for this schemer whose black soul was so attractively wrapped in petal-soft skin and hair the color of dawn. A dawn he hadn't seen for centuries, captured in the taunting waves of blushed gold across fresh starched linens. The sight mesmerized, pulling him closer to feel between the rub of fingertips what could not be seen. Like that dawn, like silver, she would burn him if he let his guard relax even for an instant. A pain such as that was never forgotten. He drew back his hand and, in his haste, the movement woke her.

He heard her sudden inhalation, a startled sharpness against the still of the eve. He didn't need to watch her depthless dark eyes widen to palpably experience her alarm. Then puzzlement crowded upon her brow as if she were wondering, struggling to remember...

"I didn't mean to wake you," he heard himself saying in words as soft as a whisper.

She stared up at him, clutching her covers up under her chin as if their purity could somehow protect her. As if anything could, should he decide to take what he desired. He waited to see the loathing, the terror, return to her expression, the rightful reaction to what he was. But it didn't come. The apprehension, the tender flush of shyness remained, but the awe, the fear she should have felt never materialized.

And then slowly, determinedly, she turned back the covers to welcome him as if he were a true husband, as if he were a man, not a monster.

Stunned by the gesture and by what it must mean, he turned away from the offer, leaving her more lonely and isolated than he could have purposefully intended.

"You didn't tell her."

Percy bolted upright within his desk chair, papers scattering all about him. His frantic gaze flashed about his shadowed office before fixing upon the metallic gleam of his brother-in-law's eyes.

"Tell her what?" he asked with a nervous lick of his lips. Shaking hands began to gather his files together.

Gerard stepped farther into the room, away from the barely opened window through which he'd gained entrance. His expression held the same foreboding as the storm clouds banking above the Mississippi. Both warned of dangerous consequence.

"You let her wed me without telling her what I was."

"I told her enough."

Gerard laughed softly, but Percy wasn't deceived into thinking him amused. "I hardly think so. When one makes a deal with a devil, one should know what he wagers. You are a wretched coward for holding to your silence."

Percy squared his narrow shoulders. "I don't deny that, but I was thinking of her welfare, too."

"Really? By placing her into my care, an unsuspecting sacrifice?"

"Laure is hardly naive, sir." In later reflections, Gerard would come to wonder over the harshness of that claim. "And she is more able to care for herself than you might guess."

"And it is your guess that she will remain with me to secure your finances even after she learns the truth?"

Percy never faltered. "Yes. I think she will. You'll find no easy way out of this bargain, Pasquale. What I lack in fortitude, Laure holds in an abundance. If you knew the entire truth, perhaps it is you who might be afraid."

"*Bastardo!* I have nothing to fear from you." He spat symbolically on the floor.

But Percy merely smiled.

"If that were true, you would not be here, and we would not be related. Knowledge is power, sir, and with what I know, I have twice your strength. If you are wise, you will give my Laure everything she desires, and you will be careful not to make an enemy of me lest you find yourself frying in the morning light. I have the advantage of daylight, which you do not. Remember that, Pasquale, and remember that you exist for only as long as my dear sister remains unharmed and my fortune stays intact."

For a moment, Gerard said nothing. His impassive features, with their unnatural lack of motion, did more to unsettle the little lawyer than any display of force. Until Gerard chuckled softly, and the chilling sound sent tremors shuddering up Percy's spine.

"I have not lived for centuries by letting insects such as you feed off me. You might remember that I am not particularly charitable to my enemies, either." His voice lowered to a threatening rumble. "Either you educate your sister...or I will."

Before Percy could respond, Pasquale was simply gone; a brief shimmer of form, then nothing. For a moment, only the lawyer's hoarse breathing sounded, then he gave a vicious curse.

Damn the man!

With a sweep of his arm, he sent all the folders flying. None of them would realize half the bounty that was close to escaping him. Pasquale's fortune was the solution to his troubles, and his step-sister was both avenue and barrier to his success. He needed more time to siphon off a tidy sum to survive on.

He sat down, calming his breathing, collecting his thoughts. He didn't want mere survival. He wanted luxury. And to have it, he would have to rid himself of two very compelling problems. Or better yet, he could conceive of a way for them to destroy each other. It would interesting to see whose survival instincts prevailed. Not that it mattered as long as the outcome was as he'd prescribed. Both of them gone.

He smiled to himself.

Leaving him alone with all that lovely money.

FIVE

Stepping through the humble double doors of Antoine's into the Quarter's most elegant restaurant was something Laure had never seen herself as doing. To stop conversation and turn heads was far beyond her conception. But stare they did, all those fine, pedigreed members of the society who'd scorned her mother before her. As she paused, holding to a dignity that couldn't quite still her trembling hands, the whispers reached her: not the dreaded hush that came with the name LaClaire in the rundown sections of town, but the awe that accompanied the mystery of Pasquale.

It was then she realized that, in her fancy afternoon dress of midnight blue overset with bows of heavy cotton lace trim, with her fair hair twisted up beneath the angular set of a bowed and be-feathered hat, they did not recognize her as other than the wife of the city's most intriguing recluse.

It was as Percy had promised, a new beginning. As long as she was willing to pay the price.

"Madame Pasquale," murmured the *maitre de* with silky deference. "Your party is waiting for you, if you would follow me, please."

Head held high and gaze straight ahead, she swept between the diners, ignoring the gawkers, refusing to hear the buzz of speculation, smiling only when Percy rose from their prestigiously situated table.

"Laure, my dear, how lovely you look," he exclaimed as she was seated. He, himself, was dapper in his exquisitely cut new suit. The pair of them looked more than a match for the glamorous surroundings. None would have guessed less than a month ago, they had been eating fried oysters out of wrapped paper on the benches flanking Jackson Square instead of oysters Rockefeller and *pompano en papillote* under the attentive eyes of St. Louis Street's elite.

"You look particularly pleased with yourself today, Percy. Is there some occasion?"

Nearly bursting with self-satisfaction, he announced, "It's a day of celebration. While we sit here sipping wine, my humble offices are being moved to their new location. In the Godchaux Building."

"Oh, Percy, such an esteemed address!"

Smiling proudly at her rightful awe in regards to the huge corner bastion on Canal and Chartres, Percy gloated, "I've got three appointments scheduled for this afternoon alone."

"I'm so pleased to hear of your good fortune." Her sentiments were genuine. Why shouldn't her hard-working brother reap the reward of his efforts? Just because she was less enthusiastic about her own change in circumstance, there was no reason to begrudge his happiness. "This calls for more than a toast. What can we do to truly celebrate?"

Settling back in his chair with a close-lipped smile, Percy had just the answer. "What's called for now, is my introduction to the higher limits of society. How goes the renovation of your home?"

Not equating the two things immediately, Laure said, "It goes well. If not a showplace, than at least not an embarrassment."

She was understating her affect on the previously decrepit manse. None who had seen it before would recognize it now. It's once neglected stone facade had undergone as dramatic a metamorphosis as Laure herself.

It hadn't been difficult.

Having nothing else with which to occupy her time, Laure spent the better part of each day combing through the shops along Royal Street looking for bargains. Aware that she had the funds to spend top dollar if she chose, it challenged her to find the best deal possible when it came to embellishing the now tastefully filled rooms of her new home. Perhaps a two-day search would yield no more than an elegantly shaped vase to compliment the foyer table, but each possession filled her with a sense of pride and permanence. If she was not happy, at least she was content. Wasn't that far more than once she'd been able to hope for?

"Then perhaps you could do me a great favor."

The hint of careful earnest in Percy's tone alerted her to what she should have suspected at once. The reason for this invitation to lunch was more than just to be seen. It was a precursor to his plan to ingratiate himself into the company of society's best.

"What is it you want, Percy?" she asked with a cautious neutrality.

"A two-fold celebration. The means to announce that we both have arrived and will not be ignored."

"And just how will that be accomplished?"

He spelled it out exactly as she'd feared.

"By you hosting an unequaled event to show our vastly elevated status."

"You mean show off, don't you?"

"What if I do?" he admitted without the slightest degree of shame. "Don't tell me you wouldn't enjoy having the *crème de la crème* of New Orleans scrambling for your invitation? Come, Laure. The truth."

Yes, she would enjoy it. Revel in it to be exact. How satisfying to earn homage from those who'd snubbed her on the street, stepping out of their way as if she carried some horrific contagion or sought to pick their pockets. Seeing the gleam in her gaze, Percy began to grin. That returned her to the reality of the situation.

"They would not come at my summons," she declared with a touch of bitter truth.

"But you shall not be issuing the invitation as Laure Cristobel, sister of Percy Cristobel. You'll be the elusive and exclusive Mrs. Gerard Pasquale for whom Percy Cristobel is a respected solicitor. How many of these fine people would recognize you as a woman in your own right? With Pasquale's name and fortune to blind them, they will never see beyond it. That I can guarantee with a few well placed words in a few influential ears."

"What words, Percy?"

"That the reclusive Mr. Pasquale is willing to invest his fortune under my dictates. That should make his acquaintance a necessity and seal my future all at once."

He saw her frown gather and quickly waved away her expected protests.

"Laure, it is not a lie. It would only be dishonest if it weren't true. You *are* Mrs. Pasquale and I *do* administer his monies. What we make of those simple facts is what will establish us in society."

Her reticence must have been clear in her expression, for Percy seized up her hands in a demonstrative press. He bent forward, features flushed with passion.

"Laure, think of what is at stake here."

She did and, finally, she sighed.

"I shall have to discuss it with my husband. He is a...private person and may not like the doors to his home thrown upon to a curious populace."

As if he'd even notice, she thought with a humbling touch of chagrin. She hadn't caught so much as a glimpse of her handsome husband in at least two dozen days. Not since the last regrettable invitation she'd made. That private humiliation still burned, adding to her reluctance to approach the stranger who shared—at least on documents—the same address.

"How could he refuse you?" Percy protested. "He needn't attend if it makes him uncomfortable to do so. You're the one they'll flock to see. The new power in their circle. Can't you feel them staring even now?"

Yes, she could. She'd been trying not to squirm under their scrutiny with each bite she took, with each word she spoke. Like a bird trapped in a magnifying bell jar, not the slightest detail went unobserved.

"I will ask, Percy. That is all I can promise."

Undaunted, he beamed. "I'll begin making up a guest list. We shall be the talk of the town."

Better than the butt of its malicious gossip, but Laure wouldn't speak of such things to her treasured step-brother. Instead, she murmured, her eyes misting, "Our parents would be so proud."

A stillness befitting her husband took hold of Percy's face for just an instant. Then he smiled wistfully. "They are never far from my thoughts. Yes, this is a fitting tribute. It's what they deserve, after all."

As she dabbed a betraying tear from her cheek, Laure missed the hard sheen that revealed itself in Percy's eyes.

A gleam of retribution.

At nightfall, Laure did something unique to her month of marriage—she purposefully sought out her husband.

It wasn't an easy thing for her. Her pride, her hopes, her feelings still ached from his brusque rejection of her as both a wife and as a companion. Seeking him out was courting more of the same, but as she'd filled the rooms in this house that was not a home, she'd become more aware of its emptiness. It wasn't the lack of decoration, it was the absence of life that made it echo so hollowly. An echo that reverberated within her heart. She hadn't gone to so much trouble to impress New Orleans society for Percy, and her own needs could have been satisfied with much less. As she waited for Gerard to appear, she realized the truth, and that truth only emphasized her loneliness. She'd toiled so meticulously to please her husband, to earn an approval he'd stingily withheld, and perhaps to create an environment where he'd be more apt to linger...with her.

"Buona sera."

Her pulse gave an unexpected leap as she turned toward that mellifluous voice, not in fear but rather in anticipation.

The sight of him stunned her senses. Now that she was accustomed to his pallor and the odd phosphorescence of his stare, she saw only the dark splendor of his looks. He was a most marvelous looking man. For a moment, he didn't advance or withdraw, giving her the chance to feast in anguished appreciation.

This magnificent man was her husband. In name only.

"Was there something you wanted, *signora*?"

As he spoke, a simmering heat kindled in his unblinking gaze, a fire suggesting that she was not alone in her feelings of need. Mesmerized by the pull of that keen stare, Laure grew light-headed, all shivery hot and cold at the same time. Strangely, it wasn't an unpleasant sensation, that surrendering of awareness to all but the sharp, hungry edge of his attention.

When had she felt it before? She tried, but she couldn't quite grasp the occasion.

But the spark of his interest quickly extinguished, and he looked away from her as if bored by her presence and the mere thought of conversation.

"Speak quickly, madame. I am in a hurry."

"Where are you going?" She hated the petulance she herself heard in that demand. As did he, for his mood chilled perceptively.

"Out."

"Is the claim upon your time such that you cannot spare me even a few minutes?"

Apparently, he responded better to the snap of her temper than to possessiveness. He regarded her indulgently. "You have my attention."

"How do you like what I've done with your home?"

He blinked. "You wish to discuss furniture with me?"

"No. Yes." She took hold of her frustration with a determined breath and forged onward. "There are many things I should like to discuss. I have no idea of your opinions or your tastes and would like to know if you approve of the changes I've made."

A long minute passed. Then another as she refused to fidget beneath his unwavering stare. Slowly, he slanted a look to his left then his right, taking in the nearest rooms and their improvements.

"Well?" Laure prompted.

"I have been accused of having appalling taste, so my opinion has no true value here, but I see nothing that displeases me." Then he turned to her again for a lingering appraisal. "Nothing at all."

Even a room away, she felt engulfed by his intimate study as if his hands were charting the same avenues his gaze was taking. She took a quick step back, unable to stop a sudden shudder. Though she'd prepared herself mentally for the possibility of contact, her body rebelled of its own volition.

True, she'd invited him into her bed. For some strange reason, it had felt natural and appropriate at that time and place. But here and now, with such distance and such uncertainty between them, nothing was less appealing than the thought of his hands upon her.

Heavy hands. Hurtful hands. A cold sweat formed upon her brow. Her stomach clenched, her teeth ground as if to stop the cries to please stop, please don't...

But that hadn't been Gerard, had it? She looked away, anxious and confused by her troubling response.

Noting her aversion, Gerard smiled narrowly.

"Was there something else?"

Recovering herself with some difficulty, Laure came to the point, since idle talk seemed only to irritate him. "I should like to give a party."

His black brows soared. "Isn't it rather late for a wedding reception?"

"For my brother," she clarified, "to honor his success and thank him for all he's done for me. I thought it only appropriate to make this gesture, if you approve."

There was no mistaking his dislike of the subject. "By all means, let's shower him with gratitude. I should like very much to give him what he deserves."

Pretending not to notice his searing sarcasm, she continued. "Not a grand affair, just a small guest list from whom Percy might benefit by acquaintance."

"Ahhh. Other wealthy fools who will be unsuspecting until he has his hands in their pockets and a knife at their throat." His mood turned surly. "Tell me, does he have other sisters with which to bargain?"

Paling at the insult, she mumbled, "Forget I broached the matter."

"But you did, all for dear mercenary Percy's sake. I'm sure he will relish the chance to glory in his new found status. By all means, turn my haven into an orgy of greed. Why should I alone be victimized? Misery loves company, isn't that what they say? Just do not expect me to be in attendance."

"I didn't mean to offend—"

"Offend?" he roared. "Everything about you and your brother offends me!"

And there it was again, the fury he'd displayed so briefly at their wedding ceremony focused upon her with an intensity that had her reeling. Wounded by his undeserved verbal assault, yet too proud to give way to the tears blurring her vision, she countered his attack with a fierce parry.

"Then why did you marry me?"

"Why?" He stared at her, angered, amazed, then finally amused. "What did your brother tell you?"

"Nothing that's proven true thus far."

"So you want the truth, my dear wife?"

A note of malicious pleasure seeped into his tone, and suddenly she wished for blissful ignorance. Whatever he would tell her would bring only pain and more disillusionment. She swallowed down the anxiety, the awful panic inspired by his widely wicked smile. He was daring her, defying her to find the courage.

And so she nodded. "Tell me."

He regarded her with a look akin to pity, and that was worse than the loathing. "Poor girl. You really have no idea, do you?"

"About what?" Her voice trembled slightly as she prepared for her world to collapse.

"I shall tell you everything you want to know and more. But not tonight. Tonight I have other matters more pressing." He dismissed her anxiety with a wave of his hand and no further explanation. "Plan your party. Invite your guests. It shall be a time for celebration...and revelation. So be prepared for both."

He knew.

She was too dazed to notice he'd gone. She found her way into the parlor where she sank down upon one of the new chaises. Her shoulders slumped until her head fit into her hands. There was no mystery as to what would happen next. She knew what would happen next from the experiences of a broken heart. This place she'd taken such pride and enjoyment in, the dreams she'd allowed herself to fragilely believe—that she may have finally found a place where she would be safe—all about to end.

He knew. Somehow, he knew. Between the time he'd agreed to wed her and the moment they first made eye contact at the altar, Gerard Pasquale had discovered the truth about who and what she was.

And now she would pay, just as her mother had paid before her. With the loss of everything.

Akin to the darkness within and without, Gerardo Pasquale skimmed the shadowed alleyways of Vieux Carre. He did so with a precision both efficient and deadly. He'd had over four hundred years to practice.

Orlean's Alley ran along the south side of the Quarter's grand cathedral. During the day, a cadre of young artists used the walks to set up the samples of their trade. Watercolors, oils, pastels, a rainbow of life reflected on canvas. But by night, those who remained to haunt the narrow street lined by wrought iron fences and closed, shuttered doors belonged to a trade much older.

She was a prostitute, probably a good deal younger than her ravaged features and sluttish dress suggested. She laughed softly to herself as her steps faltered in the heeled shoes displayed by an indecently high hemline. Catching one arm about a lamppost, she hugged to it for balance until she saw a prospective customer emerge from the midnight shadows. With a conscious effort, she shifted her shoulders back to offer a small but impressively bared bosom.

"Bonjour. Comment ca va. Etes-vous seul?"

He could smell the liquor on her, not quite strong enough to disguise the decaying scent of disease. Neither discouraged him from the richer, more potent aroma of living being. He wondered if she knew how little time she had left on this earth even without his intervention.

As he drew closer, she released the iron post to totter slightly, sizing him up for potential profit. Fine coat, clean hands, even if he was a trifle pale. Her rouged lips pouted, ripe with promise.

"You would like some company, *non*?"

"No."

At one time, he would have toyed with her first. He would have dazzled her with the beauty of what he was while acting the part of charmer, of courtly swain. He would have savored her seduction, her confusion and sudden horror as she realized her own fate, indulging in a sense of perverse power and wicked pleasure before the final feast. He no longer had the patience for, or interest in, playing with his food.

Any chance outcry was stifled by the clasp of one hand over her mouth. His other arm snaked about her tightly corseted waist, jerking her up against him with a force that left her bruised and breathless. Without pause, he got right to business, biting into the succulent flesh of her throat to feed. She stiffened at the initial shock then went limp in the thrall of his embrace. Any who happened upon them would have thought them engaged in intimacy rather than a more basic exchange of life from death.

It was over too quickly. Staggering from the satiation, Gerard held to the crumpled shell of the woman. The effects of her vitality flowed through him with intoxicating potency. Heat burned along each vein, a warmth that could be supplied by no other source. Finally the lightheadedness and euphoria faded, leaving him in control once again, stronger, eternally renewed.   After slitting the woman's neck, he draped her upon the steps of a recessed doorway. In finding her, there would be evidence of violence that was human rather than supernatural in origin. Concealment was imperative if he was to continue hunting the same streets night after night. Fortunately, New Orleans was a dangerous place to be after twilight, and there was no shortage of criminal doings to cover up the savage means of his own survival.

Leaving his victim on the cold stone steps, Gerard walked away without a second glance, without a trace of remorse. That, too, was a necessity he'd learned long ago. Never confuse them with anything other than a meal. They were not mothers, sons, wives or lovers. They had no pasts, no hopes, no futures left unfulfilled. They existed only to prolong him and those like him. As a superior being, it was his right to demand their ultimate sacrifice and their privilege to supply it, though sometimes not very willingly. After four hundred years and thousands of souls, to believe otherwise would lead to sure madness.

Of course there were some who did not hold to those callous truths. Some suffered the guilty torments of hell when forced to succumb to what they were. His oldest friend was such a being. Dear Gino, writhing in an eternal agony of conscience while Gerard boasted of not having one. A lie, he'd discovered most unpleasantly.

He was not superior. He was damned.

He continued along the shadow-washed streets, turning onto thoroughfares that were teaming with the noise and tempting heat of humanity. Though he moved among them, they could sense his presence with an uneasy chill but never quite see him. These frail, industrious humans going so determinedly about the process of living, not realizing that even as they were born, they were doomed. To what purpose was grubbing for wealth, scheming for influence, mourning the inevitability of death or the fickleness of love. It was all so fleeting, so unimportant to those who saw centuries as humans did years. Silly, greedy mortals, obsessed with possessions and pride. Had he been any different? Had he, in his youthful arrogance, in his insatiable thirst for acceptance, been any different than Percy Cristobel? He shuddered to think so, but it was true.

The sound of sultry laughter distracted him as he passed an open courtyard. He slowed then stopped to watch as two impassioned humans sought their own immortality through the rough, sweaty act of illicit procreation. A young Creole gentleman had ingratiated himself beneath the skirts of a pretty Quadroon maid and theirs was a lusty coupling.

Gerard stood unmoved by their hurried breaths, by the flash of silken café au lait legs wrapped about the young man's waist. He'd distanced himself from his humanity so long ago, it was a puzzle as to why he lingered now, curious and vaguely disturbed by the young couple's passion. It wasn't as though such carnal stirrings acted upon him. Lust for sustenance drove him now just as desire once provoked the man he was into making a fatal error. That error had ended his insignificant life. Odd to think of it now. He didn't bother himself with much reflection about what once was. He told himself he was beyond such trivialities, but in truth, the past brought only pain. Better not to look back. Better not to remember. He was what he was. What came before no longer mattered.

Yet as the rutting pair strove for their final satisfaction, he was reminded again of Gino, who mourned for his lost humanity and tried to pretend he could still pass for one of them. He recalled the mortal his friend had married. Arabella. The name played through his memory like a cherished melody. Such a rare and worthy woman. But human, all too human. And though Gino had found a brief happiness with her, the relationship had been doomed to tragic consequence. He could not wish for a like circumstance even if the rewards, though fleeting, were undeniable bliss.

He would not find such a situation beneath his own roof with the quixotic human he had been forced to wed.

As dusky cries evolved into sated sighs, Gerard walked on, bemused by his strange melancholy. It was the remembering that caused it. The bittersweet envy of what his best friend so briefly enjoyed, and his own involvement in its end. It wasn't Laure Cristobel, now Laure Pasquale, who woke those chafing sentiments within him. No. She wouldn't—couldn't—matter more than a passing inconvenience to be endured and outlived as he had all others.

He was far removed from mortal folly but not above feeling a nostalgic ache for what could never be.

His wife. A cruel irony, a joke of nature tying her vivacious freshness to one as dark and damned to indifference as he had become. He wanted to be indifferent, but as he slipped inside the cavernous halls that she had miraculously changed into a welcoming home, he was annoyingly affected by her presence. She had made it a home. That was some miracle itself. Though his taste ran toward the garish and the colorful, he couldn't deny the calming effect of her subdued choices. Tasteful. Elegant. It reminded him, not in style but in quality, of Gino's home in Florence. How he'd enjoyed visiting there, even though he had always been afraid to sit upon any of the furnishings. He smiled, ruefully, remembering. There was no harm in appreciating the attractive comforts Laure brought back into his life. He'd enjoyed fine things once upon a time, and there was nothing wrong in doing so again.

Just as long as he didn't forget who she was and what he was by thinking the two could ever co-exist as one.

He scented her before actually seeing her there asleep on a damask covered chaise, just as he'd found her that time before. The delicate floral perfume she wore, the salty warmth of her skin, the hot sweetness pulsing beneath it creating the tantalizing flush of health coloring her cheeks, and the rosy curve of her breasts above the rounded neckline of her gown, all enticements. A new dress, he noted. Fashionable, pretty, well made but not extravagant when she could have afforded extravagance. With his money. He would give her that much. She knew how to spend wisely. A trait he'd never mastered when money had mattered.

He crossed the room to stand above her, using his vampiric magic to cloak his presence as she briefly woke then settled back to sleep. So innocently trusting, as she'd been that first night when she'd offered herself to him as his bride. Silly creature, she'd had no idea. Still had none.

He touched her soft cheek, letting his fingertips trail like a whispered breeze along the gentle slope of her jaw, pausing at the junction just below her ear where her life force beat strong and steady. It didn't matter that he'd grown to admire her. It couldn't matter that he enjoyed their brief parry of words, surprised to discover how lonely for simple conversation he'd become.

That was the problem. He'd never been alone since becoming one with the night. He'd never had to face his exiled existence without the benefit of a companion. Bianca, however vile, had still amused and aggravated him. Even after she'd almost succeeded in killing him, he found he missed her startling beauty and clever viciousness. He rubbed his wrists as if he could still feel the silver shackles she'd used to bind him to a wall where he'd waited for sunlight to find him. Treacherous creature. They'd been such a dark and deadly complement to one another. But she was gone, a danger to him even in her absence, and the reason he was careful to remain in seclusion lest she decide to finish what she'd started. He'd come to New Orleans to recover from her betrayal, or had it been the other way around, him betraying her trust? It didn't matter now. At first, he'd lost himself in solitude, needing the quiet to heal in body and soul. Time, always of little consequence, had escaped him as he'd hibernated in these empty rooms, leaving them only to take what he needed from those who didn't matter. And as he'd sunk into that cocooned oblivion, that's when Percy Cristobel had found a way through his defenses.

And for that, the nasty little lawyer would die.

Gerard let a strand of spun gold hair filter through his fingers as his mood grew more complex and restless.

What to do with this one? Should it matter that she was not guilty of her brother's sins of greed? Since when did guilt or innocence make a difference in his dealings with human kind? She was in danger as long as she remained with him not knowing what he was. And he would be in danger from her once she found out that truth.

It was more than Cristobel's meaningless paper that kept him from cold-bloodedly murdering her as she slept. There was something stronger and more disturbing holding him at bay, that curl of panic and uncertainty that leveled his defenses when she'd turned those covers to invite him into her bed. Since then, he'd been careful to avoid her, though ever aware of her proximity.

What was it about her that had him at such a disadvantage?

Would that invitation still be open to him once she knew what she offered to embrace?

He smiled to himself, a slow, self-deprecating twist that mocked himself more than her ignorance.

An ignorance that would soon be shattered by a most unpleasant truth.

SIX

"How lovely you look this evening."

Laure whirled away from the cheval glass in her dressing room, startled by the intruding voice. Alarm eased to a shy welcoming smile when she saw her husband in the adjoining doorway. It led to the second master suite, one she knew he didn't use. With the darkness framing him, he created a stark silhouette of black and white—elegant evening tails to accentuate his sleek foreign looks against a snowy shirtfront and vest that made his complexion that much paler. Only the jewel-like brilliance of his eyes brought color to the image. They glimmered like fiery blue topazes.

"Good evening, sir." She sounded oddly breathless and sought to control her inner trembling with a slow, deep breath. "Does this mean you plan to attend this evening?"

He placed a hand upon the snug satin of his waistcoat. "Perhaps. And my name is Gerard. You may call me that. You are not my servant."

"Yes, of course. Gerard." Then why didn't she feel close to his equal? Even in her glamorous evening gown, she felt the awkward pretender. Anxious not to be a source of shame to him, she fingered the folds of her skirt. "Then the dress is all right? It's not too daring...too red?"

His glittering stare lowered to her hem then rose incrementally up the yards of deep crimson velvet, up the flattering flare of its skirt from heavy twin ruffles to the narrow belt of same colored satin that encased her slender waist. Up the molded bodice that seemed to be suspended in defiance of gravity rather than by the thin off-the-shoulder straps. A large velvet bow rode the dip of her decolletage, revealing a hint of shadowed cleavage. Just enough to incite the imagination. Her fair shoulders were all but bare, dramatically emphasized by red velvet gloves that rose above the elbows. Sparked to life by the glorious shade of the gown, her upswept hair seemed streaked with golden fire. Gerard's gaze lingered, not at the creamy expanse of her bosom but rather at the column of her neck, so regally unadorned.

"If you had wished to catch my attention," he murmured in a husky timbre, "you could not have chosen better."

Had he guessed that to be her intention?

He followed the flush of pleasure as it rose up the sleek expanse of her throat. His raw exhalation sounded before he glanced away. "Who are all these...people scurrying about downstairs?"

"Percy hired them to see to the guests's needs. I hope they won't be a bother to you."

"The attentive host." He held up his hand as if to stop himself from saying more. "But enough of that. I don't want to spoil your evening with my less than flattering opinion of your brother. You should not keep him waiting."

His opinion of Percy hardly phased her. It was his opinion of her that mattered. Laure took a risk by speaking her hopes aloud. "Would you escort me down, Gerard?"

"No."

His single word crushed her excitement. But he tempered it unexpectedly with gentler reasonings.

"This night has nothing to do with me. I would not distract from the cause of celebration."

"But there would be no cause if not for you."

A wry smile shaped his lips. "Perhaps I choose not to be reminded. *A piu tardi.* Until later. Remember," he stated ominously,

"I promised you truths."

She glanced nervously back toward the glass. How to admit that she didn't really want to hear him speak them aloud? It wasn't as if she'd choose to hurry her own doom. Couldn't she just wear the pretense like she wore the gown? She meant to ask but when she looked behind her the doorway was empty. Her husband was gone.

Sighing, she turned back to her reflection. Then her breath caught upon a strange revelation. The mirror clearly depicted the doorway behind her, yet when she'd first heard Gerard's voice, she hadn't seen him there. That's why she'd been so surprised to find she wasn't alone.

Surely just a trick of light.

Or so she told herself as she suppressed a shiver.

What else could it be?

The pinnacle of New Orleans society arrived in a steady stream. Exquisitely garbed, impeccably mannered and unbearably curious. In his tailcoat, nearly salivating as he estimated bank rolls, Percy was careful to dry his palms before greeting each new guest. How could the evening not be a staggering success with the attendance list so elevated. Amongst the crowd, he noted society columnists who were certain to give the affair a glowing review. He was all smiles and ready charm. His sister was undeniably gorgeous and as refined as any of them. The only missing element was Pasquale, and Percy, for one, didn't miss him. His absence would create an intriguing topic of conversation amongst the invited. No harm in that. So far, none had made a connection between his name and the long ago scandal. Perhaps it was too small a ripple in their pedigreed pool. Nervously, he hoped his luck would hold out.

And then that wish knew a terrible death at the arrival of Alain Javier.

As one of the city's wealthiest patrons, Javier had every right to be there. He was handsome, well connected and thought to be a prize any young woman of breeding would be fortunate to snare. Obviously, that's what Miss Edna Farris believed as she clung to the gentleman's arm. The Farrises owned a large import/export business and as such, were on Percy's targeted agenda for prospective clients. As such, he couldn't afford to be rude to Edna's escort.

"Percy, old man. Quite the crush. You and your delightful sister seem to have done well for yourselves."

Percy saw past the smile to the malicious spite in Javier's eyes. The man would hurt them if he could. If he dared.

"Extremely well, Alain." He allowed a slight puff to his chest. "I always knew my Laure would find the best of the best. She didn't fail me."

Javier's smile soured. "I see your ravishing sister, but where is her new husband?"

"Business matters. But don't worry. He'll put in an appearance. He is very, very anxious to meet you."

Javier's eyes twitched, and a tick pulled at the corner of his failing smile. "I should be honored."

He sounded anything but, and Percy grinned to rub in the intimidation. Good. Let the bastard sweat. Anything to keep his mouth shut.

Across the room, Percy saw his sister freeze up, her gaze riveted to Javier.

Please don't let her cause a scene.

"Your Laure doesn't seem too pleased to see me," Alain gloated. "Perhaps she is a bit jealous, eh?" He squeezed his fair pigeon's chin to evoke a wan response from the meek and not very pretty Miss Farris. Obviously, Edna was aware of her beau's roving reputation. "Come, sweetmeat. Let's greet your father and his friends." His tone chilled as he turned back to his host. "We shall have words later, Percy."

Percy swallowed hard and forced his knees not to buckle. How he hoped Pasquale *would* show up, if for no other reason than to give Percy someone to hide behind.

When he caught sight of a lovely young girl taking furs and heavy great coats from their guests, Percy's anxiousness faded as he turned to another part of his plan. He approached the girl casually, waiting

until they were alone. He watched with disapproval as she quickly
snapped the jeweled buttons off an ermine cape and slipped them into
her pocket. He gripped her arm and whispered fiercely, "Do not forget
why you are here. Watch for your earliest opportunity."

"*Oui, monsieur.* I will be ready. Do not forget the amount we
agreed upon."

"Find out what I need to know, and I may even be more
generous."

Greed became the dusky young beauty as she smiled, her black
eyes slitting with calculation. He'd chosen well for his purpose. Her
avarice would not allow her to fail him. Nor would her fear. He
turned away from her just in time to greet his distraught step-sister.

"Percy, what is Alain doing here?"

He took her hand for a hard squeeze. "Compose yourself, my
dear. People are looking."

"I don't care." Still, she gathered her fraying wits to appear more
calm and in control. But she couldn't cool her heightened color. Percy
could feel her trembling.

"I didn't invite him. He came with Farris's daughter. I can't very
well throw him out, can I?"

She drew a breath, beginning to think beyond her panic. "No, I
suppose not. Not without explanation."

"Just stay clear of the man. He wouldn't dare try anything in the
midst of company."

"I cannot relax knowing he's in the same room."

"Smile, Laure, but be on your guard. I shall keep on eye on him,
too. He will not get his hands on you again." His tone toughened. "I
promise."

Laure took comfort from his words. This was her brother's night.
She would not spoil it for him. Even a snake such as Javier would
not strike and reveal his true self to others. That wasn't the way he
did things. He would be on his best behavior as long as he was
stringing along the pallid Miss Farris as a future fiancée. She studied
the timid creature, overcome by a sudden empathy.

"I wonder if she knows the real Alain."

"It's not our business to educate her, Laure," Percy cautioned, caring not at all for the fate of the daughter when it was the father's millions he could feel running through his fingers.

"She should be warned of what he is capable."

"Do not involve yourself." This time, he spoke more forcefully to shake her from that noble intent. "Besides, whom do you think she would believe?"

She glanced back to where the obviously infatuated couple murmured with heads together. Alain could be devastating to a woman's will when he chose to be. She remembered how it had been at first: the flowers, the sweet treats, the poems, the tender smiles. All an illusion for the ugliness of the real man to hide behind. How easily she'd fallen prey to his false charms. Would the insipid Miss Farris fare any better? Would she heed a warning from one of Alain's former attachments?

"You're right, of course," she said with a fatalistic sigh. "It cannot be our concern."

But still, Laure felt a twinge of regret and responsibility as she regarded the cooing pair, well knowing that tender turtledove was a chicken hawk in disguise.

Voleta abandoned her post as soon as all the guests had arrived. Quickly, as to her employer's instructions, she slipped up the wide stairs to the quiet rooms above. There, she conducted a swift and thorough search of the rooms, most of them oddly empty and of no interest to her. Look for hidden passageways and locked doors. She'd earned the opportunity because of her skill with gaining entry to where she should not be.

Percy Cristobel had rescued her from a prison sentence in exchange for doing what she did best. Of course, he didn't hire her to steal from his sister, only to find a secret room where her husband had a treasure hidden. In return was the promise of pay. Not a bad night's work, but she meant to pad that payment wherever possible. Unfortunately, after an exhaustive search of the mistress of the house's room, she discovered that Laure Pasquale owned no valuables other than a string of unexceptional pearls. Those she pocketed.

Or, perhaps her true riches were kept with her husband's treasure.

Greed-fueled by that supposition, Voleta left the dressing room, raising her lamp high to examine the second master chamber. This one was vacant of all but a huge ugly armoire. Her attention peaked the moment she found it was locked. Locks were meant to hide behind. So what did the Pasquales' keep in their hideous painted cabinet?

Expertly, she worked the latch with the thin wires of her trade. She made an excited sound when the catch gave. She opened the door, expecting something. Anything but emptiness.

There was nothing inside.

"Disappointed?"

She turned with a gasp to find herself face to face with a dangerously handsome man. Set in a face of startling angles, his pale eyes gleamed bright, holding her momentarily spellbound. She couldn't move, could barely prompt her tongue to tell her well rehearsed lie.

"I was lost, *monsieur*."

"Yet you had no trouble finding this."

Suddenly the pearls she'd had in her pocket were in his hand. She stared at them, dumbfounded. "But *m'sieur,* those are not mine."

"That I know. They belong to my wife. Which is why I must wonder how you came to have them."

Thinking quickly to save herself from what she considered the worst scenario of going back to jail, she said, "I know that, *monsieur*. She sent me up to get them for her. She'd forgotten to put them on in all the excitement."

"Ummm. A plausible excuse. One easily verified."

He'd made no move toward her, yet Voleta seemed paralyzed by his presence. She tried to remain calm. There would be time for an escape when he led her downstairs. She could slip him in the crowd and exit one of the many doors. Surely, Percy would not abandon her, not if he wanted her to keep silent.

"Let's go ask her," she prompted, "to put your suspicions at ease."

But he still didn't move. Instead his gaze flared, growing lighter, hotter, boring into her brain as if he could read her every secret. He smiled, the gesture slow to unfurl and wicked in intent.

"I would rather not concern my wife with this. What I would like to know is, if you already had what you'd come for, why are you here, in this room?"

"I-I thought I heard a noise."

"From inside this locked cabinet, no doubt."

He advanced upon her, approaching without seeming to move, gliding across the floorboards as if borne upon a cushion of air. Voleta's hair rose in a prickle, stirring upon her arms and at the nape of her neck as she witness something unnatural, something too terrifying to comprehend.

"I am not interested in your clever lies, *signorina*. What I wish to learn is why you are here and who has sent you. Can you tell me that?"

The sudden pressure inside her head made the trembling girl gasp. She pushed her palms to her temples as if to keep him out of her thoughts, but he broke through them as easily as a cracker through the thin shell of a pecan. And, to her own horror, she heard the words tumble out of her mouth.

"It was *Monsieur* Cristobel who paid me for my services. I was to look for the treasure you had hidden somewhere inside the house."

"Treasure," Gerard mused. "Yes, I suppose he would see it that way." His gaze slitted, glittering thoughtfully. "Now, what to do with you, my lovely snoop."

He caressed her cheek with a long-fingered hand, his cold touch sending a shudder through her. Yet, for all her fright, she was powerless to withdraw, having lost her freedom of will to his hypnotic stare.

"Something that will teach both you and our friend Percy a lesson, I think."

And his hand gripped the back of her head with a vise-like strength, wrenching it to one side.

Laure hurried up the stairs, brushing at the wine spill on her skirt. Her own clumsiness was at fault, her nerves stretched taut just knowing Alain to be in the same room. Excusing herself from company, she meant to take a moment to brush out the worst of the stain before it set and to settle her rattled composure before it cracked.

For Percy.

Things were going well for her step-brother. Laure watched him work the room, moving from guest to guest, plying his smile and offering his services to receptive ears. No matter what else the future held, she embraced the knowledge that she'd been able to repay him for at least part of his kindnesses to her. Admiring his cleverness and ambition, she knew he would make the most of this opportunity. All she had to do was endure.

She slipped into her bedchamber and found a cloth with which to soak up the remaining moisture. Not too bad, she decided, if she kept the folds just right. It had been a silly accident. She'd felt a presence at her shoulder, a heated breath against her neck, and in a moment of complete panic, assumed it to be Alain. How grievously she'd shocked the elderly Mister Mountfortaine as she gasped and whirled to face him as if he meant her harm. Like a true gentleman, he accepted her apologies, but she could see the puzzlement in his eyes. As if he questioned her stability.

She questioned it herself.

She'd thought she saw her husband shot and killed on their wedding night. She imagined he cast no reflection in her mirror. And now she was feeling threat where none was due. Alain Javier had shaken her to the soul, and it was time she reclaimed it. She couldn't concern herself with him when she faced Gerard and his unspoken truths at the evening's end. That was the matter that would shape her future, not her painful past with Alain.

There were worse things than being fooled and used by a smooth talking liar.

Brushing at the velvet until the stain barely showed, Laure took an extra minute to check her appearance in the dressing room glass.

Her color was high, her eyes bright, but at least she didn't look on the edge of an emotional collapse.

She only felt that way.

If she could just get through the remaining hours until the last guest said good night.

A quiet moan from the other bedchamber distracted her. Upon closer examination, she could see a faint light glowing beneath the closed door. Someone was in the other room. Gerard? What would he be doing in that cold, empty chamber?

With worried thoughts of what her brother had said about his health, she tapped once then pushed the door open. A staggering sight greeted her.

Gerard was indeed there. And in his arms, swooning from the ecstacy of his embrace, was one of the hired girls she'd seen below.

She must have made some sound of embarrassed hurt for Gerard glanced up. His pale eyes blazed with feverish passion, a desire she'd never been able to kindle even upon inviting him to her bed. Yet he found it here, above a house full of her guests, with a servant girl.

The shock pierced her heart. And with it, one thought. What was wrong with her? What made her so lacking that her own husband would seek out another?

Before he could speak and increase her mortification, Laure fled back into the dressing room, shutting the door on the scene of her misery.

She'd taken three tottering steps when he had her by the arm.

"Laure—"

Another time, she might have been charmed by his use of her name. But the familiarity came too late, on the heels of an unforgivable slight. And it was just the cruel twist of irony needed to change humiliation to outrage.

Laure whirled to confront her husband. That his mouth was still rouged from another's kisses redoubled the insult.

"There is nothing you can say," she began in a low, furious voice that sounded nothing like her own. "But you will listen to me."

He waited for her to go on, expression neither touched by remorse or regret, but construed in a careful blank.

"If you are not interested in any kind of relationship with me as your wife, I can accept that. If you must seek your pleasures elsewhere, that, too, I can endure. But you will not, will *not*, flaunt your infidelities under my roof or in my presence. Is that understood?"

That last cracked under the strain of her anger and upset. The question quivered upon a long silence as hot tears tracked her cheeks unbidden.

"Is that what you think this is about?" he asked at last. "You think I've been unfaithful?"

"I have eyes," she returned ferociously.

"But they do not see."

"They've seen enough for one evening. Excuse me." Laure drew herself up into an imperious column of dignity and disdain. "I have guests below."

He didn't try to stop her again.

After all, what could he have said?

SEVEN

With righteous upset and a deeper ache of betrayal clouding her senses, Laure swept down the stairs, meaning to rejoin the party as soon as the telltale flush cooled in her cheeks. Because she was focused to that end, she failed to see a figure lingering in wait. A dangerous mistake. The instant she reached the foyer floor, a hand closed none too gently on her elbow, jerking her sideways into shadow, where no one from the party could see them. Terror wedged up in her throat to silence her cry of alarm upon recognizing her assailant.

"Good evening, Laure. I hadn't had a chance to congratulate you on your wedding yet. It did not take you long to land on your feet, did it?"

She dragged in air and a fortifying anger through the thickening of fear. "I'll thank you to take your hand off me, Alain. You're attention is undesirable."

"Not like it once was."

"Once, perhaps. But no more. Not once I realized the kind of man you were."

Javier leaned in close, his whiskeyed breath scorching her averted face. The pressure of his fingers bit into her arm, but she would betray no pain to feed his pleasure.

"And what kind of man is your new husband? Did Percy try to

auction off your charms to him as well? Vastly overrated charms, or hasn't he discovered that for himself yet?"

She refused to show him any reaction as he gave a nasty chuckle. He pitched his voice more intimately.

"Does he know the truth about you? I warrant he doesn't, since he's set you up here like a queen. You should have treated me better, then I would have been inclined to keep to my silence. As it is, you and your brother are going to have to find a way to secure it. Can you think of a way, my lovely?"

Combating her panic, her stomach roiling at the thought of his cruel touch, Laure returned his threat. "And what of Miss Farris and her family? Do they know the truth about you? Would they be so willing to let you escort their only daughter if they knew the delight you take in hurting helpless women."

"You are hardly helpless from what I understand. And you will keep your mouth shut, or you will suffer worse than a few bruises."

"What are bruises compared to the horrors she'll have in store if you convince her to believe you're sincere in your well pretended affection?"

He shook her, hard. The force of it snapped her head back and set her ears ringing. Before she could recover herself, Javier yanked her up roughly.

"Be careful what you say—"

"I would be careful, were I you."

The silky intrusion of a low, accented voice distracted Javier from his intimidation. He released Laure as he turned to face the unknown interloper. He had never met Gerard Pasquale, but something in the penetrating ice of the man's stare convinced Javier of his identity. And because he suddenly feared that glare more than he was intimidated by the man's money, he was quick to avert offense.

"Forgive me, Mr. Pasquale. I forgot myself. Your wife and I are old friends and—"

Gerard brushed aside his hurried speech as easily as he pushed the man out of the way. His attention fixed on Laure's pallid face. "Are you all right, *cara*?"

She nodded stiffly, careful not to make eye contact with either man.

"Good," he drawled as his gaze slid toward Javier once more. There was no mistaking the malevolence glittering in the silvery depths. "Then I will, perhaps, forgive the insult of seeing another man with his hands upon my wife. This time. You understand?"

Before Javier could finish his agreeing nod, Gerard had him by the throat, lifting him off the ground effortlessly with one hand. Dangling there, purpling in distress, Javier's eyes bugged as Gerard continued calmly.

"I will not be so tolerant should you forget yourself again."

And he let just a hint of his true nature show through, just a glimmer of the violence that would await Javier if his manners slipped again.

The instant Javier's feet touched the floor, he scrambled away like the coward he was, leaving Laure to explain as best she could the circumstances Gerard had come upon. But instead of demanding an account, he asked even more quietly, "You are certain he did not harm you? You are very pale."

"Just taken by surprise, is all."

Then she was surprised by the sudden weakness spreading along her limbs. As her knees buckled, Gerard caught her easily with the loop of one arm about her waist, turning her up against his chest. She leaned there gratefully while pindots of sickness swirled behind her closed eyes. She clutched to the fabric of his evening coat, feeling him recoil slightly, though he didn't withdraw his support. Finally, she experienced the light brush of his hand upon her hair, a brief, soothing gesture that quieted the coils of nausea and woke awareness of the man who held her in his arms. It was difficult to recall her earlier fury with him as she drew upon his silent strength.

Her cheek resting against his chest, her hand over his heart, the realization came to Laure in gradual degrees. The lack of warmth his closeness should have yielded. The utter stillness of him. No rise and fall of his shirt front. No tympani of life beneath her palm. It was almost as if—

As the incredible thought struggled to form upon a disbelieving mind, Gerard set her away from him with a gentle firmness. His expression was unreadable.

"You should rejoin your guests."

Nonsense. She was thinking nonsense. Just the strain of the moment, the hysteria of shock. Her husband was a living, breathing, man not something that had travelers crossing themselves on the road at night.

He'd come to her rescue, hadn't he? That made him no monster in her eyes. But suddenly she felt the need for people around them, for normal conversations and the sound of laughter to drown out the suspicion borne of his one time words as they came back to hauntingly whisper.

...no man at all.

"Our guests," she corrected firmly, slipping her hand through the crook of his elbow. She looked up with a patient expectation, denying their previous clash, tamping down her half-realized fears. This was her husband, and this was their home. It was as simple as that for the moment. He'd made it that simple when he'd stepped between her and Alain,and became the only man to have ever put himself in harm's way on her behalf.

And that meant more than any suspicions.

She smiled.

"Shall we?" Gerard gestured toward the double parlor, where the sound of gaiety seemed a lifetime away from the sudden intensity of his gaze. She lost herself there for a long moment, dazzled as much by his actions as by his outer beauty.

"Thank you, Gerard."

"*Non importa, mia moglie.*" He lifted her hand with a courtly leisure to press against the coolness of his lips. In contrast, his eyes burned.

That heat warmed through Laure like a thousand unmet promises.

Gerard's presence at her side created an immediate stir through the crowded room. But none were as amazed and curious as Percy.

Pasquale's genial front and his sister's obvious affection for him were more than just a little unexpected. The impossible came to him in a sudden shock of clarity. What if they formed an alliance?

How long before he was pushed out of the equation?

Anxiously, he scanned the elegant company, searching for the pretty little thief, Voleta. She was not among them. Perhaps even now, she was uncovering the leverage Percy needed to control Pasquale.

If he could discover where Pasquale lay during the daylight hours, the creature would be at his mercy.

So he continued to smile and ingratiate himself to their wealthy guests, coming away with six scheduled meetings and more than a dozen possibilities to follow up on. A successful night. But greedy Percy wanted it all. As the last of the company was filing out, he caught sight of Voleta at the far side of the room. She was reeling slightly, unsteady on her feet. The little tart was drunk!

Outraged, Percy escaped from the duties of host as quickly as possible to hurry to where the Creole girl slumped in a near swoon in one of the arched doorways.

"Fool," he hissed, giving her arm a hard shake. But the rest of his scolding came to a halt when she spilled bonelessly against him. He noticed then her extreme pallor and the dazed quality of her stare. And when he helped her regain her balance, her head lolled loosely, exposing the true reason for her lethargy. It wasn't drink...or at least, no drink she'd taken.

His gaze fixed in horror upon the puncture wound on her throat.

There was something about her husband that drew their guests to him. From his wry smile and detached humor, Laure guessed he believed his money was the magnet. But she knew differently. For the men, it was the smug confidence and power he exuded, an irresistible challenge. For the women, it was an exotic and slightly dangerous charm—a lethal combination. Though he offered little conversation, his rare comments were crisp with the bite of wit and private amusement. She realized with some surprise that he was enjoying himself as the center of attention, despite his claim to shun notoriety.

And on his arm, the frequent focus of his sultry glances, Laure floated on a cloud of excitement and pride. She was Mrs. Gerard Pasquale, accepted and sought after by the peerless gathering. It was the dream her mother once held for her, reborn. For the moment, she could pretend that she was deserving of their deference, that the intriguing man beside her had invested more than his name and his monies into their marriage. For the moment, she had a glimpse of the happiness her mother must have known, and she understood why all the sacrifices had been made. And she knew she'd made the right choice in those she'd offered up as well.

If only the illusion could last beyond the last guest's good night.

If only reality wasn't waiting when she turned on her husband's arm to see Percy slipping money into the pocket of the woman she'd seen in Gerard's room.

For what service was he paying the girl?

She couldn't help remembering Gerard's startlement when she'd accused him of adultery. Of what was he guilty then? Or had she been totally mistaken?

"Come, *cara*," Gerard crooned down softly, noticing where her attention was focused. "It is time for you to discover the truth."

Laure hesitated, perplexed by the coldness that came over his gaze in contrast to the lulling quality of his voice. What devastation was he preparing her for? She glanced at Percy. A huge welling of protectiveness demanded that she separate him from her troubles. She placed her other hand upon Gerard's sleeve, halting his advance and drawing a questioning look.

"No matter how disappointed you may be in me, please do not blame Percy. He is innocent of any wrongdoing beyond a brother's desire to see his sister safe."

Gerard's black brow canted upward in a disbelieving arch. "I highly doubt your brother is as sinless as you think."

"Can you fault him for wanting to see his only family well provided for?"

"Cara, it may disillusion you to discover that your well-being is hardly his priority."

"Of course it is. Why else would he have gone so far to convince you that I am...worthy of you? The sins are mine, not his."

Now he looked impatient, and his tone was gruff with it. "The only sin from which you suffer seems to be ignorance."

"But if you know the truth about me, then you know—" She broke off in confusion.

He stared at her so strangely.

"What exactly are you confessing to?"

She looked down in humility. "To the secrets of my past. I don't know how you found out..."

His hand forked beneath her chin, lifting her head so he could command her shimmering gaze. "I have no idea what you are talking about. I don't know what secrets of yours you fear I've exposed. This is not about you, Laure. It's about me and the bargain your brother has forced me to make and the lies he has told to get you to comply."

She began to shake her head but his fingers tightened, stilling the movement.

"You need to know the terms to the bargain you've made. You may find yourself unable to keep them."

"All right," she said at last, sounding more composed than she felt inside. Inside, her belly jumped with anxiety. Defensiveness began to build an insulating wall about her heart in preparation for the pain. He was going to get rid of her. He was going to break the vows they'd spoken and cast her back into uncertainty. "Tell me about this bargain."

"What did your brother tell you about me that made you agree to marry me?"

"That you were rich and would provide for us both," she told him.

He frowned. "That's what you think I expected to hear. What is the truth? Your truth?"

"That you were an eccentric recluse suffering from a lingering illness. That you sought a companion to lighten your loneliness."

When she spoke those things aloud, she realized how naive her reasonings sounded. But amazingly, Gerard didn't scoff at them.

"So it was pity for my circumstance rather than greed that motivated you."

Something pulled in his voice, a hint of prideful anguish that had her quick to deny his conclusion. "No. Not pity. Understanding. I thought I'd found a kindred spirit. I thought we could be...good for one another. Now you may laugh at my foolishness."

But he didn't laugh. Instead, his thumb stroked lightly across her lips before he let his hand drop away.

"You have been cruelly deceived by one you trusted. And now you are bound in a marriage mockery. As you were unaware of the circumstances and innocent of guile, I am willing to let you go without repercussions."

"Let me go? I don't understand. Do I displease you that greatly?"

A frustration of anger and regret flashed through his eyes. "I am giving you your freedom. Take it and run. While you can."

"Where would I go?" she asked in all honesty. "I have no home but here."

"This is no home. It's a prison! What you risk under this roof is more than your life. It's your immortal soul."

"I-I don't understand," she cried out. Why was he being so harsh? So fierce? Why didn't he just say he didn't want her? That would be enough to make her go. Her throat ached, and her head pounded miserably. She wanting nothing more than to go to her room and hide, to pretend this whole matter was behind her and forgotten.

But Gerard wouldn't let it go.

"You want to understand? Then come with me."

He dragged her across the room with him, to where Percy was trying to get an uncooperative serving girl into her coat. Tears burned Laure's eyes as she fought both her husband's compelling force and the facts he would make clear to her. For with that clarity, she feared she would lose all.

Who was this girl to him? Why did she stare at him so dreamily? Was this the woman with whom he spent his nights when he was not at home? Thinking it was bad enough without having the truth pushed into her face.

"Tell her," Gerard commanded of Percy as the little lawyer regarded him in apprehension and dismay. "Or just show her. It's past time that she knew the truth."

Gerard gripped the collar of the girl's coat and pulled it away. Incomprehensibly, Laure stared at the raw puncture wounds on the girl's throat.

"This is the illness I suffer from, dear ignorant girl. This is the kind of monster your sweet brother has wed you to. Now do you understand?"

She tried to shake her head in denial, but even as she began the move she was seeing her husband's unnatural pallor, the way he cast no reflection in her glass, the way he'd survived a bullet to the chest because his heart no longer beat within it. Part of her had already guessed what her mind still refused to accept.

The whispers she'd heard at her grandmother's knee, stories of the undead, stories meant to fright, not to be believed, prepared the way for the single name she mouthed in dawning horror.

"Revenant."

"My name is Gerardo Pasquale. I should have died four hundred years ago. Go while you still can," he prompted viciously. "Run from the demon you have wed."

That was all she heard as a low-pitched hum began to swell within her ears, filling her head until it overcame her consciousness.

"Run while you can."

EIGHT

Awareness came back to her in slow, rhythmic waves, lapping at her senses then easing away before she could seize upon it. There was a reason she sought oblivion. It lingered just out of reach, something dark and frightening enough to send her into hiding amid the grey mists of unconsciousness. Something she didn't want to remember.

A cool damp cloth touched to her brow. It's chill was the reviving shock she needed to coax her from her purposeful retreat.

"It's all right, Laure."

Percy?

"He's gone now. He can't hurt you."

He, who? Alain? Panic jolted through her. But no, his threat was ended by...by Gerard. Gerard, the man she'd married who was not a man at all.

Her husband, the monster who walked the night.

With a protesting moan, she pushed away Percy's well-intentioned care. Opening her eyes, she found herself in her own bed, the bed she'd never shared with the one who'd given her his name.

"Where is he?" Her words came out thick and raw.

"Where does he go when daylight approaches? I don't know. Are you feeling better?"

Feeling better? An incredibly foolish question. But gradually, she began to feel stronger, more capable of confronting the truth this night had forced upon her. Slowly, she sat up, waiting for the shivers of hot and cold nausea to settle and finally leave her. What remained was an emptiness spreading to the core of her being.

"You knew what he was." Statement of fact, not accusation. She wasn't ready to assign blame or levy guilt. Not until she understood all of it.

"None of what I told you about him was a lie," Percy said in his own impossible defense.

"But it wasn't the truth, either."

"I went to great lengths to insure your safety, Laure. Believe me, you would have come to no harm at his hands. I saw an opportunity—"

"Yes, you did. An opportunity to latch onto his considerable wealth—"

"And to save you. Do not forget that. That was not a lie, Laure. Pasquale offered the perfect solution." A pause. "He still does."

"Still? How could you think that?"

"So, you've discovered the truth. What does that really change?" He spoke as if she'd just learned that her husband walked in his sleep. Her husband walked at night. To kill to survive.

Her laugh was a bitter parody of mirth. "It changes everything, Percy. Everything."

His anguished expression was too much for her. Laure covered her face with her hands, hands that were none too steady. She tried to breathe, tried to keep her mind clear, while astounding and awful facts assailed her.

A revenant. The undead.

She searched back through the stories her grandmother had told her. The truths of her old religion didn't consider death to be a cessation of life. Rather, in death, one merely changed from one condition to another. It was the placement of the soul that mattered.

What was the state of Gerardo Pasquale's soul?

The only way she could protect herself now was with knowledge.

"What manner of creature is he?" How difficult it was to consider Gerard as a creature of darkness rather than as a man deserving of her compassion.

"He's walked as a vampire since the 1400s. Or at least that's how far back the records go. He survives on the blood of the living and hides like one of the dead during the day. That's all I know." Percy evaded her gaze, looking uncomfortable in revealing those truths. It brought the horror of what he'd done out into the open. He'd married her to a ghoul.

She couldn't control the shudder that swept through her with an ominous chill. The image of the servant girl did a damning dance before her memory's eye. A laugh strangled in her throat. Oh, to be so naive again as to think infidelity was all she had to fear.

"Tell me of this bargain you made with him. Tell me the truth, Percy."

And so he did, embellishing the nobility of his own motives until she grew impatient with them. She was seeing Percy in a new light, one as bright and clear as a fresh dawn after a long, concealing night. No matter how sincere his protestations, he had used her. He had capitalized upon her fear and innocence to make an unholy alliance. For his own benefit, definitely. For the community, that was in question. For her? Perhaps she would never know. That truth was confused by a coloring of obligation and gratitude. Whatever his reasons, she could not deny his rationale. Pasquale was a powerful force, with the fortune and influence to protect her from those who would do her harm.

But who would protect her from him?

"So what will you do?" Percy asked at last, more than a little worried by what she might say. His future hung upon the schemes he'd woven behind her back. With the pull upon one thread, she could unravel the whole of his ambitions.

"I don't know," came her honest reply, the only one she could give him. There was so much to absorb. So much to comprehend. Too much, too soon for her to make an arbitrary choice based on what little she yet understood.

"Will you stay or go?"

All hinged upon her willingness to hold fast in this unnatural home. Percy knew it, and he didn't like Laure knowing it.

She smiled faintly. She'd already admitted that sad truth to Gerard. Where else could she go? Not back to Percy. Not to her mother's people. Not to where the Alains of the world could further misuse her. Where else remained?

"Go home, Percy. I have much to consider."

"But Laure—" She could see he was desperate for some sign of assurance. And she was unwilling to give him one at the moment.

"Go home. Let me think. Do nothing rash for the moment. I will talk to you soon."

Forced to settle for that vague answer which didn't please at all, Percy nodded.

And once she was alone, Laure lay back against her pillows to think on what best to do.

A revenant.

It explained everything. With that certainty came the relief that she wasn't going mad. She had seen with her own eyes the proof of his dark existence. Only now could she admit to herself what she had guessed already within the resistant recesses of her heart.

Her husband was a vampire.

She'd been raised to believe such things were possible. She'd been taught of the *baka*, the evil spirits who roam at night to possess the unwary. The *loup garou*, the leopardmen, and those who could transform into invisible birds of prey. The bogeymen parents frightened their children with to get them to stay safely in bed at night. She knew all these things. They were a part of her hidden heritage, but she'd always thought of them as stories, folklore.

Until now.

Now the truth had placed a ring upon her finger and called her 'wife.'

But did having a new name to give him change what she already knew about her husband?

Did it change the fact that she was dangerously close to falling in love with him?

He woke as he always did, from drifting nothingness to complete awareness, with the last dying ray of the sun. Century after century, it was always the same, the first razor-sharp roar of thirst threading through his withered veins, the surge of dynamic energy, and the sense of sameness, that the moment replayed over and over to an eternity. But on this night, he woke to newness, to uncertainty, and for the first time in a long time, to anticipation.

Would she still be there beneath his roof? His bold, combative beauty. Or would the truth have driven her away in understandable horror? In his excitement to find out which, he was able to disguise his own anxiousness. He was simply curious, he told himself, not that what one silly mortal did mattered to him in the least.

But oh, how quiet the huge house would be without her in it. From comfortable home back to mausoleum again.

It wasn't as if he would miss her.

As he moved through the rooms now populated with furnishings all speaking to her taste and conservative judgement, Gerard reached out mentally to find her. When he couldn't touch upon her unique essence, an annoying agitation settled upon him.

Where was she?

It wasn't as if he feared she'd fled; he just wanted to know his situation. Would he have to pull up stakes—how he loved that quaint phrase—in order to protect himself? Or would he be better served by charming her into silence and an uneasy co-existence? He didn't consider her wishes. If her own brother didn't, why should he? He was only interested in his own survival, after all. His own interminably long and lonely existence.

Where was she if not within these rooms? Within these walls?

He prowled the house, reluctant to go out and seek his own satisfaction until he knew the way of it. She couldn't have gone far. She'd left her belongings in her room. Her scent filled that living space. Her heat lingered in delicious traces upon the bed linens, so he knew she'd slept there only recently. He breathed both in, fueling his restlessness, feeding his impatience with an unfamiliar type of hunger, one that teethed on his emotions most cruelly.

He paced the front rooms that still echoed of life and laughter. If he were to be honest with himself, he would have to admit that he'd enjoyed the room full of company. There was such amusement to be found in moving amongst the masses, indulging in their inconsequential troubles. Such irony in inviting them to dine without them knowing they might at any moment be the main course. How he'd missed being entertained over these last years of solitude. He knew, of course, that immortality was as much the will to go on as it was the cleverness to continue unobserved. His will had ebbed of late, and Laure, his unlikely bride, had restored it.

"No wonder you hated me so."

Her soft claim intruded upon his thoughts, startling him because he hadn't felt her arrival. His preternatural senses had failed to detect her approach. A failure as dangerous as it was disturbing. Yet there she stood in the black and white foyer as if she'd just materialized there. He regarded her warily, wondering how it could have happened. Did she distract him so greatly as to put himself in jeopardy?

"Where have you been?"

She didn't respond to his question as if lost to her own discoveries. "I didn't understand at the wedding," she continued in that same factual tone. "I had thought it was a mutual arrangement, not one that had been forced upon you. Like I was."

He narrowed his eyes. What was this? Apology? Was she telling him good-bye? How strongly he rebelled at that possibility. He waited, unwilling to reveal his sentiments until he'd heard all of hers.

"You must have believed I knew and approved of Percy's scheme. I did not, I assure you, though you've no reason to believe me."

"I know your brother. That is proof enough," he stated generously, willing to concede to her ignorance of the clever plot.

She shifted uncomfortably. He waited. Her features were wan, as if she'd known little sleep. Understandable under the circumstances. Yet, he marveled that she was here, boldly confronting a monster that would send most running for their lives, not calmly discussing their future options.

"You're not afraid of me?"

Her gaze rose to his, hers steady with a flicker of worry behind the sincerity. "Of what you are, perhaps. Of you, surprisingly not. I have confronted worse things and survived. Should I be afraid?"

He laughed. Should she be? Indeed. He had roamed the nights, a terror of unspeakable origin, feasting off the unsuspecting, indifferently destroying fragile mortals like herself for centuries. Should she be?

"Yes. Very."

"Do you mean me harm?"

His lip curled back into a sneer. "Do you ask if your brother's threats hold me at bay? I am contained by no natural law of man, by no intimidation from a puny mortal source."

She had the nerve to smile slightly at his arrogant speech. He scowled, brows lowering to a menacing degree.

"If you know what I am, you know what I can do. Are you foolish enough to think you are safe?"

"I am curious enough to ask why you have not harmed me thus far."

He huffed and blustered over that for a moment. Why hadn't he, if all his boasts were true? If he wasn't shackled by the fear of breaking Percy's bargain, what then kept him from ripping the two of them to shreds for their outrageous impudence? He began to pace again, searching for a way out that would reveal no weakness.

"So, you have complaints about my hospitality? Have I given you reason to believe you were not safe in your own bed?"

"Repeatedly, sir."

It was his turn to smile. "Ahhh, yes." He faced her then, expression filled with his perplexity. "Why have you stayed? Why have you returned now that you know to what you've been unfairly wed?"

"This is my home. You are my husband."

She made it sound so simple. Yet it could not be. Would not be. Could it?

He frowned and began to pace again.

"I do not understand you. You know what I am, and you are willing to remain here, beneath this roof. Are you stupid, girl? Have you no care for your own future? Do you think your obligation to your brother takes more importance than the continuation of your life beyond the next few moments?"

Still she regarded him unflinchingly, that small defiance goading his temper, as if his demands that she consider her safety gave her courage to remain.

Foolish woman. He didn't care about her safety. If she knew that, why did she remain? Why did she speak to him as if nothing had changed between them?

"This is not about Percy. My debt to him was paid last night. He deserves no further payment for his scheming. I will see to Percy."

"Then why remain? Is it the money? I could give you enough to make it in your best interest to go away."

Her voice quieted. "Is that what you wish? For me to go away?"

"Do not try to confuse the issue by being clever."

"I am not being clever. I am asking for honesty."

He made an uncharitable noise. "Is that all?"

"Yes. That's all. If you wish me gone, speak it plain, and I will be. I'll see that Percy is no further threat."

He stared at her, trying to see through her calm facade to some scheme, some insincerity. It bothered him that he could find none. "You would go, just like that, walking away from all this, from all the money?" *From him.*

"I have no wish to remain where I am not wanted. None of the rest matters. When I agreed to wed a stranger, it was not to claim his wealth or his social standing. Nor was it to please Percy."

"Then why, *cara*. Why the noble sacrifice?"

She ignored his sarcasm, her uncomfortable frankness unwavering. "Because I wanted a home, a place to belong. A rich place, a poor place, it didn't matter. I have spent my life on the outside looking in. I wanted to know what it was like to be safely inside."

Gerard looked away. Distressing memories clouded his heart and mind, memories of a young Florentine so greedy for acceptance that he would abandon his conscience, betray his friend, even embrace the horror of what he'd become. Yes, he understood that yearning all too well.

"You should have chosen a safer place."

This time, the truth of her dire circumstances escaped through her sad smile. "It is not as though I had many options, sir."

"A pity that a monster like me was the best you could do. Most would just as soon leap out into the waters of the Mississippi were their situations so grim."

"I am not like most people. And I am quite adept at sleeping in the bed I've made." She smiled again to remind him of the reference. "Even if I don't rest particularly well while in it."

He laughed. He couldn't help himself. She was so delightfully provoking, so refreshingly candid. "No, you are not like most dreary mortals. You amuse me, and that is no small feat. You may remain for as long as it suits us both. But you must make me one promise."

"Yes?" Relief was carefully tempered with caution as she waited for him to name it.

"You will not forget the nature of what I am."

For a moment, she was wise enough to appear afraid.

Slowly, she reached into the bodice of her gown to withdraw her slender silver chain. From it, dangled a delicate crucifix. As he grimaced and glanced away, she stated quietly, "I will not forget. I will do my best to protect us both from those natures we cannot always control." She let the chain trickle back out of sight.

"*Buono.*"

"And I have a promise to exact from you."

His brows made a haughty arch at her impertinence. "Yes? And what might that be?"

"That you will not avoid me. That we should take the time to talk as we are now. I will do my best to amuse you."

Again, the soft chuckle. "And so you shall."

He regarded her for a long moment and as he did, unbidden

hunger began to rise. The scent of her flared his nostrils and scalded along his veins. He let it come on, the need, the lust for life she carried with each strong beat of her heart. He allowed the subtle changes to come over him. The eerie, quicksilver brilliance heat his gaze. Taut edges of urgency sharpened the angles of his face. The points of his teeth elongated into deadly fangs. And he watched her closely as she observed his altered state. He saw the awareness widen her eyes, the terror to quicken her pulse into a rapid flutter. And yet, she held her ground.

"Can you still claim to be unafraid?" he mocked with a dark pleasure.

"No," came her faint, truthful whisper.

"Good. This is what I am, and you should fear me. Always." He cloaked the horror of his vampiric self, and her fright was quickly replaced by a wary understanding. "Now, I must go out and tend to my...appetite."

Her pallor rose with a sudden, dramatic blanching. "Yes, of course," she murmured in a tone so weak no mortal would have heard her.

"Get some sleep, *cara*. You may rest easy on this night. You have my word."

Some of her color ebbed back, along with the flash in her eyes. "And I should take it?"

"At face value," he said with a grin.

When he smiled, all that was unholy fled his features, and Laure found herself lost to his devilish charm. A deal with a devil. That was what she'd made.

But what was worse, the devil she recognized or the one that stalked unseen?

She hadn't known until these past minutes what she would choose to do, run or hold her ground. But talking with him, enjoying his wry humor, his splendid looks, she saw only her husband. She'd become accustomed to his oddness. As she would become accustomed to his true nature, given time. She was like a small animal who, once having burrowed safely into a hole to avoid the sharp talons of the hawk, was unwilling to be driven out by the badger. Both were dangerous. Neither could be trusted not to act upon their basic instincts.

But Gerard had never pretended to be other than he was. She had lived with that truth, though unsuspecting, for over a month and had come to no harm.

The truth was, she felt safer in the badger hole than exposed to the dangerous world outside it.

"Good night, Gerard," she bid him quietly. "And I will sleep well. At least on this night."

NINE

A deep, restful sleep was followed by dreadful nausea the moment Laure tried to get out of bed. She lay there, hoping her stillness would quiet the roiling of her stomach. As beads of moisture broke upon her brow, the truth had an equally sickening impact.

She was pregnant.

She just knew, without question. A new life stirred within her, created under appalling circumstance, making its presence known to her at the most inconvenient of times. How could she establish a relationship with her husband while another man's seed blossomed in her womb?

How could she follow Percy's advice by keeping her condition secret?

At least she didn't have to worry about Gerard finding her hanging over the commode each morning.

Her mind awhirl with consequence, Laure tried again, more gradually, and this time successfully, to rise. Dizziness made her progress slow, but she'd accomplished her dressing by the time she heard company knocking.

Pausing long enough to run a brush through her hair and to pinch some color into her cheeks, she made her way to the front door, surprised to see Percy there at such an early hour.

"I didn't hear from you and grew worried."

His agitation spoke more clearly than his hurried words. He couldn't stand the suspense any longer.

With a sigh, she held the door open. "Come in, Percy. I was about to have some tea. Will you join me?"

Impatient with her courtesy, he managed a curt nod. She left him seated on the edge of a parlor sofa while she went to heat the water and prepare a tray with cups and dry biscuits that she thought might settle well in her still nervous stomach. By the time she carried the service into the parlor, his fingers drummed upon knees that bounced up and down in a restless rhythm. He waited anxiously while she poured.

"As you can see," she said at last, "I am perfectly fine."

"And Pasquale?"

"He is fine as well."

"You know what I mean, Laure," he cut in crisply.

"Yes, Percy, I believe I understand you quite well." Her dry response didn't calm him in the least. She paused a moment, letting him chafe and sweat before adding, "Gerard and I have reached our own understanding. I will be remaining here."

The breath exited the little lawyer in an audible rush. "So he's no longer angry—"

"Not at me." Her cool reply gave him no comfort.

"And what is his attitude toward me?" he squeaked out.

"Justifiable, I would say. You've behaved most shamefully, Percy, and that will stop."

He regarded her blankly for a long beat, considering her flat command like an unexpected attack, then he smiled. "Whatever you wish, Laure."

A month, even a week ago, suspicions wouldn't have prickled at her nape. But then, she'd been blissfully ignorant of her step-brother's mercenary side. She would leave him no illusions that that state of grace still existed.

"You may remain as our solicitor."

Again, the gust of relief, this time premature.

"But there will be conditions."

His good humor fled. "Oh? And they are?"

"You will immediately set up a fund to help the needy from the dowry you received. It must only be dispensed from with my signature."

Percy's features tightened, a tapestry of disapproval stretched upon a merciless frame.

"You will then amend the agreement granting me instead of you power of attorney."

"Is that all?" he asked through gritted teeth.

"For the moment."

"These were Pasquale's suggestions?"

"No. He gave me leave to deal with you as I saw fit."

"And you are dealing with me quite harshly considering all I've done for you." The petulant tug of his words would have humbled her at one time but not now.

"Percy, you know you have my unending gratitude. But it is not limitless. From the contacts made the other night, you should be well on your way to a great success in the circles you desire. I owed you that much, but no more."

His eyes narrowed for a long moment then the slitted corners relaxed with forced congeniality. "You are right, Laure. I should not expect to live off your generosity. It would be most unfair. I will see to your terms as soon as I'm able."

Laure, too, relaxed, glad to have the confrontation at an end. Though she knew she was right in what she demanded, it didn't make her feel good about clipping Percy's financial wings. She did owe him her life, and now her very happiness. And she'd repaid him with the means to make his own way. It wouldn't be a difficult way, knowing Percy's shrewd mind for making the best of any given situation.

"One more thing," she added. Her somber tone warned him of her seriousness, and he was all wary attentiveness. "You will never in any way threaten my husband again. If you do, I will see that all you've gained will turn to losses. Is that understood?"

"Clearly, dear Laure. Apparently you have been paying heed to my bargaining skills, for you wield them quite effectively. Your tea is growing cold."

She sipped it cautiously and grimaced as her stomach took a nasty roll.

"Are you all right?"

"Yes," she assured him, panting into the distress. Her face once again grew slicked with cold perspiration.

Unconvinced, Percy rose up and came to her, gently easing her head down to her knees. "Breathe slowly and wait for the sickness to ease," he advised. Then came his summation. "You're with child."

Finally, she sat back and wiped her damp brow and neck with the handkerchief her brother offered. "I fear I am."

"And what have you told Pasquale?"

"Nothing yet. Oh, Percy, I don't know what to tell him. The issue of trust is so fragile between us. If I tell him of my condition now, he'll never believe I didn't conspire to trap him into providing for my—my bastard child."

"You could always go to Javier."

"Never! He must never know of this. Percy, you must promise me!"

"He'll not learn of it from me," he vowed, patting her cold hand comfortingly. "You...you don't fear Pasquale enough to consider ridding yourself of the child, do you?"

"No," she whispered in horror, then more strongly, "No. The circumstance of its conception is not the child's fault. I will think of some way to tell him."

"Go carefully, Laure." Percy squeezed her hands between his in earnest. "As of now, this child is Pasquale's legal heir unless he decides to publically disavow it. Your future is assured as long as he doesn't have that opportunity."

"What are you suggesting, Percy?"

"Nothing, my dear. I only want you to proceed with caution. Talk to me before you go to him with the truth. That way, I can make sure you are both protected. Will you do that much for me? Do you have enough faith left to give me that promise?"

He looked so unhappy with the thought of her distrust that she leaned forward to embrace him. "Of course, I do, Percy. I know you have my best interest at heart. After all you've done for me, I'll never doubt that."

Right up until the time I crush you, he thought, smiling fiercely over her shoulder.

As Percy bent to click the lock of his office door open, a strong hand gripped him by the back of the neck, propelling him forcefully into the room. Stumbling, he caught himself and turned to identify his attacker. The room was dim, the shades pulled against the slant of afternoon sun. A huge figure stood silhouetted in his open doorway. His eyes widened in alarm as he heard the man's knuckles pop as beefy hands fisted at his sides. The message was clear. He was going to take a painful beating as payment for something he'd most certainly done.

Just when Percy was considering which would be his best option—trying to flee past the behemoth or dropping to his knees for some serious begging, the giant stepped aside to let a smaller, leaner shape pass. Percy didn't need daylight to know who it was.

"Javier," he wheezed then cleared his throat. "What can I do for you?"

"Oh, you've done quite enough, Percy. I've come to decide what should be done about you."

Fear trickled down the lawyer's neck, sopping his new starched collar in a cold dredge of apprehension. "Done? Why should anything need to be done? You and I have always seen eye to eye on things, Alain."

Javier motioned to the gargantuan, who ambled toward Percy with obvious intentions. Percy darted behind his desk, dodging the inevitable long enough to plead his case.

"Come now, Alain. You can't blame me for Laure's change of heart. I pushed her in your direction with the best of intentions."

"Yes, your own, you greedy little worm. Now, your ungrateful sister has not only spurned my generous offer of support, but she's found herself another benefactor behind which she sneers at me and threatens my future aspirations. It will not be borne, Percy."

"She would never do anything to disrupt your plans for Miss Farris."

"Edna." He spat out the name. "Such a timid little sheep. If she didn't have such deep pockets, I would cast her off in your sister's favor. I've never wanted a woman the way I want her. She makes the chase interesting. I like that. There's such a greater sense of accomplishment in taming a woman with spirit."

Percy smiled wanly as his mind churned frantically for a source of salvation. When he hit upon it, it was like a light from above illuminating the end to all his troubles. Laure was now out from under his control. Unbelievably, she'd turned to that creature she'd married and away from his council. She could not be counted upon to aid in his schemes. In fact, she'd proven her intention of becoming a deterrent. A fund for the needy, indeed. He needed that money, every penny, every dollar. He'd worked for it, and he was not inclined to share with some dirty paupers who weren't smart enough to rise above their circumstances. Here was the answer to everything. A way to clip Laure's independence, a way to handle the threat of Pasquale without having to do the deed himself. His smile widened, growing crafty with self-interest.

"And what if Laure came to you with a wealth to rival that of Miss Farris?"

"You forget your sister is married. Though I can't understand her preference for some pallid recluse when she could have all of New Orleans at her feet as my bride."

Drawing confidence from Javier's arrogant claim, Percy pulled out his chair, clutching tight to hide the shaking of his hands as he sat down to assume a nonchalant pose. "You made a mistake, Alain."

"A mistake?" His dangerous drawl stated he was in no mood for criticism.

Percy waved his hand in a generous gesture. "You should have saved your heavy handedness for afterwards. Broken ribs and a broken wrist do not endear a woman to her suitor."

Javier considered this then shrugged. "Perhaps I got carried away by the moment. But what does any of this matter now? Why do I need to listen?"

"You said you wanted Laure."

Javier's eyes narrowed over a hungry gleam. "Oh, yes. That's true."

"Enough to make her your wife?"

"There's the little problem of her current husband."

"You're not listening, Alain. Laure finds herself married to a different kind of brute, albeit a very wealthy one. If something...unfortunate were to happen to the man, Laure might be persuaded to turn in your direction for comfort. And with her comes all that lovely money. But only if you mean marriage. And only if you agree to be most generous to yours truly for making the arrangements possible."

Javier was thinking. Percy could almost see the nasty turnings of the man's mind.

"Accidents happen all the time in New Orleans."

"Exactly so. But this accident would have to be of a specific nature if you are to rid yourself of the problem of Pasquale."

"I think Marcel could handle the particulars."

Percy glanced at the bulky henchman. Yes, perhaps he could, if he had the wits to do the job right. Things were looking better and better.

Then Javier's enthusiasm cooled, much to Percy's anxiousness. "But why would Laure come back to me. Those were harsh words she spoke the other night. I believe she meant them."

"Oh, I'm sure she did, at the moment. But things have changed, Alain."

"What things?"

Percy laid his final card on the table with a flourish.

"Laure is carrying your child."

TEN

Laure sat in the darkness of the parlor room. She'd spent the last hour watching twilight shadow stretch languidly across the floorboards until every corner was filled with quiet evening. Until the time she both dreaded and desired finally approached.

Sunset.

Time to decide what story she would tell.

She placed a hand upon her flat abdomen, imagining the feel of life moving beneath her palm. A life quickened by a man she loathed. Regardless of that unpleasant fact, she owed this child her protection and the right to a safe and happy future. Alain Javier would never know of the babe's existence. She could think of no greater injustice than involving that *creature* in her child's life. Born of violence, this child would know only security and acceptance. That was the vow she made as she waited for her husband to appear.

"Buona sera, signora."

Her heart hurried a beat at the quiet purr of his accented voice.

"Good evening, Gerard."

She searched for him in the thick shadow, seeing no discernable shape, but she felt his presence with a shiver. It wasn't fear, exactly. Rather an understandable caution. And a more curious quickening deep below the maturing babe.

Twin pinpoints of light penetrated the blackness, small flames akin to lantern sparks. Slowly, his human form separated from the solid void of darkness, those unholy beacons becoming his steady gaze. His smile broke with a gradual bend of greeting, both welcoming and mocking her vigil.

"Did you wish to converse before I go out this evening? I would advise you to wait until I am in a better mood for such pleasantries."

She took his meaning with a slight shudder. He was anxious to feed upon the city's unsuspecting. "Do you kill them?"

Her question gave him pause. "Are you certain you want to know?" His dire tone warned her to consider carefully before she replied.

"Yes," she insisted, then braced for his answer.

"I don't have to. I can take enough to satisfy without demanding the sacrifice of a soul."

"But do you? Do you let them live?"

"Not as a rule. It is safer for me not to leave a confused and potential dangerous witness wandering the streets with my mark upon them."

The casual way he spoke of it, of the taking of life as if it meant nothing more than wringing a chicken's neck, upset her more than the deed itself.

"Doesn't it bother you? Can't you feel for those you...you kill?"

"I try not to think about it one way or another," was his curt response. Obviously, he didn't care to have his conscience questioned. "What's brought about this unpleasant chain of questioning? Your brother? I can sense his disagreeable presence in these rooms. Has he been feeding you full of distressing nonsense?"

"Is it nonsense, Gerard? You've as much as admitted that you are indifferent to humankind, that you are able to slaughter without qualms because it is easier to kill than to preserve that which I hold sacred."

His glittery eyes narrowed. "And what is your point?"

"I am among those you despise. Would you hold me in similar contempt? Would you take my life without remorse?"

"I have told you you are safe here. Are you doubting my word?"

She wasn't fooled by his pretended affront. He was trying to steer her from an issue she was just as determined to pursue. "You've made no secret of your feelings about humankind, yet you allow me to live here with you. As what? A future meal?"

His unnatural stillness settled, remaining until she grew anxious and alarmed. Would he answer? Would that reply be truthful? Or was she ten times the fool for wanting to believe him?

Suddenly, he laughed, a loud booming expression of his genuine delight. "Oh, *cara*, there is your answer. I enjoy you. You entertain and provoke me, and both things are equally appreciated."

"And when you cease to be amused?"

He grinned at her tart command. "I do not foresee that as a problem. I am known for my sense of humor."

"But not for your self-control, I presume. You warned me of that. Does that mean you will be tempted to..." She couldn't finish, the idea too appalling to speak aloud.

"Tap into your veins?" he supplied for her with a chilling nonchalance. "Oh, my darling, that will be a constant temptation, one I will try my best to resist. Unless you wish it otherwise."

The sultry lowering of his eyelids startled a shock of erotic response. Her breathing faltered as her thoughts seized upon the possibility of his touch, of his possession. A perverse curiosity took hold of her imagination.

"What is it like? Do—do they enjoy it?"

"I believe they do, right up until the last."

The last. Until they died. Until he drained away the last of their life force in order to sustain his own. She forced herself to accept those facts, waiting for her mind to rebel in horror. But the objection still wasn't as strong as the want to question him, to learn his motives and, perhaps, to convince him to reveal his heart. If he had one.

"And if you don't kill them, what then?"

He made a casual gesture, as if the topic was one of unimportance. "Then they are mine to summon and command at will until they die. Or I do."

"Do they become like you?"

"No, not unless I wish it." His brows lowered. "I am weary of this topic."

"Oh, by all means, let me change it then to keep you amused."

Her sarcasm teased back his smile. His chuckle sounded, warm and wicked. "Good idea."

Here was her opportunity. She couldn't back away from it. He was being honest for the moment, and she couldn't afford to let his indulgent humor pass.

"Could you see me as anything more than a plaything for your entertainment?"

He walked away from her toward the window, where he lifted a heavy drape to peer out into the night. "As what? I have made you my wife."

"But will I ever be wife to you? Can you see me as a woman? As someone you might desire for more than just a meal?"

He didn't respond. His lack of movement conveyed nothing of his thoughts, of his mood. Laure waited for some sign of either while anxiety twisted about her heart. Everything depended upon his answer. If he could be convinced to give it.

"Are you asking if I could ever love you?"

His monotone betrayed nothing.

"Yes, I guess I am."

"Is that so important to you? I let you remain. Isn't that enough? Why do you insist that there be more? Why would you think I'd allow it to be more?"

He turned to look at her then, his features taut, revealing what he hadn't intended. His jaw tightened and worked silently on his displeasure. His gaze burned hot and bright with undisguised anger.

Was the idea of a true relationship with her so distasteful to him? She feared she had her answer but had to continue.

"You could never feel anything for me?"

"No," he spat out. "I could not and I would not. Such things are dangerous."

"What things? Emotions?"

"Emotions, loyalty, involvement, love—call it what you will. I'll have no part of those things. None. Do not ask again. Be grateful that you have my tolerance, for that is the extent of my *feelings* for you. Now, please excuse me. I am going out."

"To kill?"

"To dine. I shall attempt to refrain from overindulgence if that will quiet your noble affinity for the souls of those who are strangers to you."

"It will," she answered softly, but she refused to meet his gaze. Too much would be apparent in her eyes. Like the heavy ache of disappointment awakened by his cruel words.

"I shall not be long, should you wish to continue this discussion."

She didn't respond to the unexpected gentleness in his tone. Instead, she shook her head. "There's no point, is there? You've made your opinion brutally clear. Good night, Gerard. Forgive me if I don't wait up."

She rose and, with all the dignity she could muster with her heart breaking, left him standing at the window to slowly climb the stairs. To her solitary bed.

To her solitary dreams.

Gerard stalked the Quarter, dissatisfied with himself and his nighttime existence. Because of a woman. A human woman.

Such folly.

But naming it as ridiculous didn't quiet the restlessness of his mood.

Even after he'd fed off some poor drunken soul in a dingy alley off Bourbon Street, he continued to travel the crowded early evening avenues hoping to find solace in the exotic flavors of scent and sound. Both things usually enjoyed seemed soured and discordant to him now.

Because of her.

Because she challenged him to reach back for his forgotten humanity. Oh, if she only knew what she asked of him. If she could understand what lingered in the hidden corners of his heart. Such darkness. Such pain. So much regret. And he, without a heart. He laughed at himself as he came to a stop at Jackson Square. The night had lost its mysterious appeal. The only place he longed to be was home.

With her.

The need to explain himself rose like a sudden sharp pain, impossible to ignore, annoyingly resistence to his want to wish it away. Why should he care what she thought of him? Why did her tears pierce to his long-buried soul? She hadn't shed them in front of him. She was too strong for that. Yet he'd heard them in her voice.

He kept thinking of that mortal couple entwined in earthly mating. As a youth in Florence, he'd indulged in a passionate nature, but he could not remember what it was like to be with a woman in that explicit fashion. He couldn't recall what it felt like to be moved to weeping by the sweetness of a kiss or carried to the heights of delirium within the heat of a womanly embrace. Those carnal desires were absent in him now. The lust for blood filled passion's void, making him forget he once sought different pleasures with equal abandon. He couldn't remember the man he once was. He'd been the monster for too long.

What did Laure want from him that he could yet give? What remained of any value that she had not already claimed? Abruptly, he needed to ask. He needed to know.

And so he found himself back at their home, in the perfumed darkness of her room where he could hear her breathing beckoning and feel her tempting warmth, both of body and spirit.

It wasn't wise, but it was suddenly necessary to be close to her.

She stirred as he stretched out on the bed beside her. He stayed atop the covers, leaning up on one elbow as he watched her features awake to an awareness of him. At first, she stiffened, then her eyes came open, wide and wary. Until she recognized him. Then amazingly, the fear faded away. She didn't speak. Her gaze asked the question for her.

"I have dreadful luck with romance," he confided, smiling wryly as he made that humbling admission. "I've adored two women in my life, and both were nearly the death of me. And I mean that literally, not as an expression of romantic woe. The first, Bianca Du Maurier, brought me over to this existence and introduced me to desires dark and unnatural. Now I hide from her until my strength renews enough to survive her...disenchanted affection. The second was a mortal female, Arabella Radman. A remarkable woman of wisdom and education, courageous and loving enough not to wince away from what I was."

"And how did you lose her?"

"I never had her. She was my best friend, Gino's, wife. She held my heart but could only return a weak fondness." His sigh spoke volumes.

"And what happened to her?"

"She's gone now. In the end, both Gino and I lost the only woman worthy of absolute love and loyalty. I have never seen her equal. I never shall. And will never be satisfied with less than that."

Less. That summation pierced Laure's expectation. She was less than this specter from his past, this Arabella, his perfect love. Why was he telling her this? To hurt her or to warn her away? She refused to be goaded into either state.

"How lonely that must be for you."

He shrugged eloquently. "I didn't tell you this so that you would pity me."

"No? Why then?"

"So that you would know why I cannot be the husband you seem to expect me to be."

"Because you chose badly twice before?"

"Ahhh, you laugh at my expense. Perhaps you've the right to find amusement in my misery. I often do, myself."

"If I am, it's because you seem so proud of your unhappy state, too proud to look beyond it to what you might yet discover."

"And what is that?"

"That you are not alone."

"Ahhh. And you wish to apply as the next to break my heart?"

"Or renew it. Is that so impossible?"

He touched her cheek with the tips of his fingers, charting its upward curve then stroking down to her stubborn jaw. "I fear it is. To awaken what's been dead in my heart for centuries could be a dangerous venture, one I am not willing to risk. Not even for one so charming as you, *innamorata*."

She stilled his hand by covering it with her own. For a long moment, she was sure he didn't breathe or pretend to. She searched his expression for some sign of softening, for some scrap of tenderness, but all he did was smile in that devastating, cynical manner that mocked her want to see more.

"You proceed onto unstable ground, *cara*. What you wake in me may not be the type of passion you desire."

"Kiss me, Gerard."

He leaned forward, pressing his lips to her forehead. That chaste touch wasn't the gesture Laure had in mind. Impatiently, she bracketed his lean face between her palms, guiding him down to her again.

His mouth was surprisingly warm. Because no repellant taste lingered, she didn't dwell on the source of that heat, only upon how it infused her with an answering fire. Her lips parted, eager to learn the shape and supple texture of his. When the tip of his tongue skated along that moist opening, a shudder shook to the soles of her feet. She had to know more.

Her hands moved to cup the back of his head, her fingers weaving through the midnight strands of his hair. Twining to hold him a captive to her pleasure.

And it was pleasure. Deep, delicious pleasure as he coaxed her to explore his mouth as he had hers. Cautiously, she traced along the row of his teeth, finding them unexpectedly even. She felt his smile and felt suddenly foolish.

"There are some things I can control, *cara*, and some things I cannot," he whispered. The words tickled her lips as she tried to devour them. He allowed her to feast off his mouth for a few minutes more, indulging her with his response. She could have lost herself to him right then and there, except she slit her eyes open to find him staring unblinkingly at her.

There was no grand passion burning in his gaze. His eyes were as pale and pure as jewels, and just as cold. She pulled back, more disturbed by that emotionless glitter than she cared to be. Apparently, she was no Arabella Radman to stir his heart and inspire him to urgent feelings. He settled back on his elbow and watched impassively as she drew the sheet up to her chin in a denying manner. Denying her this time rather than him.

"You are angry with me now."

"No," she told him truthfully. "Just disappointed in my inability to make you think of me as a desirable woman."

He caught a wayward tress of her hair and curled it back behind her ear. "It isn't a lack of ability, wife. You are all that is desirable. But you fight a difficult battle if the goal is my heart."

"Difficult but not impossible?"

His lips pursed thoughtfully. "Perhaps not as much as I'd hoped."

She smiled, settling back into her feather pillow. "Then I am encouraged."

He regarded her curiously, head slightly cocked as if she presented an unusual puzzle. "Why is it so important that I feel fondness for you? You would return this affection toward one such as me?"

It was her turn to tease. "Perhaps."

"This *mal d'amore*, this love sickness, what if it's something you cannot survive?"

"Then perhaps I will die happy. It's better than dying alone."

She could feel him pull away from her at those flippant words, not physically but emotionally. Back behind the impenetrable stare and motionless facade. Back where sentiment couldn't betray him. "Hope that it is a choice you don't have to make. I'll not ask it of you, but I sense there is more you would have of me. What is it you want, Laure? What would you have me give to take away this provoking mood?"

"A child."

He blinked but otherwise had no reaction she could see. "You wish a child?"

"Is it possible? Do you know? Are you able?" She blushed fiercely at the intimate nature of those questions, but he answered them with an unwincing candor.

"I do not know. My friend Gino and his wife, Arabella, they made a child between them, a child that was a bit of both their worlds. But he was much closer to human than I have ever been or ever will be."

"Does the idea disgust you, then?"

"Just surprises me, is all. You would wish to have my child?"

"Is that so hard to believe?"

He laughed. "In a word, yes."

"But will you consider it, at least, before you rule out the possibility?" She held her breath, watching his smooth, flawless features, waiting to hear what direction her future would go.

"I will consider it." He rolled off the bed with a graceful twist of his body, gaining his feet effortlessly. "And you consider the consequences of what you suggest. *Buona notte, cara mia.* I fear I am the one who will know an uneasy rest this night."

After he'd gone, Laure put her hand to the covers where he'd lain, startled to find his form left no impression upon them. This was the nature of what he was, she reminded herself sternly to combat the sudden surge of her alarm. He was a being with the power to control the ordinary world. Nothing she should fear. Nothing to fear. Shivering slightly, she burrowed beneath those undisturbed covers.

It could be done. She could manipulate Gerard into believing the child she carried was his own. They would both know a secure future under his protective wing. All she had to do was pursue the act of intimacy to its conclusion, and Gerard would never be the wiser. A perfect plan.

One that burned through her with guilty shame.

She could think of few things worse than convincing a man that an offspring was his own, when actually it was the spawn of another man. Her conscience rebelled against such trickery. Her growing fondness for Gerard saw it as unforgivable treachery.

But there were worse things.

Things like struggling to raise a child alone within a hostile world. The unfriendly world that had turned its back on her and her mother.

Worse yet, having Alain Javier discover the babe's existence and claim it as his own.

She shuddered and squeezed her eyes closed. What to do? Was there a right path leading out of this imbroglio? Dare she risk the truth and jeopardize her innocent babe? Tears stung beneath her lids, but she refused to shed them. Tears wouldn't help her out of this situation. But perhaps she knew something that would.

Her mother had forbade it. But what other choice had she? Better to risk the disapproval of her mother's spirit than endanger the life of her unborn babe.

She took a deep breath and bid her body to relax. Each limb, each muscle. She moved mentally along them, soothing away the stress, the strength, until she was limp upon the mattress, until the only activity was within her mind. That, too, she commanded into a deep penetrating calm. There could be no distractions as she stretched out beyond herself, beyond this time and place in search of an answer to her predicament.

Let me see what I must know.

The visions came to her like wisps of a dream, sometimes accompanied by voices, sometimes with an eerie silence. She saw Gerard. In his arms, he cradled a tiny bundle. She tried to see more, to be sure. She needed to see his expression. Was he pleased? Was he angered? She couldn't tell, and she couldn't receive any clear emotions from him.

And then a miniature fist popped from that wrap of blankets to wave imperiously in the air.

Her child!

She strained to see more, but her husband began to turn away, concealing the sight of her baby from her anxious eyes. Where was he going? Where was he taking her child?

That sudden jolt of panic disturbed the scene even as she struggled to retain it. She needed to gather strength to hold onto its obscure message. She took a slow breath, willing herself to concentrate.

Then there was just sound, a horrible wailing, a grief beyond measure. A wailing she recognized as her own.

"Where is my child? What's happened to my child?"

Laure's eyes snapped open, the mists of the future scattering. She lay still, her breaths coming in agonizing gasps. Her cheeks grew wet with the evidence of her distress. Protectively, her palms shielded her belly. No, it could not be true. She was not going to lose this baby. Her eyes closed again as the memory of her own anguish tormented her mind. It could not be true.

As she wept quietly in her despair, she tried to bring back the images, to learn more, enough to disavow the horrible glimpse of her own tomorrow that she'd seen. But she couldn't command a quiet spirit from out of a tortured heart.

She was going to lose her child.

What part did Gerard play in the vignette she'd seen? Hero or villain? Was there a certain symbolism in the way he turned away from her with the baby in his arms, or was she trying to attach too much to the snippets given?

She'd seen into the future. But was that future set, or could her present actions change it?

Only one would know.

She would have to find Eulalia LaClaire.

ELEVEN

A child!

The very idea stunned him from his usual indifference. Gerard walked along the broad river's edge as if he were a human man trying to outdistance a problem on foot. Anyone observing him would believe him to be just that.

A child.

What a thing to ask for, and from him! The thought still amazed and alarmed him. Amazed because she would consider a union with him to create such a miracle. Alarmed by how appealing the idea sounded to one who should have no business entertaining what surely must be folly.

Was it possible?

He brought the cherished image of Nicole LaValois to mind, the only human to touch upon his soul other than her sainted mother. But then Nicole wasn't quite human, was she? She'd been a hybrid product of mortal mother and vampire father. He'd taught her about the nature of the beast inside her. And he'd loved her like a proud papa as he watched her evolve to the sleek and confident woman that she was today. A woman with a child of her own. Frederica. And what manner of being was she, one more step removed from her preternatural grandfather?

Was it right to alter the natural balance with beings of their ilk?

It was one thing to walk on the dark side and quite another to straddle both worlds. Yet Gino, lucky Gino, had the unwavering devotion of family around him, a state Gerard envied to the point of exquisite pain.

Family. He'd not thought of it for ages. What was there to look back upon that was not colored by the horror of what he was and what he'd done? Yet he'd gone on for centuries, searching for a surrogate to fill that lonely yearning for what he'd lost. Bianca had been a poor substitute, an obscenity really. When Nicole had invited him within the treasured embrace of her own brood, he'd had to decline, though it had broken his heart to do so. He could not take happiness from those to whom he'd brought such misery. So where did that leave him but alone. Alone with a suddenly amorous wife who got him thinking about things that should not be considered.

Why not?

Why not!

Why shouldn't he try to capture an eternity outside of the damned one he commanded? A child to carry on the name Pasquale, a name that had once held honor and pride. A child to love...

He shook his head as if to deny that hope. Love was dangerous. Love was weakness. It would make him vulnerable and place those he cared for in certain peril. Had he and Bianca not become a torment to Gino when he sought his own happiness outside their unholy circle? Hadn't Arabella and Nicole become innocent victims of their unnatural revenge?

He would not bring such misfortune to Laure and any child they might make between them.

And he would not open himself up to such an agony of loss again.

Gerard stopped his directionless journey. Something pulled him from his melancholy musings. He stood upon the embankment and let his preternatural senses reach out for what had disturbed him.

There, dallying just beyond his sensory grasp. Someone followed him.

He began to walk once more, this time not lost to a fog of inner thought but alert and on edge. Was it Bianca, or the creature she'd made to replace him? A cold remembered panic quickened his pace. She had left him to die a tortuous death in the embrace of daybreak. Had she discovered he'd escaped with Gino's help? Had she come to inflict some other horror upon him in retribution for his betrayal? He'd crawled into New Orleans drained almost to the death of his powers, so weak he could barely manage to do more than feed himself and hide. But he was stronger now, wiser. And he would protect himself from her evil reach. *Il nemico.* Evil one. It had only taken him centuries to realize just how black her soul was, if she could still claim to possess one.

And if Bianca Du Maurier was here for him, she would strike first through those closest to him. It was her way. She enjoyed her role as harbinger of suffering. If she was here, Laure was in grave danger.

In a casually calculated move, Gerard stepped to the edge of the levee and off, plunging down into darkness toward the cold Mississippi waters. But instead of hitting the water, he swooped along its surface, a dark night bird in search of one who would see him as prey. He made a tight circling loop, skimming the rolling wake as one of the big Gulf-bound barges lumbered toward the sea. And then he touched down lightly on the promenade once more, shaking the dampness off his coat as he scanned the nearly deserted area for the one who tailed him. Whoever had remained in stealthy shadow was now gone.

An ominous shiver passed over him, though he could not really feel the cold that seemed to stroke along his senses.

Laure.

In the time it took for a human heart beat, he was home. Nothing felt amiss as he strode through the rooms in search of his wife.

Nothing, that is, until he realized that she was gone.

Laure sat in the bow of the shallow draft pirogue. The torch she held illuminated the still, black waters of the bayou. Behind her, a silent figure plied the oar in a tireless rhythm, pushing them deeper and deeper into the swamp.

She'd forgotten the smell. Rich, dark, verdant with abundant life, decay and inevitable death. The stagnant scent of her childhood.

Dawn colored the waters with strips of gold against depthless green before they approached her destination. Ahead, crouched low on the weedy shore, sat a lowly cabin, small, inhospitable and all alone against a background of wilderness. But to Laure, who'd played there as a child, it had all the charm of coming home. Home to family, home to a culture her mother had disavowed. Home where her answers could be found.

The boatman angled the wooden hull up against a rickety dock that stood like a water bird on spindly legs amongst the thick lily pads. He held to one of the old mooring posts to steady their hand-hewn craft as Laure stood to disembark. She turned toward the somber-faced black man and extended a coin. Without even checking the denomination, he shook his head and gestured for her to go. Gathering up her skirts, she stepped up onto the warped planking and, before she'd even smoothed down the crumpled fabric, her transportation had disappeared back into the sudden clouds of fog hugging to the water. There was nothing for her to do but go on.

As she picked her way along the uneven boards, other odors reached her. Some of the brewing herbs were familiar. Others held a vile, noxious bite. Whatever was cooking was strong medicine.

Again she shivered. Premonition or simple dread?

She shouldn't be here.

But the instant her mother's memory gave that mental warning, the door to the cabin opened.

Too late to go back.

"Laurette, *infant*, is that you?"

"It is. I've come for your council, Aunt Eulalia."

Eulalia LaClaire was as dark as her sister, Laure's grandmother, had been fair. In fact, they were opposites in every conceivable way. Moira had been graced with beauty and a gentle spirit. Eulalia was her shadow. Her face had been pocked by a childhood illness; the scars outside evident but not those of the scarring within. Unlike her sister with her benevolent soul, Eulalia regarded the world through a bitter slant, borne of being younger, less attractive, less sought after and second choice. Even when Laure's mother, Jeanette, turned from her heritage and refused to let Laure learn their ways, Moira hadn't let Eulalia take the reins of power until all hope was buried with her only child. She'd only assumed full control of the *societe* after Moira's death.

Now, Eulalia ruled unchallenged. Her power stretched across the swamps, touching the lives of those who would never admit to believing.

Those like Laure, whose faith had nothing to do with logic or understanding, springing instead from an instinctive knowledge from deep in the recesses of the soul.

Belief and a reverent fear went hand in hand.

"What troubles bring you here, child? Come inside and shake off the chill. We've much to catch up on."

With a slight shudder of premonition, Laure followed the bent figure into the dim interior. No images, no murmuring messages from beyond, just a damp chill raising the hair along her arms as she crossed that once forbidden threshold.

The inside of the shack had changed little since Laure's grandmother had practiced her spells and mixed her potions. As a child, she'd sat on the three-legged stool before the fire while her *grandmere* explained the powers of each of the herbs she sprinkled into the pot. Laure had pushed the knowledge away at her mother's insistence, but she never forgot any of it, any more than she'd forgotten the lyrical cadence of her grandmother's voice or her somber warning.

*Only for the good, Laure*tte. *Only to help your people.*

Looking into the cold gypsum of her aunt's eyes, she didn't know what Eulalia LaClaire practiced. But she'd heard the rumors. Rumors that haunted her mother and now shadowed her own existence.

Dark magic.

If only she weren't so desperate.

"I had a dream, *Tante* Eulie."

"Just a dream, child? There's nothing to fear from dreams." Her shrewd gaze fixed upon Laure's face, reading the anxiety that roiled beneath the surface. "Or was it more than a dream? Tell me, child. "

"It was more," she admitted with a guilty duck of her head. "Now I need your help to discover what it means."

Eulalia's voice came in a whisper. "You called upon the sight?"

"Grandmere taught me, only I'm not strong enough to control the visions."

"What did you ask and what did you see? I must know." The elder woman leaned toward her, expression intense, almost frighteningly so.

"I wanted to see my child's future—"

"You're with child?"

She nodded, not elaborating on the circumstances. "I wanted to make sure my husband was happy with the babe. I am not sure it's his wish, and I've been uncertain as to how to tell him of the child."

"And what did your sight tell you?"

"That's what's troubling me. I saw him holding the child, and then it was gone from me."

"Gone? How?"

"I don't know," she cried out in anguish. "Gone. Ripped from my arms, my heart. I must know what happened. I must know...if my husband is a danger to the child."

Eulalia seized her hand, dragging it toward her so the firelight pooled within her palm. Her fingertips charted the networks of lines, crawling over them in a spider-like dance. Gooseflesh rose along Laure's arms, and she fought not to pull away. She had to hear what the old woman saw.

"The child is not of your husband's loins."

Laure's startled gasp was answer enough.

"I see darkness all about him, all about this man you married. A strange mixture of death and the beyond, and power, much power."

"The child," she prompted worriedly.

"The child is in danger from one who is closest to you. I see the sacrifice of a life for a life."

"Whose? Can you tell whose?"

Her fingertips traced from the swell above Laure's thumb, around the plump curve which ended before her wrist. Eulalia frowned. "Your future..."

"What do you see, *Tante* Eulie?"

She pushed away the younger, softer hand and exclaimed gruffly, "It is unclear."

"What am I to do then?"

"I can call upon the loa and ask again. If you believe, that is."

Laure hesitated. Her aunt granted a thin smile.

"There is much of your mother in you. Jeanette threw away the truth, and she would have you do the same. Child, the situation is grave. You cannot afford to turn from the answers you seek."

"All right, I'll hear them."

"In two night's time. You know where to come."

She nodded slightly. "And until then?"

"Do not place your trust unwisely. A dark force is at work in your life, child. It threatens both you and the unborn babe. Come home. Come home to where we can protect you."

She sat in deep shadow, her arms wrapped instinctively about her unborn child. Her troubled thoughts were well reflected by the gloom.

"Where have you been?"

Laure jumped at the sudden explosion of her husband's voice. Without being aware of it, she shrank back into the cushions in response to the fierce emotion pulsing through his words.

"I've been here."

"You were gone when I returned before dawn. I feared—" His tone fractured then after a deep breath, he began again with his usual indifference. "I was concerned."

Laure studied the man she'd married, looking beyond the glorious features, past the practiced calm. What had he feared? That she'd left him? The question woke her to the truth. He wasn't angry. He was afraid.

"I went to visit my aunt."

"At four in the morning?"

"It was a distance to travel, and she rises early. Besides, I was wide awake. I am growing used to functioning at odd hours."

He didn't return her faint smile. "Have I given you a reason to be concerned by my absence?"

He did smile then, a smooth gesture meant to placate in lieu of the truth. "No reason, *cara*. But should you go out at such an hour, I would prefer you let me know. As a courtesy. I can provide you with escort. This is a dangerous city at night. I should know. I am one of its dangers."

"I had not thought you'd want to be bothered with my affairs."

Did she imagine the sudden shift of his expression to one of intense displeasure and back to bland indifference?

"It is no bother. You will do as I ask, then?" Again, the subtle press of anxiousness.

"If it pleases you, Gerard."

Why the sudden worry? She had to wonder as she watched him glide across the room with his unnatural grace. It was as if he feared to have her out of his sight during the nocturnal hours. But what threat existed after twilight that was not there during daylight? Other than him.

"Would you like to walk with me? It is a balmy night." He turned to grin at her, dazzling her with his quixotic charm. "I will be more considerate this time."

Had her company become enticing, or was he unwilling to leave her at home, alone? Whichever it was, she found herself equally dissatisfied with the thought of separation. In the empty house, she had too much time to think, to fret, to assume. But until she spent time with Gerard, learning more about the man he had once been, she would be no closer to the answers she'd sought at her aunt's door.

Their gradual pace led them into the Garden District where huge mansions sat back from the avenue in arrogant pride. Wearing comfortable shoes and clothing more suitable than her wedding gown, Laure enjoyed the exercise. And she enjoyed the company.

Choosing to be gregarious, Gerard chatted about the places he'd visited over the centuries and the changes he'd seen, preferring to mock the ridiculous aspects of each time rather than its successes. He seemed relaxed and good humored, and she would have believed it if he wasn't so casual about the frequent glances he cast about them. Almost as if he expected them to be followed. He kept her close to his side, he who had always seemed so adamant about maintaining a safe personal distance now tucking her arm though his in a possessive loop. Or a protective one. She would have appreciated his courtly behavior if she'd been certain of his motives.

"How much you must have learned over the centuries," she mused, listening to his travelogue. He laughed at that, at himself.

"Learned? You would think so, eh, *cara*. All those years, those decades, all the chances to improve. But not me. I never learned anything. I rarely appreciated anything." He lifted her fingers to his lips, brushing them with a kiss as his light eyes danced above them with some hidden mischief. "This being one of those rare times."

If he chose to play the flirt, perhaps now was the time to pursue her own agenda.

"Have you given any more thought to our discussion of last evening?"

He glanced away. He might pretend a polite interest, but she felt the muscles of his forearm tighten. "You are aware of what your suggestion would require? It's not an immaculate creation you have in mind, is it?"

"I know what's required." Her reply was a bit more brusque than she'd intended, but then perhaps he was too preoccupied to notice.

"And you understand the dangers involved with such an intimate relationship? They do not frighten you?"

He stopped her then, pulling her up tight against him, so that she was trapped against the power of his form, so he could stare down into her eyes, his gaze full of potent meaning. And while she was intimidated, her heart picking up a hurried beat, she refused to feel afraid.

"There are worse things, husband."

"Really?" he drawled out, eyelids dropping with veiled menace. "Worse than me?"

"Yes."

Her curt tone must have amused him, for he stepped back and continued to stroll with her by his side. "An intriguing proposition. Would you be so willing to experiment, I wonder, if your brother's marriage agreement didn't provide for all I own to go to my heir?"

She stumbled slightly as she craned her neck to see his face. Did he believe that? His silky tone gave nothing away. Her own answer held a brittle defense.

"I was not aware of that."

"You should be. You should make it your business to understand all that concerns you and your future. That way it's much harder for those you trust to surprise you."

"You speak from experience?"

He laughed. "Most definitely."

Abruptly his humor died. An aura of tension snapped through him like a sudden lightning strike.

"What is it, Gerard?"

"We are not alone."

Even as he spoke, she saw three hulking shapes separate from the deeper shadows. A quick glance about them confirmed that they were very much alone on the wide dark street where an expanse of wrought iron fence kept them from seeking shelter from the nearest home.

"This is not another test, is it?" she demanded, her bravado shaking slightly.

"Test? Ahhhh, no. Unfortunately not. Stay behind me, Laure. You are in no danger if you trust me."

It was difficult to take comfort in that claim when two of the three brutes produced wickedly glittering blades, machetes from the length of them. Gerard's arm swept her back into his shadow.

"Take his head, boys," said the one who was as yet unarmed. "And don't be hurting the girl, or none of us'll get paid."

"You are making a very foolish mistake, gentlemen," Gerard

warned good-naturedly as he pivoted to keep himself between Laure and their assailants. He had no faith in their assurances. And they, foolish mortals, apparently had none in his potential as a threat.

"No mistake."

And the two with knives lunged.

If he'd been able to move freely, they never would have gotten close to him, but he was hampered by Laure's presence. He felt the tug of the first blade as it sliced through his coat and into the meat along his ribs. He reached past the blade, his fingers circling the man's beefy wrist. With a quick twist, a snap of bone sounded, followed by a shrill scream. Gerard shoved the wailing man to the street cobbles, his attention already on the other. This one was more careful in his approach. He shifted the vicious weapon from hand to hand with a practiced ease while searching for an advantage. And that advantage was Laure.

With a quick feint, the attacker drew Gerard off balance so he could slip his guard in a dodge to the opposite side. Laure cried out in alarm as she was dragged from hiding to become a shield behind which the other could bargain.

"Any more fancy dancing an' she dies." The sharp blade touched to her throat to emphasize the point. Both Gerard and Laure went still.

"Let's finish this," the third man said as he bent to pick up the machete dropped by his moaning companion.

"A good idea," Gerard seconded with a genial smile.

Laure felt a brush of motion move by her like a breeze. A sudden warm spray struck the side of her face, and then she was free to stagger forward. She heard the machete clatter to the stones as she turned to the horrific sight of Gerard ripping through her assailant's neck with his teeth. Unable to voice her shock, she sank down to the cool cobbles on legs that would no longer support her.

Equally alarmed, the third man decided it was time to cut his loses and forget about the pay in deference to his life. He whirled and began to run wildly down the center of the broad avenue. With a single, effortless bound Gerard was on him, like a savage predator, bringing him down. He hunched over the flailing man to feed. The figure went abruptly still, and there was silence.

It was too much for Laure. In a near swoon, she supported herself with palms upon the cold stones as she struggled between the needs to wretch or scream in hysteria. Through the haze of her vision, she saw Gerard rise to his feet and turn back toward her and the remaining attacker. His clothing was bathed in blood. His pale gaze seemed to swim in it. And his fangs gleamed as he smiled.

Seeing his fate fast approaching, the last man cried out in terror and tried to crawl away. Gerard overtook him without ever breaking from his easy stride. With one hand fixed to the back of the man's neck, he knelt down beside him to converse almost pleasantly.

"Now, perhaps you will tell me who sent you so inadequately informed to murder me."

The man began blubbering like a babe.

"Come, come, *signor*. You were brave enough behind that blade. Where is your courage now? Tell me what I wish to know, and I just might let you live."

"It was Javier. Alain Javier. He told us to bring back your head but not to touch the woman if she was with you."

"How gentlemanly of him. Thank you for the information. If you are a man of prayers, I advise you say them now."

"But you said you'd let me go!"

"A slight exaggeration on my part."

Shrieking frantically, the crazed thug attempted to strike at Gerard with his good hand. He was abruptly silenced when Gerard twisted his head to face in the opposite direction.

Laure moaned weakly as the gore-drenched creature who no longer resembled her husband bent over her.

"Are you all right, Laure?"

No sooner had he spoken his concern than a tremendous force knocked him backwards. He stumbled then stared. His own surprise melded into an awed disbelief as he started toward her only to again encounter the impenetrable barrier he could neither see nor breach.

"Laure? What trick is this?"

She was crouched low, her hands raised, fingers splayed wide as if to resist him.

She was resisting him until her strength faltered and failed her. The moment she slumped unconscious to the walk, the invisible field disappeared from around her.

Gerard stood were he was, stunned by the power of his own 15th century superstitions. The name for what he'd seen whispered from him as he made the instinctive sign of the cross before his blood-soaked chest.

"Witchcraft!"

TWELVE

Laure awoke to a pounding head and a nauseous sense of disorientation. For a moment, she thought it was her usual morning malaise, until she saw Gerard basked in mellow candlelight. Everything flooded back with a jolt.

She was on the parlor chaise beneath the light drape of a bed robe. The stickiness of her attacker's blood had been washed away. Gerard, too, had bathed and changed into a bulky shirt of some soft fabric that hung to the middle of his thighs. Beneath it he wore snug black tights that hugged the elegant strength of his legs. The outfit made him look like a poetic troubadour. He was watching her with a cautious degree of concern.

"We need to talk."

She began to shiver at his tremendous understatement. "What did you do with...with those men you killed?"

"A tragic event. A falling out of thieves. 'Tis what can happen when one follows that wide road of the damned. I should know, eh?" His smile was thin and not up to his usual mockery. "Now, satisfy my curiosity. You knew what I was and now you've seen what I can do. The question is, what exactly are you?"

When she didn't reply, he began to pace. His stride wasn't the elegant, almost effortless glide he usually effected but rather a light, agitated step, as if he were walking on broken glass.

"Come now, I know sorcery when I see it," he goaded, his tone harsher now, his attitude more aggressive. He watched her through eyes that glittered, sharp and dangerous. "This is what you were talking about earlier when I, in my innate stupidity, overlooked the obvious. Of course, you would be accepting of a creature such as myself. You and your kind deal with demons all the time."

"No."

He paused at her soft objection. "No? I believed they burned your kin at the stake in my day for making such associations."

"I am your wife."

"Ha! Now I understand why a blood-sucking night walker was the best your brother could find for you. What a bargain I've made. I must admit my admiration for Percy is soaring. Pairing the damned with a demon conjurer, what a marvelous match. I am surprised you have not turned me into a toad by now."

"I have little control over what powers I have."

"A sorcery apprentice, eh? Is this something you go to a university to learn? Enlighten me. Really, I want to know. I insist."

She could sense his anger, his fear and distrust. He exuded waves of it as palpably as a storm-scented breeze. He who had only recently sprung the terrible truth of what he was upon her now shied from learning of her past. Should she tell him the truth or keep him in doubt for her own advantage? Knowing how fear oftimes backfired to deadly results, she decided it best to speak candidly about secrets unknown outside her circle.

"My mother's family were slave holders on St. Dominique. It is from there that their Catholic beliefs mingled with those of the African Yoruba."

"Voodoo? I have heard it was practiced here but have not seen it. You turn men into the walking dead, what are they called...zombies...and stick pins in little dolls. Is that what you do? Your little trick this evening was more than some native hocus pocus."

"The Vodun religion came to New Orleans with my ancestors and others like them. There has been a woman in my family serving as *mambo* for our *societe* for generations. Until my mother. She fell in love with a Creole planter, Antoine DuVey, and though they could not marry because of their backgrounds, she gave up her position as the next *mambo* to live with him. I was raised in his home until I was eleven, learning my letters and educated as if I were his legitimate daughter. When he died, my mother preferred poverty to returning to the family fold. Our situation was quite dire when she met and married Simon Cristobel. And then he died and my mother shortly thereafter. Percy took me in as if I were true kin."

"And he knows of this history?"

"Yes."

"Ahhh!" Now his odd statements about his step-sister made perfect sense. "So he deceived us both about the true nature of what we were."

"So it seems." She continued to study him, her emotions held close, her mood just as cautious as his own.

"So you practice none of these black arts?"

"No. I don't practice them, but I did learn much from my grandmother Moira LaClaire. She was the one who brought the flavoring of sorcery to the *societe* from her native Ireland. You see, a *vodun societe's* beliefs vary hugely from community to community, based on what the priest or priestess brings to it. She brought what you call witchcraft. Though my mother forbade it, I would sneak away for hours to listen to *Grandmere* speak of the old ways."

"And you were a prize student."

"Yes. A student not allowed to exercise what she knew for fear that it would bring disaster to our home."

"And that's what your friend Javier was threatening you with, exposure of your dark beliefs."

"He is not my friend, and they are not my beliefs. That is, I don't think so."

He grimaced. "You certainly fooled me with that display on the street."

"You frightened me. I was upset and used my skills when I feared that you would—"

"What? Harm you?"

She looked away instead of answering, which was an answer in itself.

"Who is this Javier, and why would he wish me killed?"

"Percy tried to match us up together, but he found out about my past and would not marry me."

He paused to examine her more closely, noting the rise in pallor, the downward cant of her eyes, the tightening about her mouth as her breaths grew quick and shallow. "There's more you're not saying, Laure."

His soft summation set her trembling. "That's saying enough." Still, she avoided his gaze until, suddenly, he was kneeling before the chaise. She couldn't escape the intensity of his stare when his presence engulfed her.

"What did he do to you?"

She hugged her arms, rocking slightly as the words came forth. "He hurt me. He hit me. He said I deserved it for making him play the fool for my affections. And then he offered to set me up as his mistress. After my broken arm and ribs mended, of course. He thought me most ungrateful when I declined."

"Why didn't you protect yourself against him?"

"He caught me by surprise." She massaged her wrist as if even now she could hear the bone snapping, feel the pain spearing up her arm to pierce her mind and render her powers useless.

"And then you turned to me after rejecting him. Imagine the insult."

His voice was little more than a rumble. She jumped when his hand touched her cheek, but she allowed him to draw her head down onto his shoulder. She buried her face in the plush fabric of his shirt until the burn went away behind her eyes and the panic ceased its loud beating within her breast. There was no more time for weakness. She'd stripped too much of herself bare already with the things she had revealed. And there was so much more she would never say.

So she leaned against Gerard, drawing upon his strength to replenish her own flagging supply. As she took comfort from the curl of his arms about her, she tried to erase the sight of him with his blood-crazed eyes and terrible fangs. An unwitting shudder shook her.

The danger of Alain Javier was far from over.

The hawk or the badger. Her fingers clutched the loose folds of Gerard's shirt. There was no question in her mind. Time was running out, and she was no closer to establishing herself permanently within her husband's house. They were at an uncomfortable impasse now with all their secrets exposed and awaiting judgement.

Except there was more she was not saying.

The sins of the past were fast catching her, and she was all but exhausted from running in place.

Wordlessly, Gerard scooped her up off the chaise. Bearing her weight as if it were inconsequential, he carried her up to her bed. There, he settled her atop her covers and bid her to sleep. Part of her longed to plead for him to stay, to remain with her until that elusive rest arrived. But another part yet saw him with a blood-smeared face, as a vengeful creature of the night rather than her trusted rescuer. So she let him go without a word.

It was hours before sleep claimed her restless thoughts. A sleep troubled by fitful dreams, dreams of running through the fog-draped streets of New Orleans with a wailing infant in her arms, being pursued by a demon with glowing red eyes. And suddenly the baby stopped crying. She stopped and looked down to find her arms cradled emptiness.

Her own cries woke her.

She lay upon the twisted sheets, squinting her eyes against the weak threads of morning. Her heart pounded madly as if she were still being pursued. The pounding grew more persistent until she realized that it was someone beating upon her front door.

Still in her rumpled clothing, Laure tottered to her feet and made her way downstairs to where an anxious Percy waited at the door. He had no greeting for her, just a breathless announcement.

"Alain Javier disappeared last night. The police have already been to see me. They suspect foul play."

She saw his frantic gaze come into a narrowed, horrified focus. She glanced down to see the unmistakable signs of violence dried in dull splotches upon her gown.

"Tell me you had nothing to do with it," he pleaded.

"I haven't seen him, Percy," she said, needing to contradict what he thought he had learned from those damning stains. "Gerard and I were set upon by three robbers while we where walking. There was a struggle."

"And?"

"Gerard chased them away."

Percy's face gleamed like a pale moon, his eyes swimming upon that milky plane, huge and disbelieving. "You had better change your clothes before anyone comes to question you."

"Why would they do that? No one knows about me and Alain. No one but you."

"And perhaps the grieving Miss Farris, who saw the two of you arguing here the other night."

The seriousness of the situation sunk in, cold and filled with dire consequence. "I'll change."

"While you do, I'm going to help myself to some of your husband's brandy."

By the time she rejoined him, Percy was slightly reeling but notably calmer and thinking fast. He gave her a quick appraisal, nodding his approval of her frilly feminine morning gown of benign apricot lace. Not at all the garb to suggest a guilty murderess.

"So you have not seen or heard from Javier?"

"Not since the night of the party. Oh Percy, do you think something terrible has happened to him?" She hoped so. Fiercely, uncharitably, for her own sake and for that of Miss Farris and of those who would follow, she hoped so.

"He was on his way to play a late game of chance with some

business acquaintances, and he never arrived. Gone without a trace."

"Gerard."

She spoke her suspicions aloud without thinking.

"You think Pasquale killed him? Why?"

Wearied by the stresses of the previous night and by the chasing torments of her dream, she couldn't keep silent. She blurted out the details, causing Percy to blanch even whiter at their graphic nature.

"But why would Javier send men to kill your husband? It makes no sense."

"He was insane, Percy. He didn't need a reason."

"And Pasquale? Did you tell him about the child?"

"How can I now?" she cried out in despair. "If he murdered the baby's father because he beat me, what chance is there that he will be accepting of it as proof of Alain's greater abuse? He is not charitable by nature."

"Are you in danger, Laure? You must tell me if you fear he'll do you harm."

"I don't think so. But I fear for my child." She could no longer contain her weeping. It burst forth in an emotional tide, flooding past her reasonable logic, sweeping away her want to believe in the man she'd married. The image of him in the midst of his killing frenzy kept intruding. The image of her empty arms forbade control. "What am I to do, Percy?"

Called upon for calculated plotting, Percy didn't fail her. He seized her hands, holding them tight, becoming once again her confidante, her protector. "You must convince Pasquale that the child is his. You must do it for the child's safety and for its future. It must be accepted as your husband's heir."

Whispers of conscience held little rational sway over fears for her unborn babe. Laure nodded.

"And you must do something else, Laure, something to protect yourself against him should the need arise."

She dried her eyes with a flutter of one hand, fixing upon the gravity of her step-brother's expression. "What?"

"You must find out where he rests during the day. You must find out and tell me."

"W-why would you need to know that?"

"He's most vulnerable when he's hiding during the daylight hours."

The horror of his suggestion struck like an unfair slap to the vows she'd spoken.

"No!"

"Laure, it's just a precaution. Just to use as leverage if we need to. You must do it. And you must tell me what you discover. Say you will. For your safety and the child's. Say you'll do it."

Still shivering with fright, and too numbed by consequence to immediately question her brother's motives, Laure nodded once again. She would think of it as Percy said. A precaution. For the child.

"Smart girl," Percy praised, patting her hand. "Do it as soon as you have the chance. Now, I'd better go in case the police arrive. It wouldn't do for them to think that we had prepared some story."

Laure nodded. "Of course. Thank you, Percy. I don't know what I'd do without you to take care of things for me."

"It's my pleasure, Laure. I'll see to everything. Don't you worry."

After he'd gone, the horror of all she'd been through began to dull into the unreality of a numbing dream. Laure found herself standing at the bottom of the stairs, thinking of her brother's words.

Where did her husband rest during the daylight hours?

Someplace near. Somewhere in the house.

A rapid knock at the door startled her from her dark musings. She put a hand over her heart as if to quiet its anxious racing. And she went to answer the official questions about Alain Javier.

But it wasn't the police upon her doorstep. There on her porch, behind the concealment of a heavy veil, was Edna Farris, his fiance.

"Miss Farris, this is a surprise. Please come in."

The timid creature looked about as if she feared being seen. Her voice was fragile with strain. "No, it's better that I not stay."

"I heard about Mr. Javier's disappearance. I am so sorry for what you must be going through." It wasn't a lie. Edna Farris had her deepest sympathy.

"I wanted to let you know what I told the police about you and Alain."

Laure froze, a chill of dread settling in her belly. "What about me and Alain?"

"Nothing. I told them nothing at all."

"I don't underst—"

Then Edna rolled back her veil, and Laure understood completely. A huge, dark swelling stood out on the young woman's cheek. Laure recognized Javier's touch.

"That bastard." Tears of empathy sprang to her eyes. "Please forgive me for not warning you earlier."

"I wouldn't have believed you. I can hardly believe it now. He was leaving me, you see, leaving me for you."

"Me? But I wanted nothing to do with him!"

Edna smiled, that thin gesture conveying a grim satisfaction. "Yes, I know. I figured that's why you killed him or had him killed. I just wanted to say thank you and to let you know that it will be our secret."

"But I didn't have anything to do with Alain's disappearance."

"That doesn't really matter now, does it? Just as long as he stays gone." Such a harsh summation from the meek Miss Farris left Laure speechless as the woman pulled down the thick netting once more. "I must go. Good-bye, Mrs. Pasquale. I will enjoy seeing you again socially."

It came to Laure as an unexpected insight as she shut the door behind her unexpected ally.

The cabinet.

She held her breath as she turned toward the stairs.

Of course.

That monstrosity in the master suite was the only piece of furniture in the house when she'd arrived. It was kept locked. She'd discovered that servant girl in Gerard's dark embrace there in front of it. A coincidence? Perhaps not. Perhaps Gerard had caught the girl snooping about his hiding place, possibly sent by Alain. Or Percy.

She started up the stairs, her legs shaky at first then growing stronger as they carried her forward with purpose.

Just a precaution.

For her child.

The room was dark. The cabinet stood in arrogant command of its emptiness. An ugly thing, possibly from the Orient. Hadn't Gerard spoken of his visits there? Perhaps this was more than a sentimental souvenir.

She approached, refusing to think beyond the moment to the consequences of her deeds. She tried the latch. Locked. Fueled by determination, she went into her room and returned with her silver hand mirror. Wedging the handle between the cabinet doors, she used it as a lever to break the lock. It gave suddenly, causing the mirror to bump the molding. Laure stared at the shattered image of her own face.

Bad luck.

She shook off the chill of premonition and opened the heavy doors. She studied the empty space inside seeing it as a challenge rather than a dead end. Thumping the walls and floor, she heard the same hollow thud of teak wood. Puzzled, she stepped outside to reassess the situation.

What if the lock was to throw off suspicion? What if what she was looking for wasn't in the cabinet at all?

She knelt down, rubbing her fingertips across the floorboards for a clue the dim lighting wouldn't reveal. The boards were scuffed by uniform scratches. As if something had been dragged across it repeatedly. Laure stood and went to the rear of the cabinet where it seemed to be solidly attached to the wall.

Or just hinged to it.

Gripping the sides, she pushed, nearly falling over when the cabinet swung away from the wall with surprising ease. She stared at the narrow turn of stairs set behind the wall, suddenly reluctant to go on.

Would he know? Would he be aware of her prying into his

secrets while he was at rest? Could he sense a disturbance in his safety, feel her presence if she were to continue on her quest?

How could her child rest easily in her womb until she discovered her husband's hiding place?

She started up the tight wrought iron spiral, holding the rail with one hand and a lantern high with the other. The stair led to a small, separate attic space in the center of the house, away from any penetrating daylight rays. And in the middle of that airless area Gerard Pasquale lay in state within a plain wooden coffin.

She stared at the box for a long minute, a trembling rising from deep inside her. Swallowing down her fear, she crossed to the simple casket and slowly raised its lid.

Seeing Gerard in his vampiric form, feasting off the blood of others, had somehow been less upsetting then viewing him in this unnatural repose. Though he lay there as still as he would be in death, his features retained their chiseled beauty—his pallor flawless, his eyes closed in a parody of sleep. There was no rise and fall to his chest that would suggest breathing, and she knew if she placed her palm upon his snowy shirtfront, she'd feel no heartbeat beneath it. The phrase sleeping like the dead assumed a whole new, horrific meaning.

In sudden recall, she remembered seeing his side laid open by their attacker's machete. Yet when they'd last spoken, he'd betrayed no sign of injury. Gingerly, she opened his coat, his vest and finally lifted his shirt to expose the sculpted perfection of his abdomen. No bandaging to protect a gaping wound. The only evidence of injury was a thin line of scarring curving along his ribs as if a remnant from an incident years past.

His body had healed itself with remarkable rapidity.

That's how he'd survived being shot in the chest on their wedding night. It had been no trick, no deception, just the dark nature of what he was. Immortal. Virtually indestructible. Unless caught in this unprotected state of sleep. Here, he could be killed and sent to a mortal rest.

Was this why Percy was so eager for her to bring him the

information? The shock of that question woke her from her compliant daze. Was her brother's intention not to control a possible threat, but to put a definitive end to the only thing standing between him and her husband's fortune?

All her past fondness and familial feelings rebelled against this revelation. Surely Percy wouldn't be so cool-blooded in his thinking, so callous in his dealings.

But she knew he was. She'd always known that beneath his acts of kindness and compassion lay a deeper self-interest. She'd dismissed them as weak character flaws not as dangerous faults. Surely he wouldn't expect her to help him slay her husband for a rich reward. Would he?

Just then, she knew he was capable of that depth of treachery, and she knew just as strongly that she could not stand by and let him destroy a life, even a life he didn't consider in terms of its humanity. Not out of greed. Not even out of worry for her safety.

She placed her fingertips upon Gerard's motionless chest. How cool he felt to the touch, yet the vibrant power within him was unmistakable. On the edge of life but not quite beyond it. Not quite safe from its limitations.

Vulnerable.

That notion surprised her, for she'd never thought of him that way. It made him...more human.

That's what she had beneath her hand with the knowledge she now possessed. His life was in her keeping to do with as she would.

And if she told Percy where he lay, her brother would have him slain. She felt it without his confirmation. Percy saw Gerard as a threat. But how did she see him?

He'd slain Alain Javier because of what she'd told him. He'd defended her honor with a quick and viciously efficient vengeance. Unlike Percy, who'd begged her to do nothing, say nothing, for the sake of her own safety. And for his. Gerard hadn't thought of consequence. He had ruthlessly killed the man, not because he'd sent thugs to threaten him, but because Alain Javier had dared harm her. His wife. She knew it with a sudden certainty.

He'd done it for her.

And her love for this not-quite-human man she'd married burst forth with a marvelous and unplanned splendor, shaking her to the soul.

"Sleep easy," she said aloud, not knowing if he could hear her. "Rest well knowing your secret is safe with me."

THIRTEEN

She'd stood at his open coffin staring down at him as he slept.

He'd been maddeningly aware of her, of her scent, of her fear, of her hesitation. He'd felt her touch against his skin, hers so warm against his so cool. He could think of no position more vulnerable, other than perhaps having one's head on a block with an executioner's axe raised high. No where to run. No way to resist whatever would follow. He was completely helpless to her intentions. And not knowing what they were was the most frightening of all.

That she'd found him was a testament to her tenacity and intelligence. That she'd wanted to look stirred more complex questions as he lay waiting for the crippling daylight to fade away so he could be free. Only then could he act upon what preyed on his mind.

Could he believe her?

Was he safe now that she knew where he spent his days? Was he safe even now as minutes ticked toward twilight with his secret exposed? If she told her crafty brother, he could expect a sharp stake through the heart at any second. He'd no doubt of that. But would she tell him? Was he so caught up in the little vermin's lies that she could not see the true black color of his villainous soul? Perhaps not, because suddenly he was free of his sunlit stupor and on his feet, wary, shaken, but no worse for wear. And alone.

He stuffed in his shirt tails and rebuttoned his vest, feeling disconcerted and oddly invaded by her intimate touch. And curiously aroused as well.

Would she touch him with such tenderness if she feared him? Would she close the lid and walk away if she meant him any harm? Or was he just being naively hopeful and she, just biding her time?

She was in the parlor waiting for him as if nothing had changed, as if nothing was amiss. For a moment, he just stared, wondering if she'd always been so strikingly lovely, or if it was just the form-fitting gown of deep wine-colored velvet decorated with swirls of gold bead and lace. Or the way the firelight played through her upswept hair where it made a sophisticated knot upon the top of her head. Or maybe it was the way she smiled when she saw him, the gesture so small, so sweet, so uncertain, he knew his heart, that hadn't garnered a natural beat for four centuries, was in danger of tripping over itself in its flustered hurry.

He was in danger of breaking his own cardinal rule.

Don't get involved with what might become your next meal.

"You killed him, didn't you?"

There wasn't so much a note of accusation in her tone as there was a whisper of awe. That confused him all the more.

"Whom, *cara*?"

"Alain Javier. He's missing."

"And is there anyone who really wants him found?"

"What did you do with him?"

"Not that I'm confessing to having done anything with him at all, I fear if it's proof you want, you would have to slit the gullets of half the alligators in the bayou. Only they can say how well he's settling into his new surroundings."

Her smile brightened. "I'd say he's in fitting company then." A softening he could only identify as tenderness came over her expression. Her voice was rich with it. "You did it for me."

"I am not so pure of motives, I assure you. He sent men to murder me, after all."

She continued to look at him in that melting fashion, obviously preferring her own twist to that truth. "You must care for me then, just a little."

"I care to preserve my own life, silly girl."

She wasn't swayed by his selfish claim.

With a sigh, he held up thumb and forefinger, spacing them an inch apart. "*Un po'.* A little. But do not get too carried away. I am still not convinced that having a human roommate is always in my best interest."

"But having you for one is in mine."

She came toward him then, moving with a slow deliberation, a purposeful stride that had him wishing to retreat for every one she took. What was it about her heavy-lidded gaze that had him so uneasy? She didn't stop until they were toe to toe, until he could see the faint pulse at the base of her bare throat when she swallowed. Her hands rose, coming to rest upon his shoulders.

"For whatever reason, thank you."

Her palms slid so that his jaw was captured between them. She compelled him to bend down. He couldn't have resisted.

He should have resisted.

Her lips were wooingly warm upon his. Their subtle shifting provoked a riot of sensation so foreign he didn't recognize it for what it was. Desire? Oh, there was the lusty hunger cutting its sharp teeth upon his restraint, but this was something different, something deeper. Something that urged him to clasp her willowy waist within his hands, not to hold her prisoner, but to pull her closer. The taste of her kiss was as sweet as life itself. He could not get enough of the feast. Only when she broke away to catch her breath, her cheek pressed to his, was he distracted by the proximity of her unguarded neck. And then she stunned him beyond the power of coherent thought.

"Make love to me, my husband."

Her whisper, so husky with urgent passion, prompted a self-preserving response. He stepped back so quickly she almost fell forward. Her eyes blinked open. Color rose to her face as he continued to stare at her through a blank of distress. But she fast recovered from her embarrassment. She straightened, hoisting her shoulders back and her head high.

"I'm sorry. I thought you said you didn't find the idea repellent. Apparently, you've had a change of heart."

Yes, a change of heart. How aptly she put it. How hugely she misunderstood the reason for his pause.

It wasn't that he found the idea distasteful. On the contrary. He was in danger of committing the ultimate folly, allowing his emotions to rule over reason. She was not of his kind. She was a weak mortal whose life was housed in a temporary shell. In her realm of finite years, she could never begin to understand the concept of an eternity alone without her.

You have no heart, Gerardo, Bianca had been so fond of saying. At this moment, how desperately he wished that she was right.

"I must go out," he told her tersely.

"Would you like me to go with you?"

"No, *cara*, that would not be wise."

Now that he knew the source of the threat had not been Bianca but rather Javier—a threat that had been effectively removed—he had no fear of her being left alone. Not as great a fear as he felt for her safety while within his company.

"I will see you later?"

The hope snagging her voice was nearly his undoing.

He forced a wry twist of a smile and a nonchalant, "We shall see."

Her features never altered to reveal her heart, but he saw her body sway and slump before her indomitable courage shored her up. The evidence of her disappointment landed like an unfair blow to the mid-section. He braced against the aftershocks while performing a mocking bow. And then he escaped into the night where he understood his place in the natural world, as predator not as a procreator.

What had she done wrong?

Laure paced her solitary bower as she turned that question over and over within her mind. She knew he had feelings for her. He'd admitted as much. She'd seen them spark in his pale eyes for a brief moment when he'd entered the room. What had so quickly extinguished those promising flames? Was it her impetuous request?

That request had come as just as much of a surprise to her as to him. She hadn't planned it. But she'd meant it.

She'd wanted him to say yes for no other reason than being in his arms. A romantic notion, considering her desperate situation.

Time was growing too short for subtlety. Within a month, the conception time would not be long enough to convince him that the child she carried was his own. The month after, she would no longer be able to hide her condition.

She had to think of the child.

She could not bear the thought of him turning both of them away. Not now. Not after she'd discovered how much she...what? Loved him? She needed him. That's all she should concentrate upon for the moment.

But how to seduce a four hundred year old vampire who claimed to have forgotten what it was to feel desire?

If only she knew more about his precious Arabella, the mortal who'd managed to move his heart of stone. He'd called her smart, brave, beautiful. But Laure herself was not lacking in any of those areas. What had made this one woman so special? Perhaps her unavailability that kept her from being a true threat.

How to persuade him to trust her? Hadn't it been enough just vowing to keep his hiding place a secret? She'd placed herself fearlessly into his arms to seek his kisses, knowing she was only a heartbeat away from death at any given instant should he decide to yield to his basic nature.

What more could she do?

Did she trust him? Could he sense her underlying hesitation? If she had so much faith in his goodness, why wasn't she telling him the truth about her condition instead of playing harsh games? For the child, she told herself. But was it her own fear holding her back from complete candor?

Each man she and her mother had placed their future with had failed them. A cruel judgement perhaps, since no man chose his own death. But the matter remained, they'd been abandoned to make their own luck, their own way, and that's all she truly believed in. Gerard may be offering her a haven, but it was up to her to keep it. For that, she would do whatever was necessary. Even lie, if that was the only course available.

But was she using her own best abilities to make a place for herself and her unborn child?

There were other ways to melt a man's heart.

Her grandmother had called her an unequalled talent. Perhaps that's why her mother was so afraid to let her visit, afraid she'd be enticed by the taste of that power, afraid she'd be unable to break away once she felt the touch of her destiny. Instead, she'd gone through life with no identity, no confidence in who she really was or what she could accomplish. Was she ignoring her best avenue for success by turning away from her special gifts?

Was it wrong to use her powers to gain what she most desired? Her mother believed so. And her mother had lived a life at the mercy of others and had died alone. That's not how she wanted to end her days. If it took a bit of special magic to invoke her husband's humanity, where was the harm?

Could she do it?

Had she learned enough to command the loa? Was she wise enough to control rather than be manipulated? Time was the answering factor. There was no time for doubts or guilty hesitations. She had to act out of faith rather than fear, for it was belief that would sustain her power. Belief that she was doing good for all to establish a future without threat and an accepting home for her baby.

For those reasons, she made her way up into the attic room to prepare.

The instant he entered the house, Gerard knew something was out of balance. He'd stayed away purposefully until minutes before dawn so now was not a great time to address any new surprises.

"Laure? *Cara*?"

No answer. No welcoming sign of her. But she was in the house. He could feel her. He followed those homing sensations up the stairs, then with an increased apprehension into his empty bed chamber. Alarm jolted through him.

The cabinet was pulled away from the wall. The first few steps of the spiral staircase were revealed behind it.

A trap? What would he find at the top of the stairs? Percy Cristobel with a mallet in his hand? He couldn't afford to wait and wonder. It was almost daylight.

After closing the cabinet behind him, Gerard started up the stairs. He didn't require any light, but noticed it pooling softly in the room above. An equally soft scent reached him as he climbed. Gardenia. A scent that was Laure but somehow intensified. His nostrils flared with anticipation.

Four branches of candles cast a mellow glow that stretched out for the darkened corners of the room. Nothing seemed changed except for a model ship suspended from the ceiling beams. Laure sat in the room's center. He didn't focus on her until he'd made sure they were alone.

Then, he could not look away.

She knelt upon a pallet of red satin, an angel all in virginal white. In the candlelight, her slim silhouette was outlined beneath a loose-fitting nightdress of thin lawn and lace. The golden blaze of her hair spun down over one shoulder, tied beneath her ear with a slender length of ribbon. Though nothing was left uncovered by that neck to wrist to ankle gown, the effect was startlingly feminine and pure seductive heaven. He was stripped of all defenses.

"What is this?" he asked. The words he'd meant to sound slightly teasing came out as a husky rumble through the tightening in his throat. "It is not a good time for games, *cara*. The dawn is almost here, and I must seek my rest."

She bent to pat the sleek gleam of satin sheets with one small, fair hand, the gesture unbearably sensuous. "Rest here with me, husband."

For a long moment, he couldn't move.

Her gaze as innocent as the dawn, and possibly just as deadly in its ability to do him harm, she asked, "It's just that I hate the thought of you in that box alone. It's so...upsetting. I would like to rest with you, if it's possible. Or must you sleep in there?"

He glanced at the casket, finding none of the appeal that he saw with this sudden siren. "It's habit, really, from the old days. Few were willing to violate the grave in search of us. But no, it isn't necessary. As long as the sun can't get in, I can rest wherever I like."

"I'd like you to sleep here beside me."

He would have argued. Should have argued. But already the lethargy that came with the sunrise pulled at him. And the idea of lying beside Laure was equally hard to resist. His wife. When she stretched her hand up to him, he could not deny either thing.

The pallet was as enticingly soft as Laure's stare. He sank into both and was lost.

"You have been busy, *cara,* "he murmured as he settled upon the feather ticking. "When did you manage all this?"

"While you were out. I spend too much time in this house alone when I would prefer it be spent with you. Since you'd rather I not go out with you, I thought we'd spend these hours at least staying in together."

His eyes were already closing, their heaviness impossible to ignore, even when he wanted to continue looking at her as she leaned over him.

"I will not be much company for you," he warned, too groggy to respond with more than a faint smile to the stroke of her hand upon his face.

"Let me worry about that." And she kissed him, tenderly, a kiss filled with the promise of more delights. A promise he couldn't collect upon as he drifted into his unnatural sleep with the taste of her yet on his lips.

Laure straightened to gaze down upon his spectacular features. The danger of what she was about to do was offset by how very much she wanted to make a future with this man who was more human than he would admit. She'd have to be brave enough to go through with the required intimacy. Yet the only experience she'd had evoked terror rather than anticipation. It would not be like that with Gerard, she knew, because he'd never handled her with anything but care. But she was still nervous. That too was a reason for what she had planned.

They would make love tonight, here in this dusty bower. In his somnolent state, she could control him and therefore not be so terribly afraid. She wasn't as frightened of the monster as she was of the man. And he would have to be human enough to believe he had fathered her child. That trickery played a sour note within her carefully orchestrated plan. Deceiving him was necessary. But so was making that deception as pleasant for him as possible. Pleasant for both of them. All would depend upon how well she could perform this impromptu ceremony, and whether the loa believed she had the power to command. If they didn't, they could snatch the situation from her for their own selfish purposes.

"*Papa Legba, ouvri barrie pou nous passer.*"

While Gerard lay upon her makeshift altar, Laure went about the rituals needed to evoke both the guardian of the gate between her world and that of the spirit and the loa deity who would act on her behalf. Chanting softly in a broken rhythm, she prepared the way as her grandmother had done before her.

On a piece of white paper she'd placed upon the floorboards, she used a powdered ash, the farine *guinee*, to draw the symbol of Erzulie, the loa of love and the moon. Her *veve* was befittingly the shape of a heart, for it was Gerard's Laure needed to reach. Upon the design she laid her offerings to the embodiment of the perfect female—sweet cakes, flowers, candles and a pot of the perfume she herself wore. The words she spoke changed from traditional Catholic prayer to African liturgy, the *langage* of the loa.

Laure held to her fear as the untested power trembled through her. In this unusual forum with no spirit helpers to aid in her request, she risked much in calling upon the *Petro* loa. Unlike their mild and benevolent counter-balance, the *Rada*, the *Petro* were dark loa which rose up during the days of slavery imbued with all the rage, passion and violence of that suppression. For all their power and their ability to make the big cures that were beyond the gentler *Rada*, the *Petro* were also ill-tempered and demanding, for their spirit was born of death and vengeance.

Pulling the edges of the red satin covers up over her shoulders like a scarlet cloak, Laure continued to chant and clap in the off-beat tempo. The longer she called, the more anxious she became. What if she made a mistake? What if, instead of reaching the loving side of Erzulie, she brought forth the traits of jealousy and discord. Erzulie could be malicious to the women who called upon her for assistance. Would she be cruel or kind on Laure's behalf? She needed the loa to guide her, to give her confidence as she charmed her husband. She would ask the loa for her secrets of love and for a way to touch her husband's hard heart. She would take the advice Erzulie gave, then put it into practice herself. If she could find the courage.

She cried out as a sudden sharp blow struck the back of her neck. Her body responded with an uncontrollable spasming. Possession. No! That wasn't what she wanted! But even as she protested, Erzulie displaced her life's energy.

Laure remembered nothing more.

"Husband, awake."

The gravely purr brought Gerard's eyes open with a snap. His mind told him it was impossible. The sun was up. Yet he was alert in all his senses and suddenly very aware of the woman straddling his hips.

It was Laure and then, it was not. The woman who pushed her palms up and down his bare chest while grinning like a hungry predator about to devour him whole was not his sweetly innocent wife. Even the way she wore the modest sleep dress, unbuttoned nearly to her belly and hanging off the creamy slope of her shoulders, was not his Laure. He'd experienced this kind of sexual temptation once before, at the knowledgeable hands of another demon, Bianca DuMaurier. This time he realized the danger before it was too late.

"Who are you?" he demanded, catching at those eager hands as clever fingers plucked his nipples erect.

"What's a name? Does it matter. I am Laure, she who wishes to mate with you, she who desires your seed."

He turned his head from her open-mouthed kisses but couldn't fight her off, not really. He could already feel his body stirring in a surprising, traitorous response to the way she moved above him.

"Where is she? What have you done with her, demon?"

"Not here, but not far away. She bid me to make you burn with passion, and so I shall."

A wave of powerfully charged intensity rode through him, a sharp-edged pleasure, excitement raging fever-hot from inside out. Flames of desire cored his veins the way his hunger would upon waking, leaving him weak and shaky, helpless to resist what he wanted so fervently.

What he wanted with Laure.

Not with this ghoul.

He was no stranger to demons. When a boy in Florence, he'd seen one of his sister's friends possessed by a brazen spirit. It caused the girl to run wildly down the streets, offering herself to any man who would look her way. Her eyes held that same blank glitter as those of the creature above him. The poor girl had been burned at the stake even as she pleaded her innocence, while the demon within laughed in hysterical delight. He'd seen it and had been mortally afraid for his soul. But the experience hadn't made him wise enough to recognize that same evil when it came again in the guise of a gorgeous blonde destructor.

But he did now.

He seized her shoulders roughly as she swayed over him, a provocative Salome. He shook her until her head snapped back and forth like a flower on a slender stem. "Begone, she-witch. I want no part of your evil tricks. Return my wife to me before I make you sorry."

She laughed at him, the same shrill taunting sound ringing in his ears since childhood. It was silenced when his hands closed about her throat. Tight.

"Fool!" she gasped, writhing like a serpent in his grasp. "You'll kill her."

"Better she be dead than a vessel for your contaminating use. Be gone before you are trapped here in this lifeless body forever."

With a hard shudder, Laure collapsed above him, her breath coming in hard, uneven gulps. Her eyes were wild and disoriented. She hoisted her gown up around her neck in a defensive gesture, protecting a modesty that had already been compromised. She looked to Gerard, who was wide awake and frowning, fearing to ask, but needing to know.

"Laure?"

"W-what happened?" A tremendous fatique crept up her limbs, making her struggle not to swoon dead away out of sheer exhaustion.

"You surrendered your marital rights to some she-demon. I am afraid I found that unacceptable."

She remembered then, Erzulie taking possession of her body against her will. But would Gerard believe that was what had happened, or would he think she'd sent an other-worldly entity to seduce him in her stead?

As she looked on in fear, he scattered Erzulie's altar with the brush of his forearm. She caught her breath, alarmed by his act of sacrilege. Almost immediately, his natural daylight stupor returned, giving him only enough time to situate Laure at his side, trapping her in an inescapable embrace, before he sank deep into undisturbed slumber.

They had things to discuss when he awoke.

FOURTEEN

Laure awoke to a ridiculous degree of weakness and to a darkness that was almost complete. Several candles guttered in the last of their wax, casting wild shadows across the walls of a room that wasn't familiar.

Until she became aware of the man beside her.

What had she done?

A soft moan escaped as she pieced together the disastrous past hours. She'd tried to manipulate Gerard into a relationship he didn't want. She'd used untested skills under unwise circumstances. She'd broken countless vows made to her mother and fractured many of the rules her grandmother handed down. Erzulie had mocked her summons, and after possessing her, had tried to seduce Gerard for herself. What else could have gone wrong that hadn't. Was there any mistake she hadn't made? All due to selfish desires. All to protect her security. Without a moment of consideration for the man who'd given her a name, a home and a sense of pride.

He would never forgive her.

She had no excuse for her shameful behavior. She couldn't blame her past for making her desperate for a place to call her own. She couldn't cite Percy's anxieties as the cause of her faltering goodness. She couldn't even point a finger at the late Alain Javier for reenforcing her distrust of men. She'd known exactly what she was doing and had done so with a single-minded purpose. That of her own protection.

He was going to hate her.

And he had every right, she thought with conscience aching. She despised herself for her ill-conceived actions. She'd wanted his trust. The scattering of altar items condemned that sham. She closed her eyes in misery. She'd be lucky if he ever believed another word she said.

Having deceived her husband and disgraced her heritage, what kind of future would be left for her now?

"I had the most intriguing encounter."

The sound of Gerard's voice was a lightning surge to her system. It took all her courage to glance beside her. His eyes shone, blue fire, in the dimness. His bare chest gleamed, pale and flawless in its powerful proportions. Her bravery crumpled with her first words.

"I have a lot to explain."

"Indeed you have, but first I have made a discovery I wish to share with you."

She glanced up through the fringe of her lashes, afraid to hold to any hope of his charity. He'd vowed to be a man of little mercy. So this was how they would say good-bye, and he would cast her, deservingly, out into the night. She braced to bear it with dignity if not integrity.

"And what is that?"

He shifted suddenly, rolling up so that he covered her without really touching at any physical point. He didn't have to. She felt him everywhere.

And amazingly, was not afraid.

"I discovered that a heart of passion still beats in this ancient form."

"It was a trick," she confessed wretchedly

"Yes, it certainly was. A good one, too. But it never fooled me. I was fooling myself."

She met his stare fully then, searching for more meaning in the iridescent eyes, for proof that he wasn't mocking her in the soft line of his smile.

"It was not your she-demon that woke me to the truth," he went on in a tone as silken as the sheets beneath her. "I have known a demon or two in my time, and there is no great appeal there."

"What then?" she asked, daring boldness because she had nothing to lose, except the man she loved.

"It was a vision of heaven, though I may never see it myself." He fingered the ribbon caught untidily in her hair then pulled it free. "It was a glimpse of what I might have had if I hadn't been distracted by those demons long ago. What I might have now if I can find the wisdom. Let me see if I can remember how this is done."

He was going to make love to her.

All wasn't lost.

That startled thought barely had time to cross her mind with a wondering excitement.

He brushed her nightdress off the cap of her shoulder and touched his mouth there against her flushed skin. An exquisite shudder swept through Laure as his kisses trickled down toward the gentle curve of her left breast. Instead of pushing the barrier of fabric aside, his lips moved over it, seeking the beaded peak the way a mountaineer looked for the right spot to place his claiming flag. She gasped. Through the hug of dampened linen, he drew sensations of sharp achy fire with his first deep suction.

And Laure realized that what she thought she knew about the act of love was nothing at all.

With an uncertain flutter, she settled her hands upon the hard flex of his shoulders. As she stroked along them to learn the powerful terrain, an awed breathlessness beset her. Surely no beast from the wild was as sleek and strong, and for the moment, captured by passion. A passion for her.

His hands scooped behind her back, lifting her into a sitting position between the straddle of his thighs. He straightened and paid homage to her lips with a series of elegant, open-mouthed kisses. Melting into them, she was too distracted by the delicate dueling of his tongue with hers to notice that her nightdress pooled about her waist forgotten. Until he leaned back. The icy hot blue of his gaze sketched over her inspired curves with the exact detailing of an artist immortalizing his idea of perfection upon the canvas of his mind's eye.

"You are *magnifico, cara mia.*" He highlighted that claim with the revering brush of his fingertips along the underswell of her breast. "My *amico del cuore* Gino said I had no appreciation for life's finer things of beauty. You prove him wrong, *bella*, for I have never seen anything quite so fine as you. Let me see all of you."

With the support of his palms beneath her elbows, he raised her up to her knees. Cloaking fabric floated free, revealing the gently sculpted charms of her womanhood to his intense scrutiny. Surprisingly, Laure felt no shame, no guilty want to cover herself. His attentiveness nurtured the confidence she'd never allowed to flower. Now it bloomed gloriously as he smiled.

"Perfetto."

With that husky endorsement, he bent low, his next kiss adoring the sweet indentation at her navel. When she started slightly, he cupped her bottom with his hands to tilt her toward him. Then he dipped down to nuzzle kisses against soft, red-gold curls. Laure's shock dissolved as a shiver of sensual awareness rushed from that point of intimate communion. Trembling fingers clenched in silky black hair, fisting and relaxing with the rhythm of her body's tumultuous awakening. A cry of discovery escaped her even as her restrictive boundaries burst beyond their known limitations. She spoke his name in wonder as the flood of unbelievable sensations eased to a splendid relief.

But it was not enough.

She lay back upon the tangle of red satin, shifting her legs to free them from the bonds of her gown, kicking it aside. Her movements were languid invitation, her uplifted gaze sultry with the loss of innocence. For even though her body had been taken, it had never been given or gifted with such sweet release.

"Be husband to me, Gerard."

Never had his senses been so acute, so focused upon a single goal.

Gerard drank up the dusky scent of her, the taste of her an aphrodisiac. Urgency roared through him, a penetrating pain as sharp as his nightly hunger, but this was centered low, pulsing with its own insistent beat.

Stupefacente!

Miracolo!

Exquisitely alive with the needs of his nearly forgotten human self, he stripped off his remaining clothing to be quite frankly astounded by just how ready he was to reacquaint himself with mortal desires. *Madre dio*, why had he surrendered up such pleasures? The pleasures of life had fallen before darker needs. Time to rediscover them. Time to reach for the glorious light his Laure represented.

She stiffened slightly when he layered himself over her, but her invitation was not withdrawn. She was afraid of this intimate juncture, and he charmed those fears away with courtly kisses. Her body responded to his clever touch, arching, opening, urging him on. Splendid madness, irresistible magic. He moved against her, reveling in the contact. Now he remembered. Now he knew what had the couple in the courtyard so entranced that the world around them ceased to be a distraction. He wanted that blissful oblivion for himself with this amazing woman he had wed.

"Don't."

The protest burst from Laure, surprising her as much as him. He read panic in her confused gaze, in the tightening of legs, though she did not deny him.

"Don't what, *innamorata*?" he whispered into her hurried breaths, quieting them with soul-shaking kiss.

"Don't hurt me."

Her plea was so poignant, so unexpected, it pierced his heart before he could find a way to protect it. Hurt her? Never! Not ever!

A chuckle vibrated through him, low and impossibly arrogant. "*Cara mi amore*, there will be no pain in the paradise I bring you. This I promise. Will you believe me, or shall we stop this now?"

He rode her deep inhalation then gratefully accepted her urgent kiss as an answer. Passion rose, hot and swirling about his brain. He sought to temper it by leaving the lure of her moist lips to scatter kisses across her fevered cheeks and heated brow. But once begun, the fire refused to burn less brightly. It roared.

Her body bowed up, absorbing the hard impression of his own in willing abandon. Control faltered as instinct surged, confusing his purpose with its own dark needs. His mouth trailed from the delicate cut of her jaw down the tempting curve of her throat, lingering with fatalistic yearning where her pulse beat strong and fast with eagerness. Another beast came to life inside him, one that would not be kind or patient or care if she found pleasure. A beast that perished the instant he plunged into the hot secrets of her female form.

He gasped, lost to sensation. For a moment, neither moved, nor even breathed. Then Laure curved her palm to fit the dramatic angles of his face, drawing him down to claim the luxury of her parted lips.

And he was right. It was paradise.

With each welcome advance and reluctant withdrawal, she found unparalleled delight. Her body learned the tempo quickly, eager to partner him in this dance of delicious pleasures. Pleasures that built and built and built inside her, until she could no longer contain the expanding pressure. She breathed her amazement into his mouth, satisfaction shuddering along her slender frame. Almost immediately, he sucked in her sigh with a disbelieving gasp of his own. His arms tightened around her, constricting so powerfully she feared he would break her in half before his tension gave in a spectacular rush.

Wonderfully mashed and wearily content, she carried his lax weight upon her well-spent form, holding him in the cherishing circle of her arms as his head rested heavily upon her shoulder. His face was turned away so she lightly kissed the back of his head.

Why had she ever been afraid?

She allowed herself the hedonistic joy of the moment, exulting in the aftermath of his possession, drifting upon the gentle tide of sated peace. She smiled as he lifted one of her hands to his mouth to express his contentment in courtly fashion. She sighed as his lips caressed along her knuckles, not noticing in her daze of happiness how chilled they'd become.

And when he turned her hand within his to press his kiss to her inner wrist, no alarm disturbed her sense of equanimity, especially when his tongue stroked over that sensitive site to elicit a sensual shiver.

And then she felt the sharp pierce of his teeth.

It wasn't her startled cry as much as his own dismay that had Gerard casting her arm away from him. He bolted upright to a saving distance, his face averted from the object of his desire and near abuse. He was breathing hard and fierce in denial of his true nature, the struggle evident in the harsh delineation of muscle across his back and shoulders. The taste of her, so rich, so sweet, wreaked havoc upon his shredding control. It would be so easy to turn back around, to bend down and take her.

She probably wouldn't even struggle.

He threw off that vile, insinuating thought and ground the heels of his hands against his temples as if to squeeze out other similar suggestions. Unholy suggestions.

What a villain he was. What a monster!

Reflexively, Laure rubbed her wrist where it ached from the brief stab of penetration, fighting down her own panic. She didn't know what to do, what to say to him now that the bliss-filled moment was broken.

"I told you," he snarled without turning toward her. "I told you never to forget what I was."

"Gerard—"

Before tears of fright and remorse had a chance to form, she was alone on her makeshift marriage bed.

FIFTEEN

Laure rushed through the cleaning of Gerard's hidden chamber, removing all evidence that they'd been there together, as if it was some dirty secret to be quickly concealed. Her heart pounded fast and furious as she held back conflicting emotions along with the dampness wobbling along her lashes. The fact that her senses yet hummed with the feel of him made his absence echo more emptily. She didn't dare consider what had happened within the scope of her future. They'd made love. They were bound as man and wife in every definition. Except love.

When only the perfume lingered as a reminder of her passing, Laure went to her own chamber to wash and change her clothes. Her hands and knees shook, making the task complicated. She couldn't meet her own eyes in the mirror so could only guess whether she looked presentable. Presentable to whom? Who would care? Her days, her nights stretched out before her in a great wasteland of despair. If Gerard couldn't be made to care for her, what did the rest matter?

If only the babe stirring in her womb was his.

She went downstairs, too absorbed in her own confused melancholy to even suppose that Gerard might yet be home. Of course he'd gone out—out to see to his preferred passions, those for blood and death. She took a faltering breath and blinked hard before turning into the parlor. And there, she stopped, uncertain and suddenly afraid to move.

Gerard stood at the window, hands clasped behind his back, knuckles defined with tension. Not knowing what to say or how to approach him with this new distancing intimacy between them, Laure stayed where she was, waiting for him to give some sign that he knew she was there. Of course he did. With his superior senses, he'd felt her long before she was aware of him.

Silence stained heavily across the space between them. Laure clutched her skirts to keep her nervous hands still. And she waited, studying his lean, dark silhouette there against the night.

"I've killed them all."

His opening statement carried the impact of a shot. Her heart jumped then began to race wildly.

"Who?" That single word quavered with the wish not to know.

"Everyone I've ever loved. Everyone who has gotten close to me. I am not what you call a good investment for a long-lasting relationship. You must take my word for that. That's why you must go."

Go? Panic superceded hesitation. Panic, followed by a sudden fierce denial. He wasn't throwing her out. He wouldn't rid himself of her so easily.

"No. This is my home, and I will not leave it."

"You and your brother may have the money. Take all of it. Just go."

She had no patience with his wearied martyrdom. "How dare you make that offer to me? How could you think that is the important issue here? I don't want your money. I want my home and my husband."

"The issue here is your life. Have you no idea how close you came to losing it tonight?"

The quiet gravity of that question made the truth of her peril sink deep and cold like the death he warned of so somberly. Yes, he could have killed her, easily, quickly, so simply. But he hadn't. That strengthened her petition.

"Here I am, Gerard, unharmed and unafraid."

He turned toward her then, a fine dramatic sweep punctuating his anger and frustration. She took an involuntary step back because what stood before her wasn't the tender lover of less than an hour ago. Here was the beast that warred within him, the dark soul that sought control.

His eyes glowed with a lurid light, gleaming red and silver. The angles of his face jutted above sunken hollows, leaving a pale, cadaverous shell instead of a handsome man. This was the monster she'd seen kill without discrimination, with lustful pleasure. The other half of what she'd wed.

"This is what I am, Laure." As he spoke, his words hissed past his elongated teeth. They shone, sharp, white and horrible. "This is all that I am, yet you look foolishly for more. There is nothing else, no mortal lover, no genial companion, just a demon who would slay you, without a flicker of conscience, to feed an appetite he cannot control."

"If it were that easy to slay me, you would not be telling me this now."

Her somber logic took him aback. With a blink, his gaze reverted to its normal blaze of pale blue. His features seemed to fill out and grow less frightening. And the dreadful teeth had evened out with the others as he fretfully ran his tongue along them.

"Laure, you don't understand the risk you take even standing in this room with me."

"I'm willing to take it, Gerard."

"I'm not!"

His venting roar forced her to clasp her hands over her ears. Though he drew no closer, his presence filled the room, menacing, enraged, and undeniably dangerous. Still, she wouldn't withdraw or betray the slightest fear.

"Good God, woman, don't you realize what I am? I have lived off the blood of centuries. I have stolen thousands of souls so my own black one can survive. I've heard the weeping of hundreds and have gone on unaffected. I am not good, nor decent, nor kind. And though it may amuse me now to play the doting courtier, the time will come when what I am will rise to tear the throat from you and feast upon your blood."

Laure paled but didn't falter. "I love you, Gerard."

He recoiled as if in horror. "No! You don't love me. You fancy some fantasy hero who has rescued you from poverty's grasp. You confuse gratitude for the one who brought you to this house and let you make it your home. You adore a savior who saved you from a wicked figure from your past. You think an interlude of passion equals an eternity of devotion. You are a fool, and you will be dead if you don't wake up and see the truth. I do not love you."

A shudder shook through her, but she braced against further weakness. "I don't believe you."

"I cannot love. I cannot feel what was human inside me. I will not. Do you understand? *I will not.*"

"Gerard—"

"Leave this house while you still can. Leave my life while I'll still let you."

"No—"

"I am not a man, Laure. I am not a husband, a lover, a saint. What I am is a killer who feeds on those like you in order to survive. You may deny what you are. You may pretend that your past does not influence your future. You may dabble with your powers when it suits you, then claim you have no control. You may live that lie without ever harming a soul. I cannot. To try would be dangerous folly. I am a monster who slaughters for a selfish cause, and you cannot change that. Try as you might, you cannot change me."

"And if I could?"

That soft-spoken question knocked him back on his heels for a moment of silent, troubled thought.

"If I could," he replied flatly, "I would not."

"Why?" she cried out in disbelieving anguish. "Do you enjoy the life you live so much?"

He shook his head and turned away, but not before she saw the depth of pain in his expression. "Yes," he told her, and she knew it was a lie.

"Now who is pretending?"

"Yes," he said more strongly. "Because as this creature, I am immune to the trivialities of a human existence. I am above the suffering. I am beyond the reach of consequence. I don't need to concern myself with the petty nature of mortal man. I am a god."

"You are alone. And afraid."

He closed his eyes, refusing to admit to those truths.

"And I am not tortured by the faces of those I've slain. You think this is a damned existence? I can imagine no greater hell than to have those ghosts upon my soul. I can ignore them now, but if I were mortal, I would be driven mad by the memory of deeds I've done. You cannot know the horror I've caused. I won't feel responsible. I won't live with those reminders."

"And if you could change things?"

He glanced at her over his shoulder, his eyes narrowed into wary slits. "What things? How?"

"If you could change the past, so you could live without guilt—"

"Impossible." He made a denying slash with his hands. "One cannot wipe away one's sins so easily."

"If you had the opportunity to change, say three things, would that be enough to give your soul peace?"

His luminous stare darkened, haunted by the suggestion, by even daring to hope it could be so. "How?" he whispered. "How would this be done?"

"I'm not absolutely certain that I—"

"You?"

She regarded him with a cool disdain. "Yes, me. You have challenged me to reach out to my destiny. My mother tried to keep me from what was in my blood. Perhaps by facing it, we can help each other."

He stared unblinkingly, having nothing to say, so she went on.

"My grandmother told me I was born with special powers, an unusual reception for the loa, which are the deities we worship. She told me of things she heard were possible if the *mambo* has sufficient strength. I have that strength. I know it. If you will trust me, tomorrow night we can see just what is possible."

Trust her. There was the ironic rub. Gerard returned to the window to stare out into the void of darkness which was like peering into his soul. His soul. Did it exist? Was there anything left, after all the centuries, that would be worth saving? Was he ready to put a limit of mortal years upon his life just to live with a woman? He didn't need to close his eyes to bring the image of her face all passion-flushed to mind. It was etched there for an eternity.

"I have never made good decisions for myself," he stated, watching his wife's reflection in the window glass as she approached him. "I am not particularly wise." He chuckled softly, a sound filled with his frustration and inner pain. "You see the result of both before you."

He didn't flinch when she slipped her arms around him. In fact, an odd constriction formed in his chest when she laid her cheek against his back. Part panic, part pleasure, he didn't know what to make of it or what to do about it, so he endured both the confusion of feelings and her embrace.

"Laure, what would you have me do?"

"Let me help you put an end to your regrets. Let me clear the stains of guilt from your soul. Let me prove how much I love you."

He shook his head, unable to accept those words, those concepts too foreign, too frightening to him. "I have always viewed love as the weakest of human emotions, the one that brings the most pain."

"You're wrong, Gerard. You must have once loved deeply to have hardened your heart to the very idea."

He heard the tease of his sisters' laughter, saw the sweetness of his mother's smile. As much as he tried to cling to those cherished memories, others swelled up upon a crimson tide, washing them away with the sound of screams. He took a jagged breath. Better not to look back at all. Better to have no past and an endless eternity laid out before him than to risk the return of that spectacular pain.

But if he could change things...

He covered Laure's small hands with his own, absorbing their warmth, seeking out the life-giving pulse in her wrist with the rub of his thumbs. His future was tied to that vital beat, to that heated flow of blood within her veins. Nothing else existed to equal that power. Or he would have believed so until tonight. Until she sent his heart and soul rocketing to another sort of paradise within her loving arms. She did love him. He couldn't make light of it within his own tumultuous thoughts. But was her love strong enough to heal one as ravaged by wrong-doings as he was?

Trust her. Did he have any choice if he wanted to keep her in his life—without taking that very life through the vileness of his own dark nature?

"What must I do?"

She clutched his hands exuberantly, but her voice was calm. "Tomorrow night after the sun sets, you will come with me to a meeting of the *societe*. We will discuss your situation with my great aunt Eulalie. With her guidance, I will free you."

"To be what?"

"My husband."

Lightning strobed over the sluggish waters of the Mississippi, leaving a suspenseful sizzle in the air, a sense that things were about to change. That same disquieting mood of expectation chafed through Gerard as he hunted the rain-dappled walkway in search of his evening meal.

The hour was late. A cold downpour discouraged loitering, so pickings were unusually lean. What few fools braved the inclement night traveled in huddled groups. Like a stalking wolf, Gerard preferred the lone straggling sheep to a bunched flock.

There was no music in the air, no laughter, just a dreary patter on the brick pathways. Rumbling thunder lent to the oppressive feel. It was as if heaven wept upon its lost souls. And none were as unforgiven as his own.

Though his hair slicked back to hug his head like black satin, and his coat provided scant protection, Gerard felt neither wet nor cold. Just hunger. But even that gaunt, gnawing appetite wasn't foremost in his thoughts.

What if she could do it?

What if after tomorrow night, he could right the wrongs he'd done and live amid humanity instead of preying on its members like a curse. A curse. Yes, that's what he'd been living all these hundreds of years. It took Laure Cristobel to remind him of it.

Until meeting her, he'd been satisfied with his nocturnal existence. Until her, he'd not truly felt alive. Or quite so alienated. He'd been content to shadow the midnight streets, a dark spectre, reveling in his own power as he fed upon the insignificant.

And then greedy little Percy had shaken him from his placidity.

Gaining a wife and a conscience in such a short period of time was exhausting. His mind reeled with the consequence. How he'd taunted his friend Gino for his fits of guilty melancholy while he considered himself far above such moral anguish. Gino would laugh if he could see him now.

A sharp scent snared his focus from his own ruminations. He went still, testing the breeze, letting his primordial senses find his unsuspecting victim along the darkened avenue. A single set of footsteps, light with youth and vigor, breathing quickly with hurry, and heartbeat strong—hypnotic. All vestiges of what one might recognize as human fell from Gerard as he became a creature of pure instinct.

That instinct was to kill and feed.

He swooped down the puddled street, a blur undetectable by the human eye. Hunger directed him. There, ahead, a slight figure raced along the levee, a newspaper held overhead to ineffectively ward off the rain. Gerard struck from behind, bowling the frail form to the wet ground. He tore back the collar of a thin coat, and with a predatory snarl, his teeth came down, only to stop a scant inch from stealing away a life.

Such a slender neck. A child, not even close to adulthood. Soft sobbing sounds reached him through the roar of his need. A child.

Why did he hesitate?

He'd shown no particular mercy according to age in the past. Yet, when he bent, intent on feeding, he could not force himself to rip the future away from one so young and innocent.

What was wrong with him?

He left the dazed youth in a disoriented huddle, and was gone before his victim could grasp the source of the attack. As if anyone would believe him.

Gerard put several blocks between them before the raging hunger could best his sudden panic. He paused, doubled up in distress with hands gripping his knees, insides clenched against the twist of want. He'd never walked away unsatisfied, except from Arabella and now, Laure. But he felt emotional ties to them and none to this faceless child in the rain.

Why spare one inferior human at the cost of his own discomfort? He didn't understand. What was Laure doing to him with her taunting offers of mortality? Why was he even considering her scheme? He hadn't been reluctant to join the legion of the night, nor had he ever been ashamed of what he was. True, it hadn't been his choice, and if he could turn back time and make things different...

Would he?

Should he?

His head ached with the unknowns of it.

How he wished he had just a trace of Gino's intellect or Bianca's ruthless self-interest. Something to sway him one way or the other before the tug-of-war tore him in two.

"Eh, you be all right there, mister?"

Gerard exploded upward with a roar. The good Samaritan's answer was brutally concise, stabbing into his throat and leaving him with scant breath in his body upon the slick grass within view of Jackson Square. Where someone was bound to find him and see he got help in time to save his foolish life. Why that should matter to him, galled the four-hundred-year-old hunter as he finally made his way home.

What had she done to him? What magic, what charm placed confusion between heart and mind?

As he stood at the foot of her bed, watching her sigh in the throes of slumber, unwelcomed knowledge of his plight came with a cruel thrust.

Love.

He was in love.

He was doomed.

SIXTEEN

Eulalie LaClaire regarded them through slitted eyes. To her, they both must have seemed decidedly nervous, Laure's impassive-faced husband particularly. Was there something about him that gave her pause? Did she sense the eddies of raw, dangerous power beneath the elegant drape of his clothing and European *ennui*. She'd introduced him as husband. Did Eulalie wonder what else he was?

"Our rituals are not for the eyes of unbelievers, Laurette. You know this, yet you bring this outsider here when there are those who will not accept you as one of us."

"I know *Tante* Eulalie. But we had nowhere else to turn. We need the strength of the *societe* if we are to succeed in what we must do. I need your help."

"What is it you mean to do?" She leaned forward, intrigued despite her reservations.

"I want to perform a *voyage*."

The old woman's eyes flew open wide in shock. Her voice faltered. "*Voyage*? I've never known of anyone attempting to travel."

"*Grandmere* said I had the power, but I'm not sure I know how to control it."

The old *mambo* said nothing for a long moment, assessing the situation with both interest and understandable apprehension. And envy. "Did she? I understood from your mother that you had never been formally trained."

"Not formally. My mother didn't approve."

"But Moira showed you the ways. How like her to do so without permission." A trace of bitterness crept into her tone, making Laure wonder if the rivalry between the two sisters, Moira and Eulalie, over control of the *societe* was just a story as she'd been told. But then Eulalie smiled. "How fortunate for us. Perhaps she gave you the secrets she did not have the time to tell me before she died."

"Whatever she gave, I'd gladly share another time, but tonight we must prepare for the *voyage, "*Laure said. " Tonight is *casse canarie*, the breaking of the jugs to deliver souls from purgatory."

"And whose soul are you attempting to free? Moira's? Your mother's?"

"My husband's."

Shrewd black eyes fixed upon Gerard, who up until that point had been as immobile as one of the ceiling support posts. He endured Eulalie's scrutiny without a flicker of reaction.

"What is the state of his soul?"

"His *gros-bon-ange* was lost long ago. I seek to send his *ti-bon-ange* back in search of it."

"Such separations of the soul are dangerous to the living, Laurette."

Gerard bestowed a narrow smile and a wry, "I am not exactly living, *signora*."

Eulalie's gaze flew to Laure in demand of an explanation. There was no time to broach the truth gently. "My husband is a revenant—a vampire."

"A—" Eulalie blinked owlishly, struggling to believe the unbelievable.

"His *gros-bon-ange* was lost to him four hundred years ago. I want to send his spirit back to reclaim it."

Eulalie recovered her breathing and attempted speech again. "A vampire. A *baka*. I have heard of such things but have never seen one."

"Be glad of that, madame," Gerard told her.

"Laurette, dealing with the spirits from the dead should only be performed by a fully initiated *mambo*. You have the knowledge, perhaps, but not the experience. You could endanger all my people if evil spirits escape before a benevolent loa can be summoned to drive them off."

"I know, *Tante* Eulie. That's why I come to beg for your assistance. I may have the knowledge, but you have the power. Together, we can heal his soul."

"It is unusual," Eulalie mused, rubbing her pursed lips with her thumbs. She looked to Gerard again, this time, as if seeing something totally different. Something alien, powerful beyond understanding. Then she nodded. "We shall try. But you must promise to do only what I tell you, Laurette. You must trust me, or I will not place all at risk."

"I trust you, *tante*."

"And you?" The ancient *mambo* demanded the same admission from Gerard. He smiled.

"I trust her."

Laure slipped her hand over one of his for a slight squeeze and was surprised when he slid his fingers between hers, curling them into his palm.

"All right, Laurette. Let me go advise the others of what we will attempt this evening. If we succeed, word of our *societe's* power will spread throughout New Orleans."

"No."

She glanced at Gerard, affronted by his slashing tone. "No?"

"No. Word of this goes no farther than the three of us. I may trust my wife, but I am not so foolish as to place my fate in the hands of a faceless mob. I will not have my identity exposed so recklessly."

Laure looked anxiously between the two of them. "Is that a problem, *tante*? Can't they perform the ritual without knowing who he is or what we plan to do?"

Eulalie scowled in displeasure but said, "I suppose. But there will be questions."

"And you will answer them to everyone's satisfaction," Gerard concluded, "without giving me away."

"Yes." She stood abruptly. "Prepare him, Laurette. I will come for you when all is ready."

When they were alone, Gerard slid his hand free and rose to pace the confined space of Eulalie's cabin. Laure read his nervousness in the clutching movement of his fingers.

"What is this *bon-ange* you speak of?"

"The *societe* believes that the soul has two parts, the *gros-bon-ange,* which is the life force we share with all living things, and the *ti-bon-ange,* which is what makes each of us unique. When you became a vampire, your *gros-bon-ange* was separated from you, which is why you are not truly living as a human being but have not died. We call this *dessounin.* Your *ti-bon-ange* can safely leave your body during dreams or when the body is possessed by a loa. That is the part of you I will send back to collect the other half of your soul."

"And when it returns, I will be human?"

"That is our hope."

"And this has been done before?"

She paused, considering the benefit of a consoling lie, but could not tell it. "Not that I've seen. But my grandmother spoke of it being possible."

"Possible. Ahhh, there's a comfort. And if something goes amiss and neither part returns? What then?"

"You would be trapped in your own past, forced to live it over again." And they would never meet or marry. That she didn't tell him. That was her own private pain.

"These changes I can make to the past, how are they accomplished?"

"You will have time to touch upon maybe three events within your past. There will be one moment where you will be at a point of choice or conflict. If you can catch that moment and alter its outcome, you can mend what you wish never happened."

"Will these changes affect me?"

"Just those around you. You will still be here in body and, therefore, cannot alter your own fate by any changes you make. But those you know, those you've loved, could live very different lives. This will be a dangerous time," she warned, "for while your *ti-bon-ange* is absent from your body, you will be vulnerable to sorcery."

"But you will protect me." His steady gaze demanded that assurance from her, and she gave it with more confidence than she felt.

"I will. I will be with you in spirit. I will follow you back but may not interfere with your actions. I cannot guide you or advise you, but can only protect you from the effects of evil and bring you back when the time is right. You must be ready. The time will pass quickly, and our chances will not come again if they are missed."

He stopped, pulling himself from his own concerns to regard her. "And you? Is there danger to you?" When she didn't answer right away, he crossed to her, lifting her chin in his palm until she couldn't avoid his penetrating stare. "Is there, Laure? I must know. Tell me the truth."

Laure smiled thinly. "My aunt will shield me from any harm. I'm not worried for myself." If she couldn't bring him back, it didn't matter what happened to her. It was that simple in her own heart. This was her chance for the happiness that had somehow always evaded her. Nothing else held any importance. They would be a family, or they would not exist. While she could find the strength to go on without him if she had to, there was no will within her to do so. Gerard was her future, and that future was tied to his past. Healing the one would make the other possible. No matter what the risk to herself, she would give him the chance to free his soul from its dark stains.

"And if it does not work? If nothing is changed, what then?"

Laure waved that worry away. "We will talk of it if it comes to pass. We'll be no worse off, will we?"

Gerard didn't return her smile.

Eulalie's return ended further discussion when she said, "It is time."

They traveled by shallow pirogue over glassy black water and through areas so stagnant one might be tempted to walk across them.

Their boatman was the same silent man who had brought them to
Eulalie's, and he had no more to say on this trip. He poled the boat
to a rickety dock that seemed to disappear into sinister darkness.
Eulalie climbed out so they followed, finding a narrow, well-traveled
path which led deep into the bayou. The usual cacophony of night
songs from birds and frogs and beasts was hushed until a low,
throbbing beat could be heard, calling the faithful to ceremony.

The only rituals Laure had attended were in worship of the Rada
loa, the gentle deities who were summoned for harmless service.
These were held in the low-walled *hounforts* in the open air beneath
a roofed *peristyle*. There, offerings were made at the center post
surrounded by the bright-colored flags symbolizing each of their loa.
The devotees were charged with a positive energy within the embrace
of community, and Laure had felt safe and good when witnessing the
rites.

But the moment they entered a small, torch-lit clearing, Laure
experienced no such serenity. As she had feared, her great aunt was
not a devotee of the peaceful Rada but rather a *bokor* in league with
the dark *Petro* forces. Red-clad believers circled a chest-high stone
beneath a gnarled tree where symbols of the lion and white sheep
named it as Legba's altar.

An eerie silence fell over the crowd as Eulalie stepped forward to
call upon the keeper of the crossroads.

"Papa Legba, ouvri barrie pou nous passer."

Water was presented to four cardinal points then poured three
times before the altar and before each sacred drum. LaPlace, the
master of ceremonies whom Laure recognized as an elder cousin,
came forward with two devotees to perform salutations with flags and
the ritual sword. When this was done, candles were lit in a circle
while Eulalie drew the symbolic *veves* on the ground. Once these
designs were completed, she blew the remaining *farine* to the four
cardinal points. Laure watched, chilled despite the humid night air.

At her side, unaware of the significance of these acts and probably
highly cynical of their power, Gerard was unmoving. She couldn't
tell if he felt awe or apprehension. If not, she felt enough for the both

of them.

The *houngenikon*, another cousin, this one female, led the chorus of fully initiated members in unison chant, beginning with Catholic prayer. Gerard crossed himself out of habit then went still once more when the liturgy shifted into an ancient African tongue. Drums punctuated the song, not in a pleasing tempo but rather with a sharp, off-beat pulse both discordant and disturbing. Hands clapped to the same broken rhythm that called to the body to move and sway in irresistible accord. Laure wasn't immune to the twitching cadence. Her insides vibrated with it. Soon, Gerard was the only one who stood unaffected. Eulalie, in trancelike ecstasy, struck her calabash gourd rattle atop the symbol of Baron Samedi, loa of the dead.

The *houngenikon* held up two live black chickens. Their beating wings and frantic cackling added to the confusion of noise. The birds were laid upon the *veve* shaped like a coffin where, one at a time, *LaPlace* slashed their throats and drained their blood into a hollow gourd. A low rumbling sounded from Gerard. His lips parted slightly, and his eyes took on a metallic glitter. Laure touched his hand, alarmed to find the skin cold, him unresponsive.

Eulalie beckoned to Laure, bidding her to lead Gerard into the circle. The ritual chanting rose to a fevered pitch, the drumming an angry throb of violent passion.

"Very dramatic," Gerard murmured, glancing about with a disinterested calm. "This isn't the part where they sacrifice me, is it?"

"Shhh!"

Eulalie waved her hand across the top of the altar stone, and that's when Gerard balked.

"Please," Laure whispered. "You must lie down upon it. You will not be harmed."

"I don't like this. I don't trust her."

"Gerard, it's the only way we can be together. Please. Trust me."

His nostrils flared at the scent of blood, from the blade, from the ground, from the gourd. It clouded his thinking, just as the insistent sound battered at his ability to reason. He focused on Laure, seeking the sincerity of her gaze, so deep and beseeching. He couldn't deny her, as much her captive as these weak followers were to their vicious gods. He laid back on the hard slab of stone, forcing his body to relax and his mind to clear.

He couldn't afford to fall prey to their madness if he were going to save himself.

As torchlight cast wildly distorted images upon the untamed bayou backdrop, Eulalie lifted the gourd to her lips and drank deeply. Her head fell back, and her eyes closed for a long moment before she regained control. And carried the gourd to Laure.

"Drink and share the Divine energy."

Laure took the gourd in shaking hands and tipped it up for one swallow, two. The thick salty warmth made her gag at first then went down smoothly. As a swirling dizziness came over her, her thoughts touched briefly on that irony.

This was what sustained Gerard.

She drew a deep, shuddering breath and leaned against the altar as if intoxicated. There, upon the foot of the stone by Gerard's feet, was a clay pot inscribed with fanciful designs. Her gaze fixed upon the *govi*, made to hold the spirits of the dead, and she was struck by a sudden clarity.

Though an anxious Eulalie tried to hold her back, Laure pulled herself along the length of the altar. Her knees were wobbly, her vision unsure. Had there been something besides blood in that gourd? She reached out for the *govi*, cupping it in both hands as tears blurred her gaze. The *ti-bon-ange* of Moira LaClaire was imprisoned within the vessel, keeping it from finding peace in the land of the dead.

"*Grandmere*," she called down into the neck of the pot. "Who has banished you?"

As if in a dream, she could hear the dear old woman's voice speaking inside her head.

"Laurette, I warned you not to be trusting. Danger is near. Take heed, or sorrow will rule."

These vague prophesies told her nothing beyond feeding her own subconscious dread. "*Grandmere*, I need your help to make the *voyage* for my husband. Help him rejoin his soul, then I will free yours. Give me the knowledge, the skill and the faith so I might perform this task."

"You have always had it, child. Relax and be one with the Ginen. Let the strength of our cosmic community guide you. Let their knowledge be yours, their skill and faith fill you like this vessel of clay. Trust only in your instincts and let not your heart lead you."

"What does she say, Laurette?"

Eulalie's strained words pulled Laure from her silent communion and back to the dark circle of the *bokor*. She pushed past Eulalie as if she was of no importance. She took Gerard's pale face between her hands and bent to kiss him, letting him taste the sacrificial blood upon her lips. Even as she lifted up a scant inch, close enough to feel his breath mingling with her own, she began to chant.

The language was unknown to her, as was the meaning. The words poured forth from some unseen well of purpose as she fixed Gerard with her unblinking stare. The trembling of her hands transferred to him, a vibration of power, a displacement of time and space and distance.

The *batterie* of ritualistic sound became a humming within her head, its pagan tempo a heartbeat to match her own, and the echoing pulse of Gerard's joined in. And then she could feel him, at first just the blur of confused emotions, then more clearly his thoughts as they played out a tableau within her own mind. She was aware of nothing but the two of them, psychically joined both physically and mentally.

"Are you ready?"

The words flitted from her thoughts to his and returned with a, *"Yes."*

"Picture the time and place you want to go. Recall the sounds, the smells, the textures. Make it real. Tell me, are you there?"

"Yes."

"Then let go of this solid flesh and form. Let go and rejoin the other half of your soul. Become one with it again. Become one."

Gerard sampled the blood on his mouth left from Laure's kiss. Instead of kindling his hunger, the metallic taste made him faintly

queasy. He wiped the back of his hand across his lips but came away
with nothing.

"What's wrong, *amico mio*? Lose your appreciation for fine
wine?"

Gerard blinked his eyes into focus and stared with unabashed
disbelief at the young man beside him. He drew a shaky breath,
sucking in the scent of fresh bread and garlic, of leather and horse and
city. There was no fragrance like it. He was home, seated in an *al
fresco* café at twilight, drinking wine and talking youthful nonsense
with his best friend.

It was, wasn't it?

"Gino?"

His friend regarded him with a quizzical amusement. Luigino
Rodmini just as he'd last seen him only...not. This was Gino when
his face had still shone with purity, his green eyes with innocent
wonder at the world around him, and his smile with a philosopher's
tolerance for the flaws of man. Before he'd become a monster.

It was hard to remember back when they'd been the dearest of
friends, practically inseparable, the solemn aristocrat and his
entertaining, lower-class companion. Gerard swallowed hard as a
wealth of memories overwhelmed him. He couldn't recall the
significance of this particular meeting, but he knew their time of
innocence was almost at an end. As was their friendship.

Gino, his dear naive friend, who never understood the lure of his
wealth or the charm of his own generous simplicity. How
shamelessly Gerard had taken advantage of those things back then.
He'd been envious and petulant but always a loyal *amico del cuore*.

Right up until the time he'd tried to kill him.

But he could end that. He could break the tragic chain of events
that may have gotten their start on this balmy night. But first, he
wanted to enjoy the moment.

"*Madre mio*, how I've missed you." With that glad cry, Gerard
threw his arms about his friend for a squeezing hug and enthusiastic
kisses on either cheek.

Gino smiled, slightly embarrassed and bemused by his friend's passionate behavior. Gerard was the demonstrative one, the one who was free with his favors and with his faults. "Yes, it's been what, an hour, maybe two?"

"Too long," he exclaimed slumping back in his chair to absorb the shocked delight. "Too often we don't appreciate what we have until it is no longer there before us."

Gino cocked his head. "Is this my frivolous Gerardo speaking of such somber themes? I must be a bad influence on you."

"A good influence, Gino. I just never understood that. I never had a chance to tell you how much your friendship meant to me. I was...I am such a fool." Gerard's voice fractured, and he turned away, eyes welling with unexpected sentiment. How long would he have here? Minutes, maybe an hour? It wasn't long enough. There wasn't enough time to savor the goodness of this simple pleasure—talking, laughing, drinking as if there were no tomorrow. He had to tell him. He had to warn Gino of what was to come.

Gino clasped a hand behind his head and gave him a slight shake of fondness. With him, everything was always easily forgiven.

"You're telling me now, aren't you? How odd you're acting, your normal state of late. Are you sure you're all right? How much wine have you had—"

Gerard looked up as his friend broke off, then followed his hard glare toward the door leading into the café.

And was mesmerized, just as he'd been four hundred years earlier.

There wasn't a man in sight who didn't find himself suddenly breathless with desire. She did that so effortlessly, with just a toss of her pale blonde hair. For a smile, they would do anything to please her. For a word, there was no price they wouldn't pay. She was the most beautiful woman in Florence—perhaps in the world. And she was pure evil.

"Bianca," Gerard whispered through the tightening in his throat.

"What do you see in her, Gerardo?" Gino grumbled.

The goddess glanced about the candlelit terrace and settled her gaze upon the two of them. She came toward their table as if no other existed.

"What does she see in me?" was Gerard's reply.

Gino's grip was painful on his forearm. His tone was low and compelling. "Come away with me, my friend. Can't you see she toys with you the same way she does with any foolish other who falls under her spell?"

"Except you, eh?"

"There is something unwholesome about her, *amico mio*. I want nothing to do with the creature. And you'd be wise to follow suit. Gerardo, she has no affection for you. Let's go. Turn your back and walk away."

Turn your back and save your soul.

He heard his own warning echoing clearly within his head, but he sat there, as stunned and enchanted as he'd been the first time the wicked temptress looked his way. She'd lost none of her power to captivate him, even knowing what she was, what she would do.

What she would do.

No! Stop this! Turn away!

But the vicious Bianca Du Maurier was already at their table, her sultry, knowing smile spinning his passions out of control.

"May I join you?"

May I join you?

He gasped, feeling himself jerked from the scene by some unseen hand. There'd been no time, no chance to stop the inevitable force of Bianca in their lives. He was spinning through a blur of lights and sounds and scents until an abrupt, piercing agony brought him to a halt. He looked down in almost comical surprise to see the thin blade of a rapier imbedded in his belly. His knees buckled, his vision blurred as he collapsed hard upon them.

"No! No! Gerardo!"

He pitched forward into his best friend's arms even as Gino withdrew the fatal thrust.

"Aiuto! Chiamate unmedico, subito!" Gino shouted, choking on his sobs.

"There is no hurry, Gino. No doctor can help him now. Look

what you've done. How will you ever forgive yourself for taking your best friend's life?"

Gerard blinked hard against the stabbing brightness to see a sinister shape standing in the glare of his final minutes. She was smiling, still as naked as she'd been when he'd burst in upon her and his friend tangled in carnal pleasure.

He'd gone mad at that moment, reaching for his blade, demanding satisfaction even though he knew—he knew!—the fault was not Gino's. The burn of betrayal, the sting of being made a fool, goaded him to draw steel. The insult of being second best, because it was Gino she'd been interested in, not him. Never him. Poor Gino, he was only trying to explain, to apologize, to plead for forgiveness as he parried Gerard's fierce attack. It had been an accident. A fatal accident. Almost...

None of that mattered now. Nothing mattered except stopping the grim series of events that would hurl them both down to damnation.

"Gino..." He could barely manage speech, his mouth full of blood.

"No, no, you cannot die! Don't die! Gerardo, please, stay with me!"

Then came the purr of Bianca's dark bargain. "I can save him, Gino. All you have to do is ask."

"No, Gino...no! Let me die...you don't understand what you're doing."

But Gino was weeping wildly, trying to staunch the terrible flow of blood with his palm, guilt and grief etched eternally upon his features as he looked up to cry, "Help him! I'll do anything, just don't let him die."

"He won't, sweet Gino."

Such truth wrapped about a damning lie.

And Gino believed her.

He won't...

SEVENTEEN

Soft, feminine laughter drew him out of the shadows. For a moment he didn't know where he was. Or what he was. He felt so strange. The laughter came again. How could he have forgotten? Music of angels. He closed his eyes to listen, lost to the sweet sounds. His sisters. Bouncing, bothersome, teasing, beautiful...how he loved them. In their joyous spirits lay the answer to the confusion in his own.

"Ladies! You forget the time. Your papa will be home any minute, and you would greet him looking like urchins from the street?"

His mother.

"Mi dispiace, madre mia."

"Mi scusi, mama."

"Go quickly then. Work miracles."

Giggles, then a small delighted cry from the youngest, Sophia.

"Look, there is Gerardo. *Mio fratello*, did you remember to bring me ribbon from town? You didn't, did you? You forget everything except your cheap wine and your expensive lady friends."

"Sophie, shame," his mother chided.

Three expectant faces turned his way, expecting to see loving son and brother. Oh, how he longed to feel those embraces, those fragrant kisses upon his cheeks and brow. But they didn't know what they welcomed with their smiles and opened arms.

He needed to get away, to flee before something terrible occurred, the nightmare that had haunted him over the centuries, but he was powerless to escape. Fever fed upon his brain. His body shook with chills. He took a step forward, into the light, wincing as it pierced his gaze with needles of brightness.

"Run." The single word croaked from him, raw and frightening.

"Gerardo, *mi bambino*! What is wrong? Are you ill?"

"No! Mama, get away. I am not myself."

"Mama, there's blood on his shirt. Wait until Papa finds he's been fighting again. Probably over some sloe-eyed *signorina*."

"Hush, Sophie. Gerardo, come sit down. Are you hurt?"

He wanted to deny it, to send them away, far away where maybe, just maybe, they would be safe. But coils of pain twisted tight in his belly, making him double over. And then his mother was bending over him, her gentle hands on his shoulders, her soft scent enveloping him like an embrace.

"Mama, don't..."

"What is it, darling?"

"I don't know. I don't know. Something has happened to me. I don't understand. Gino..." Tremendous agony swelled in his mouth and gums, impeding his speech, blinding him to clear thought.

"Tia, go find Luigino. Quickly. Perhaps he knows what has happened."

"No, Mama, you must leave me." He went down to his knees, his mother following, her arms around him, cradling him like when he was a child. He soaked up that sense of comfort even as he sought a way to discourage it. Before it was too late. "Mama, it's plague. Take the girls and run. Run!"

His sisters shrieked in panic, but his mother's embrace never faltered. "I will not leave you, darling. Girls, fetch the doctor and find your father. Don't just stand there like silly goats. Do as I say."

"Mama, his eyes!"

Shuddering as the last of his humanity was wrung from him, Gerard looked up into his dear mother's face, his last mortal memory that of her dawning horror as she recognized what she held to her breast. Not her son. Not any more. She had time for one shrill scream before he broke her neck with a strength that was all at once incredible and awful. The girls wailed and tried, too late, to obey her last command. His speed was incomprehensible. They hadn't a chance, falling in flutters of pastel silk that rapidly discolored with splashes of crimson.

From her impartial distance, Laure watched it happen, saw Gerard awaken to the beast within, a beast he could not then, could not now, control. Only centuries had taught him finesse. In the beginning, and this was the beginning, he was a brutal killer, savage and senselessly vicious as he discovered what he'd become under the most horrifying of circumstances.

As he lay in the blood of his slain family, Laure's soul wept for him, for the mother and sisters who had perished so shockingly.

Moaning in disbelief and intoxicating satiety, Gerard wobbled to his hands and knees.

"Nothing has changed," he cried out in agony.

"*Madre Dio!* What has happened here?"

Gerard pulled himself up to his knees, extending his stained hands before his shattered father's gaze. "Look what I've done. Forgive me. Kill me, please."

"You? You did this?" Gaspare Pasquale's voice wavered, and tears filled his eyes.

"End it now, Papa. Please."

Not understanding what possessed his only son to bring about such carnage, Gaspare unsheathed his blade, praying to himself, shocked beyond the ability to forgive. Trying to block out the horror scattered all about him, he focused upon his much-loved child to cry, "Demon!"

But as he began to pull back for a killing stroke, his son was no more. What knelt at his feet was a creature devoid of sympathy, empty of mercy, untouched by sentiment. Moved only by dreadful instinct and voracious hunger.

Gerard sprang with a hideous snarl.

"Laurette, you must return. Quickly! You've been betrayed."

Tearing herself from the gruesome spectacle, Laure obeyed her grandmother's command. She shook off the dazed, dreamlike effects of the *voyage* to return to the present where she was slumped across Gerard's still form, too weak to do more than gaze around her in confusion.

"Take her."

Her arms were gripped at Eulalie's order. She could only struggle impotently as she was dragged away from the altar stone. The drumming reached a fevered pitch, the frenetic sound snapping the faithful to and fro like an ecstatic palsy. Eulalie took the ritual sword from La Place and raised it for all to see.

"What are you doing?" Laure cried, pulling against those who held her as her aunt bared her husband's arm.

"With his eternal lifeforce as a part of me, I will be invincible." Making that claim, Eulalie slashed the razor-sharp blade across Gerard's wrist. La Place was quick to slide a calabash gourd beneath it to catch the vital flow spilling from him.

"No! No! Gerard awaken!"

"He cannot hear you, foolish girl." Eulalie chuckled, watching with worshipful anticipation the blood fill the gourd. "And to think I feared you. You are no threat to me and my power of command. Moira was wrong to believe you were next in line. You are too easily deceived. Both of you were wrong to trust me with your secrets and your souls. Tonight you will join your dear grandmother, my beloved sister. Your *ti-bon-ange* will live in a pot beside hers, forever my prisoner. You should have heeded your mother, girl, and not meddled where you don't belong."

Panting in panic and despair, Laure strained against those who held her away. Fear for her own fate never touched her as she watched Gerard's face go startlingly pale. His eyelids never quivered. There was no sign that his spirit had returned, and if it didn't soon, there would be no vessel for it to come back into.

"You're killing him!"

"That is the purpose of sacrifice, dear Laurette. His sacrifice will lead to my succession as rightful priestess of the *societe*."

Fury overrode distress, a deep cold anger at being lied to, at being used. With it rose a powerful objection. She would not lose her husband's life to this evil woman's ambitions.

"No!"

Laure flung up her arms, casting off the grown men who imprisoned her as if they were spindly children. She launched herself at Eulalie, who howled in rage as the gourd went flying from her hands before she had the chance to drink. The *mambo* tumbled back into La Place as Laure leapt up onto the altar stone, straddling Gerard's all too still form.

As other believers rushed her, they were thrown back by the same unseen barrier Gerard had encountered earlier. Despite Eulalie's orders for them to overpower her, her followers hung back, muttering between themselves in superstitious awe. Their leader had never displayed anywhere near this degree of control over the elements. They weren't prepared to challenge it.

They began to whisper amongst themselves that perhaps this was the one, this daughter of the daughter of Moira LaClaire. And those whispers made Eulalie wild with fury.

"Kill her! Kill them both!"

Maintaining the field around them rapidly drained Laure's strength, but she couldn't relax it and escape with either of their lives. Gerard was cold as monument marble, and there was no way she could lift him, let alone tote him safely out of the bayou under her own power. Not alone.

Without pausing to consider her actions, Laure cut her own wrist with the sword Eulalie had abandoned. Gritting her teeth into the pain, she pressed the spouting wound to Gerard's chill lips, rubbing hard so that the hot fluid would penetrate.

"Come back to me, Gerard. Drink and grow strong."

There was a slight movement to his throat. Then another. Suddenly, a searing heat streaked through her veins. With a cry, she swooned upon his chest, the protective force around them momentarily buckling.

"Take them!"

With a valiant effort she couldn't sustain for long, Laure reestablished the field. Her body shaking with strain, she pulled her wrist free of Gerard's feasting. His eyes flickered open, glazed and unseeing.

"Gerard! Help me. You must help me if we're to escape here alive!"

He reached up for her, banding her loosely with absurdly weak arms and drawing her close against him. He whispered, his voice faint and thready, "Help us."

She thought he was calling upon her, which made no sense at all, since she was powerless as her crippled barrier began to crumble. Then the air about them began to hum and shimmer. The very particles she breathed were charged with static electricity. It wasn't her doing, nor did she think it was his. She had only enough time to grab onto him tightly, her eyes closing involuntarily as a great surge of energy jolted through them both.

Laure must have lost consciousness. That's the only way she could explain shutting her eyes to the wild tableau in a dank Louisiana bayou and opening them someplace else. Someplace far away from a *vodun* sacrifice but perhaps not that far from danger.

She awoke with senses prickling. Not alone. Not in the bayou or even in New Orleans. The air was different, hot but a sultry rather than a sweltering heat, touched with the sea but crisp instead of brackish. She could see palm fronds and white-washed lattice work and, beyond, the glitter of a silver moon reflecting upon a quiet sea. Not the stagnant Mississippi or the commerce-crowded Gulf, but water uninterrupted as far as she could see.

"Gerard!"

She sat up quickly, too quickly. Her equilibrium roiled for a sickening moment as gentle hands braced her shoulders. A woman's hands. She gave her a fleeting glance, registering startling green eyes in a lovely face framed by a cascade of black hair. Then she concentrated on Gerard.

"Help him," she cried out in dismay. "Don't let him die."

The woman touched a hand to Gerard's still cheek, the gesture tender, almost intimate in its familiarity.

"He'll be all right," she assured in a French-accented voice that was European instead of New World patois. "Your quick thinking has saved him. Let me look at that."

Laure surrendered her injured wrist into the woman's care. She showed no shock at the nature of the wound. Though the ministrations were unfailingly gentle, Laure couldn't help detecting a hard sheen of brilliance in the cat's green eyes as the wound was carefully wrapped.

The woman was a vampire.

"Who are you?"

"Forgive me. There's been little time for pleasantries. I am Nicole LaValois. You are safe here at my home."

"How did we get here?"

"I heard Gerard's call. In the nick of time, I see. Come, let me help you up."

She took Laure by the elbows, lifting her off the bed where Gerard lay as if in state. She didn't want to leave him, but there was surprising strength in the young woman's grip.

"He will sleep for some time, and so should you from the looks of you. Consider yourself welcome. You are on the island of Martinique."

Another time Laure would find the energy to ask how they'd managed to cross half a continent and an ocean in what must have been seconds. Now, she was more concerned with Gerard.

"He'll need a place to stay...during the day."

The woman, Nicole, the vampire, understood without furthe explanation. "We'll see to it. He's among friends."

But was she?

"I'm Laure Pasquale."

"Pasquale?"

"Gerard is my husband."

The beautiful Nicole looked so genuinely startled, Laure began to frown. What was so shocking? Then Nicole shook her head in amazement.

"Gerardo Pasquale, married to a mortal. You must be an exceptional woman, Laure. I think I will like you very much. Come. I'll show you to your room. You needn't fear for your safety. We're quite civilized. And besides," she said with a dazzling smile, "you are family."

EIGHTEEN

Gerard opened his eyes, the effort enough to exhaust him. One look at the man seated at his bedside led to his pained assumption.

"I am in hell."

Marchand LaValois, his century old adversary, only smiled in wry amusement. "I may yet send you there, but I have no plans to join you."

"No you won't. You would be doing me a favor, and that would not please you." He sighed heavily and looked away from the stocky Parisian who had bedeviled him so in post-Revolution France. His gaze indifferently swept his surroundings. "What is this place?"

"My home. That would put you at the mercy of my hospitality this time. You may expect a kindness similar to what you've shown me."

He was doomed. Gerard managed a hoarse chuckle. "I would expect no less from you, patriot."

Marchand bristled at the title. "Those days are past."

Gerard's look chided him for that claim. "I cannot see you without a flag-waving crusade."

"I've found peace here with Nicole and our daughter. Something you would not understand."

"A funny thing about peace, Frenchman. It's such a transient state."

"Perhaps for one such as you." Riled and showing it, Marchand drawled, "Tell me, how is that blonde bitch you travel with?"

Gerard's mood darkened like a summer squall. His tone rumbled with approaching thunder. "You would be wise to be careful how you refer to my wife, lest you end up with your head on a plate."

"Wife?" His bored manner fell away in his astonishment. "*Mon Dieu*, Pasquale, not even you could be so crazy."

"You do not know her—"

"Know her? That meddling witch all but destroyed my life and my family."

"Laure?"

"Who is Laure?"

"My wife."

"What about Bianca?"

Gerard recoiled, for a moment in full agreement with Marchand's disgust. "Why would I wish to wed myself to that woman?"

"That's what I was wondering."

"I have not seen *il nemico* since that business in New York, and if our paths never cross again, all the better."

"So, this Laure, who is she?"

"I'm sorry, my darling," came the breezy intrusion of Nicole's voice. "I had no time to tell you. Gerard has brought his mortal bride with him. A lovely girl."

Marchand blinked. "A mortal?" Then he threw back his head to issue a huge boom of laughter. "Gerardo Pasquale, taken by a mortal passion. Oh, this is too entertaining."

"I'm so glad you are amused." Gerard turned his cheek to accept Nicole's fond kiss, attempting, badly, not to show how much her affection meant to him. It was the only thing keeping her surly husband from finishing the job the voodoo priestess had started.

Gerard's recall came flooding back.

"Where is she?"

"She's resting—"

"I am here."

All turned toward the speaker, senses quivering with the scent of live blood.

Laure hesitated in the doorway. Though she'd slept through the past day without interruption, she knew it would be foolish to step into a nest of potential vipers without due caution. The three of them were vampires. She could spot the unnatural signs of it now: the stillness, the glitter in the eyes, the pallor to the skin, the way the hair rose at the nape of her neck in the presence of danger. And here was danger, no matter how congenially wrapped.

Her hostess was seated on the edge of her husband's bed, her pale hand resting familiarly upon his chest. The intense featured man she'd not seen before, and she was wary of the way he stared at her as if she were some strange puzzle to solve. From Gerard there was nothing, no clue as to what he was thinking or feeling. The woman, Nicole, had called them family, but her glimpse into Gerard's past led her to believe that all his family had perished. So who was this gorgeous woman to her husband? She was unprepared for the jealousy tightening within her at the thought that they shared an intimate relationship, especially when her own link to Gerard was fragile at best.

Nicole smiled at her, rising up to take her hand and lead her to Gerard's side. "There you are. Looking much better, I'm happy to say. Laure, this unfriendly-looking fellow is my husband, Marchand."

As she nodded in greeting, Laure remembered Gerard speaking of them. This was the couple who'd born a child between them. This was Saint Arabella's daughter. She wasn't sure if she should be relieved or feel further threatened.

Nicole tugged at her husband's arm. "Come, Marchand, let us leave them alone. We can get better acquainted later."

When the supernatural pair had gone, Laure regarded her own husband with a cautious care.

"Are you all right?"

"Why didn't you tell me you were with child?"

Of all the accusations he could make concerning the past twenty-four hours, that one took her completely by surprise.

"Is it mine?"

She'd thought herself prepared for this moment. She'd rehearsed the answer to that unexpectedly poignant question. She could hear Percy's pressuring voice. *Yes. Tell him yes!*

One word, and her future and that of the child's would be secure. For an instant, she considered all her carefully planned lies, but in a heartbeat, abandoned them all in favor of the truth. A truth that could cost her everything.

"No. I wish it was."

His expression faltered, giving her just a glimpse of how that news devastated him.

"I was afraid to tell you sooner," she hurried on. It didn't matter. She could tell by the glaze coming over his eyes that her excuses wouldn't matter now. She spoke them anyway in hopes that he would understand if not forgive. "I feared you would think I tricked you into marriage in order to make you believe this babe was your own."

"And isn't that exactly what you've done?"

She canted her gaze downward, unable to withstand the cold cut of his stare. "I found I couldn't go through with the deception."

"And I am to applaud you for that sudden bout of conscience?"

"No." She hung her head, well aware that she was damning herself with her own words. But what defense could she offer that would make any difference now? Her lack of honesty condemned her, and to plead for mercy at this late date seemed somehow reprehensible. "What I've done is unforgivable, I know. So what happens now?"

She lifted her gaze to meet his, willing him to see that she would accept whatever punishment he deemed appropriate for her duplicity. He'd admired her for her bravery before, but she didn't feel particularly courageous as she awaited his judgement. She was scared, too scared to think or pray or even to consider what his decision would mean to her and her child. She was too afraid of losing him. That was the truth she didn't speak aloud in her defense.

He would never believe that she loved him.

Gerard placed a hand wearily across his eyes, blocking out the sight of her as if it offended him beyond endurance. "I cannot think just now. Go away, Laure."

"Go where?" She couldn't keep the panicked tremor from her voice.

"Anywhere but here within my presence. Nicole will see to you. She is more charitable than I find myself to be. Just go."

Biting down on the want to throw herself upon him to beg for his understanding, Laure turned quietly and left his room. She had no right to ask for it when such entreaties should have been made before they had lain together. Her silence since they'd stood at the altar grew into a greater confession of guilt with each day that passed with truths unspoken. She could not blame him for not wanting to listen now. Nor would he hear what her heart was saying. Not now. Not after she'd done what she'd promised never to do.

She'd failed him.

And as she stepped out into the hall and closed the door behind her, a mighty roar of pain and rage echoed behind it.

A child.

She was having another man's child.

Gerard closed his eyes against the terrible pain of that knowledge. What a fool he was. To think that for one brief, eternally blissful instant of misunderstanding he'd believed himself the father. And in that moment, that sliver of precious time, he'd known how much the idea meant to him.

He hadn't given it much credence when she approached him with the notion. He truly hadn't believed it to be possible. But then he hadn't thought himself vulnerable to desire, either, and she'd proven him handily mistaken there.

He was Italian. Nothing was so revered amongst his people as motherhood. And here was his beautiful Madonna telling him she was going to present him with an heir. A Pasquale. A way to make amends for the family line he'd torn asunder. A chance to redeem himself through new life, new hope.

His child.

And then she'd ripped that naive assumption from him the way he'd ripped out his own father's throat.

A low moan of despair welled up inside him, becoming a harsh, self-mocking chuckle. Oh, how stupid he was. How incredibly blind. *Make love to me, husband.* He could picture her lovely face, so innocent of anything but love. Inviting him to lie with her, to join with her, to plant the seeds of what was to be the most amazing plot ever devised to scheme a willing fool from his fortune.

And he'd believed her!

He'd believed her bashful inquiries about conceiving a child between them. He'd swallowed whole her story about needing family, about wanting to belong. He'd plunged right into her insidious deception by taking her hand, by taking her body without ever guessing how well used it had been before him.

Liar! What a liar she was! And he a fool for wanting so desperately to believe.

He rose, ignoring his own weakness of body when the pain of soul overwhelmed all else.

If not his, whose?

Whom had she lain with to conceive the lie she carried? What mortal had she rutted with in mindless human lust to beget a child so carelessly? Or was it careless? When was this clever conception done? Before or after their marriage? Had she wed him to cover up for her mistake, or had she taken a lover after they'd spoken vows in order to deceive him?

In order to present him with an heir.

Like brother, like sister. His broken heart allowed his rational mind to cast Laure in that unlikely mold. Were they two of a kind? Scheming, deceiving, lying to rise above their means? And he'd been the perfect vehicle for their brilliant plan.

How much of it was a lie?

How good an actress was his sweet wife?

Had she pretended the responsiveness that bloomed beneath his kisses? Had she pretended to adore his touch? Were her sighs and little urgent cries signs of passion, or born of necessity in order to convince him of her lie?

Did she care for him at all?

Did she see man or monster?

He flung off the sense of injury by cloaking it with ire. What difference did that make now? The truth was told. Their relationship was a lie.

So why had she thrown herself upon him on that altar of stone, protecting him with her own life and that of her unborn child? If he were merely a stepping stone to a life of comfort and plenty, why hadn't she let her ghoulish aunt drain away his blood and slay him, ridding herself of his existence and freeing the way to all?

There were no simple answers, and he was too agitated to deal with complex ones. He needed time, his eternal companion, to sort out the situation.

A child.

What *would* that mean?

Beyond his longing for his own progeny, there were other issues, dark, destructive issues preventing him from claiming mother and child with open arms.

She knew.

Laure had been with him in his travels to the past. He'd felt her there as witness to his fall. She now knew why he preferred an empty heart and a blank soul.

She'd watched him kill his family. Not just murder. That was too clean, too forgiving a term. He'd slaughtered them—his mother, his father, his beautiful little sisters. Like an animal, without conscience, without care, without hesitation or remorse. Then. Not then. He'd been lost to the violent thrall of his new existence. He hadn't realized what he'd done, the consequences of those actions. Not then. And for four centuries, he'd hidden from his guilt by pretending to be above the reach of culpability.

Now who was the liar?

Laure knew what he had done. He couldn't pretend with her now.

When she looked at him, she would see those savaged bodies, and she would know she'd never be safe with him. Never. Nor would her child.

"It will be dawn soon."

Gerard didn't acknowledge Marchand's statement or his presence. He had no fondness for Nicole's brusque and humorless husband. The man took everything too personally for his taste. He knew how to hold a grudge. Theirs had survived better than a century, so Gerard knew better than to think himself forgiven now just because he had arrived, uninvited, weakened and not alone. But perhaps he would be more tolerant.

"We need to discuss the conditions for your remaining here, Pasquale."

That did get his attention. He turned toward the little Frenchman with a disdainful air. "Conditions?"

"Nicole has asked that you stay on as our guest, and I will not challenge her invitation. But I will see that you do nothing during your stay to endanger her."

"I would never do that."

"Not overtly, no, I don't believe you would, or we would not be having this conversation at all. This is our home, Pasquale. We live here, comfortably, happily and no one bothers us. We like it that way. We draw no undo attention to our odd habits and we—"

"Do not leave a trail of bodies leading to your door." Gerard made an irritated hand gesture. "Do you really think I am so stupid?"

"No. I think you are vain and impulsive and arrogant. I think you believe you can make your own rules and others will abide by them. I think you believe yourself beyond mortal reach and that, my friend, makes you dangerous to us."

Gerard said nothing for a moment, affronted by the blatant way Marchand thrust his failings into his face but unable to deny them. "So, what am I to do while I am under your roof? Sip tea and feed on rodents?"

"You will not kill."

Gerard blinked.

Marchand pressed on more passionately. "You will not take a human life as long as you are on this island. It will not be allowed or tolerated. When you go out to feed, you will go with Nicole or me, and you will do as we tell you, take from whom we tell you and only as much as we tell you."

Gerard regarded him stoically for a long moment, then chuckled. "I can see your father-in-law has had an effect upon you. He views these humans with a compassion I cannot quite comprehend."

"You will while you are here, or you will regret it."

Another time, he might have taken pleasure in arguing with the autocratic Parisian. He would have called him a petty Napoleon or an idealistic Robespierre, both of whom had failed to see the irony in their despotic rule. But now was not that time. He was weary.

And he needed LaValois's charity.

Rubbing his temples as if he were bothered by a mortal malady, Gerard grumbled sullenly, "Oh, very well. I shall be the model guest. You've my word on it. I will follow your rules and cause no trouble."

Marchand stared at him narrowly. "Really?"

"Yes, yes. And I—appreciate—your hospitality." He gritted out that last.

Amazed, Marchand could think of no way to mock him for that surprising bit of humility. "Come with me," he instructed instead. "I'll show you where you'll rest."

Beneath the stylish island home was a deep, stone-walled cellar. A series of false fronts and clever latches secured the spot from unwelcome intrusion, so that they might sleep undisturbed. In that cool darkness were two chambers, one housing a simple coffin, and the other a large mahogany bed. Seeing it, Gerard recalled the Frenchman's aversion to lying in a closed casket—something he had initiated, along with a long ago bite. One of those small misunderstandings that had forged the unbreechable distance between them.

He gestured toward the box.

"Is that your daughter's?"

Marchand looked uncomfortable. "No. She doesn't require it. It's for Nicole's father when he visits."

Doesn't require it? Gerard lifted a curious brow, but Marchand's glower advised him not to pursue it.

"And Gino? How is he?" Gerard tried to sound nonchalant in his interest. Tried but failed. "Still with that...what was she, a reporter?"

"You know very well what Cassie does. She owns her own newspaper. And they are both very well. Frederica is visiting them in England. Louis has made their home there after that, what did you call it, business in New York."

"Louis," he mused, thoughts taking a wistful turn. "I cannot think of him by that name."

Marchand's response was less kind. "I'm surprised that he doesn't think of you by many."

Gerard made no comment to that wry observation. "And where will my wife sleep?"

"She'll have rooms above. Nicole has already seen her settled in."

"She and Nicole will like one another. They both have rather odd tastes in husbands."

Marchand's chuckle bordered on genuine amusement. Amazing, thought Gerard. A sense of well-hidden humor. Perhaps he's not such a total bore after all.

"One thing, Pasquale." Marchand's grip would have broken a mortal's arm as he called him to task. "Do you bring any trouble with you?"

"What do you mean?" he asked, knowing very well what he meant.

"Nicole has made me promise not to pry in your affairs. She's afraid you'll leave if I do." No loss, was his apparent conclusion. But he did love his wife fiercely. And Nicole, for whatever reason, was genuinely fond of Pasquale. "So I won't ask for particulars, but I must insist on knowing if your presence here will put us in any danger."

"I commend you for your concern for your family, and I share it. I swear to you, if I believe there is a threat, we will be gone without question."

Marchand nodded, for once believing him sincere.

No, Gerard considered cynically, he and Laure didn't need to import trouble from New Orleans. They didn't need scheming relatives armed with treachery and swords. They didn't need greed or voodoo to cast suspicion and fear. Their trouble was here, between the two of them.

And he had no idea how to resolve it.

"How is the room? Are you comfortable here?"

Laure gave a start. She hadn't heard Nicole enter. But then, of course, she wouldn't, would she? She smiled wanly at the other woman.

"It's fine, thank you. It's very good of you to take us in like this."

"Is there anyone I can contact for you, to tell them where you are and that you are safe?"

"No! No, it's better that no one knows we are here."

Nicole waved a hand as she walked to the full length windows and opened them to their spectacular view of the sea.

"This is my favorite room. Such a breathtaking vista, don't you think? I bet the sunset is glorious."

How casually she spoke of it, of the condition that kept her relegated to the night. Not with regret, Laure noticed, but as if she were truly accepting of her fate. And how easily she accepted the mystery of their arrival, not with questions or curiosity but with respect to their want of privacy.

The tangy air wafted in, along with the heavy floral scent of the exotic blossoms growing beneath the terrace. Laure grimaced at the sickly sweet scent and sat heavily upon the bed to wait for the queasiness to pass. She glanced up to see Nicole's dark gaze upon her.

"How far along are you?"

Laure started again. "What?"

"The child you carry, when is it due?"

"In less than five months' time."

"A splendid time, motherhood. The only period in which we don't have to worry about our figure. Second only to the joys of marriage. How long have you and Gerardo been married?"

A clever way to ask if the child were his. Laure didn't mind answering. "A little over a month."

"You will need clothing and necessities," Nicole chatted easily, skipping over any further curiosities she might have about the parentage of the child. Laure was grateful for that courtesy. "If you feel up to it, we can go into town at sunset tomorrow and buy you some things to make you feel more at home. For tonight, I'll lend you one of my nightdresses."

"Thank you. You are very kind."

"Gerard is very special to me." She saw Laure's expression and laughed. "Like a favorite uncle. He and my father were best friends until they had a falling out over a woman."

"Your mother," Laure supplied without thinking.

Nicole gave her an odd look. "No. Over the creature who is responsible for making them what they are. Why would you say my mother?"

"Gerard has spoken of her fondly. I must have misunderstood."

Nicole placed a gentle hand upon her shoulder. "No," she said sofly, "you didn't. He was in love with her. Of course he will deny it if you ask him, saying he has no heart with which to know love." She chuckled indulgently.

"But you don't believe him?" Laure prompted.

"I know better," she confided. "He is a soft center surrounded by a hard shell. But do not tell him that I told you so."

"You sound as if you know him very well." She couldn't keep the pang of envy from her voice. That didn't escape her lovely young hostess.

"Yes, I do. We've been through some trying times together. He was not always inclined to be as agreeable as you see him today. He's haughty and pouty and sometimes cruel, like a little boy, really, who wants everything and gets angry when you tell him he can't have it. I would tell you to run far and fast to escape him, but I can't. I just love him dearly. For all his faults you'll find no one as loyal or protective. He would not think so, but I know he'll make you a wonderful husband."

Laure supplied a faint smile.

"No, eh? Shall I speak to him for you?"

"No! Please. There's no need. We have some differences to work out is all."

"Ah, yes. How does a mortal adapt to our lifestyle, I imagine."

Laure took a chance with the generous stranger. "How do you do it?" she asked. "How do you justify what you must do to survive?"

"It was hard at first. It was Gerardo, in fact, who helped me understand what I was, but Marchand and my father who taught me how to live with it. I must take from mortals to survive, so I give back to them whenever I can in return. We have funded a hospital and a library here on the island. I organize and support many charity functions. It is my way of dealing with what I am."

"You don't kill?"

"Never! Well, only if I or my family is threatened. I am not an animal. I can control my...desires. I have a wonderful family, a loving husband, a doting father and step-mother, a beautiful child. It does not have to be an ugly thing unless that ugliness is all one has inside. I find a comforting beauty in the night, not darkness. I guess it's all in how you perceive things."

Indeed. Laure sat quietly reflecting upon that. Having seen into her husband's past, she knew how he looked at things. Through the discoloration of blood and death and guilt.

And she, despite her immodest boastings, had failed to take that stain away and set him free.

NINETEEN

"You love her."

Gerard didn't respond to Nicole's observation as she came up behind him on the wide veranda. He didn't want to think about the subject preying upon his mind these passing weeks, now months. Time had neither helped nor healed his troubled heart. He stared out over the dark sea, seeing his future reflected in that empty expanse of blackness. He flinched away from the young woman's touch, but being Nicole, she wasn't discouraged by his moodiness. Her arms banded his middle and her cheek rested upon his shoulder.

"It's been almost three months," she chided gently. "Don't you think you ought to at least talk to her."

"There's nothing to say."

"You could ask her about the child."

It would do no good to declare the topic off limits. She'd already been silent on the subject for far longer than he'd ever dared hope. One truth would answer all her questions.

"It's not mine."

"But it's part of her. Doesn't that mean something?"

"No."

Why had he thought she'd understand?

He shook off her embrace to vault lightly over the retaining wall. Within a minute, he'd negotiated the thick underbrush without a scratch and started down the beach. The sand gleamed like wet diamonds set in dark velvet. Heat from the day still shimmered up from it. The beauty of the setting was lost to him. He saw nothing but Laure's face as she spoke her most damning lie.

I love you, Gerard.

"You can't hide from her here forever."

He shot a severing glance at Nicole as she fell in beside him. "Are you asking me to leave?"

Her arm looped through his in a show of unappreciated devotion. "Of course not. You married her. You must care for her."

"She tricked me into the marriage, she and her scheming brother, for my money and to give her bastard a name."

"Harsh words for one who is always the soul of honesty."

"I have never lied to those who matter to me."

"There are things worse than lies. Things like indifference. You are an expert at that, too."

"If I am so reprehensible, why do you tolerate me? Why not send the both of us on our way?"

"Because I don't know what brought you here. Laure won't tell me, but my guess is that it would be dangerous for you to return to New Orleans. You are like family, Gerard. You will always have a home here with us."

"And that thrills your husband to no end, I'm sure."

"Marchand would do anything to please me. Even put up with you." When he didn't smile, she squeezed his arm. "I cannot help if you don't talk to me."

"Who asked for your help?"

She ignored that growl to say, "You did when you called to me on the psychic link we share. That Laure shares as well."

"Thank you for that assistance, but it doesn't give you leave to meddle in affairs that don't concern you."

"I am concerned, because the woman who bears your name is wasting away in misery. It's not good for the baby. She doesn't eat, she doesn't sleep. If you want to punish her, fine, but don't involve an innocent life with your selfish sense of justice."

"Selfish? I am the one who was wronged. That makes me

selfish?"

"What of Laure? What do you know of her plight? Whose child does she carry?"

"It was begat by some mortal. Some mortal who could give her what I could not. She pretended to be satisfied with our arrangement, but only because she was carrying another man's seed. No, that's not right. A mortal man's. I am no man who could fill her with child. I can only give her things of no importance."

"Like what? Trust? Love?"

"Love." He spat in the sand. "A vile emotion reserved for fools."

"I am a huge fool then because I am surrounded by it—from my father, my husband, my daughter...from you." She waited for him to deny it. Pleased when he didn't, she continued. "Does that make me weak? Does that make me somehow inferior to you of the hardened heart?"

"Don't laugh at me, Nicole. I have no use for love. It has always betrayed me. Or I have betrayed it. You know nothing to offer such advice to me. If you knew the truth, you would not chastise me so. You would know that I do the right thing by staying away from Laure and her child. I only bring misfortune to those I care for."

"I am happy and well."

"Not through my doing!"

She stopped him, turning him toward her. "Yes, as I recall, it was."

"How? By almost murdering your Parisian? By stealing away your father's chance to be truly human again and know happiness?"

"My father has no regrets. He has forgiven you for the past."

"But I can't forgive myself. Nor would you if you knew the truth."

"Tell me this awful truth that makes you suffer so."

He tried to pull away, but her grip was strong, unbreakable. But not so, he knew, her heart. "I can't tell you, Nicole. I value your affection too greatly to lose it."

"You won't."

"You don't know. You don't know what I've done, or you

wouldn't say so."

"Yes, I do. I do know."

He drew a strangled breath and stared at her through a glaze of guilt and regret. "How could you?"

"My father told me. Long ago."

"That I killed your mother?"

"That she was old and suffering and begged you to end her pain when my father could not find the courage to do so. I have always been grateful to you for performing that final act of compassion."

"I am not brave, Nicole. Do not paint me to be. I am a selfish coward clear through. I cannot find your father's strength to love a mortal unconditionally, knowing that she will grow old and die and leave me to go on without her. I cannot add that sorrow to the others I already carry. It is better that Laure make another life for herself away from me. I will provide for her and the child. I would not be so cruel as to deny her that comfort, just because I was foolish enough to believe her when she said— "

"Said what?"

"It doesn't matter now."

"I think it matters greatly. You need to say these things to her, not to me. If she is the greedy schemer you say she is, anxious only for what your money can buy, she should take your offer without hesitation. And if she is not... That's what you're afraid of, isn't it?"

"I am not afraid of any mortal."

She smiled in the face of his bluster. "Then convince me of it. She's on the terrace. She often goes there to be alone. I don't think she'd object to your company."

Gerard frowned, seeing how neatly she'd trapped him into doing what he'd been avoiding for so long, confronting the female who'd stolen his heart.

Laure leaned back on the chaise, closing her eyes to appreciate the night's scents and sounds. This foreign clime felt familiar to her now. She enjoyed the lush abandon of it, the vivid splashes of color, the depthless shades of green and blue. And she liked the

LaValoises. Nicole was kind, anticipating her every need. Marchand was an avid debater who liked nothing more than a well-matched argument on any subject. She'd fallen into their reverse pattern of life with surprising ease, sleeping the daylight away to rise at twilight. They filled her hours with entertaining conversation and tours about the French-flavored island where they were welcomed and obviously respected. Marchand was involved in law enforcement. She hadn't been able to figure out his role, but there was no mistaking the awe and reverence the villagers held for him and the love they displayed toward his wife.

If any questioned the nocturnal pairs' habits, no one voiced them openly.

It was truly a paradise, a place where superstition made the unbelievable commonplace. But to Laure, it was a beautifully landscaped prison.

"Nicole tells me you are not taking proper care of yourself."

Her eyes flew open in tandem with the leap of her heart. For a breathless second, she could do no more than stare, her gaze devouring the sight that had been denied her for so long.

"I see she has not exaggerated. Come. Dinner has been prepared for you, and I will see you waste none of it."

Laure's smile wavered. "Do you mean to hand feed it to me, then?"

"Why not? You have forced me to eat my own words often enough. Come."

He extended his hand in an invitation too tempting to refuse. For the chance of his company, she would have consumed the insects that the locals swore by. She struggled to lift out of the low chaise, awkward with her burgeoning girth. And he was there to gently cup her elbow and take her hand, guiding her to her feet. Too quickly, he withdrew the contact she savored more than the thought of a warm meal. For that was what she was starving for.

He escorted her inside, where the ocean breezes created a cool refuge. Laure groaned at the sight of the feast laid out upon the dining table the LaValoises never used. Gerard pulled out a chair and gestured for her to sit. When she did so, as gracelessly as a cart bearing too great a load, she stilled him with a hand upon his forearm.

"You'll join me, won't you?"

"It's not exactly my kind of fare."

She nodded, trying unsuccessfully to hide her disappointment.

"But," he added, "I suppose I can keep you company, just to make sure you are really eating. Fair enough?"

She beamed, earning a tightening to his expression. "Fair enough," she agreed more sedately.

She'd never enjoyed the exotic island tastes as fully as she did beneath Gerard's indulgent goading. Chicken basted in mango juices, coconut breaded shrimp with a peppery sauce. Since he seemed to take pleasure in every bite she took, she pushed beyond comfort just to relish his presence. When at last she couldn't force another bite, he nodded and stood.

"I am satisfied."

"And I am stuffed like a Christmas goose."

"A most attractive one."

She held her breath as he lifted her hand to his lips. The kiss he brushed there was all too brief. A gesture of courtly courtesy was not what she wanted from him, but it was a start, just as this mostly silent meal was a beginning.

"You'll join me tomorrow night as well? To make sure I clean my plate?"

"If that is what it takes, I will be here."

And after he'd gone, she refused to wonder over his sudden agreeability, certain it was Nicole's doing. If it took worry over her health to force him into her company, she would not question it. The moments spent with him were too precious. And if this meal yielded little other than an aching stomach, she would try to make further progress the next night. And the night after. Until their polite facade crumbled and honest speech was freed.

Only then could she ask his forgiveness

Only then could she dare to dream.

Early July heat beat down on the island jewel, wilting everything upon it. Laure, now huge with child, spent most of her time dozing, for it was too uncomfortable to sleep, or she walked along the beach where an occasional cooling breeze made existence bearable.

After the first few months of sickness, her pregnancy progressed easily. She was healthy and strong, continuing to stay active despite the insistence of the house servants that she should be resting. She didn't want to rest. When she rested, she worried. When she worried, she couldn't rest.

So far, there'd been no contact from either Percy or Eulalia. She hoped they'd managed to fall off the face of the earth and not to be found. That's what she hoped, but she wasn't entirely certain. She felt bad not writing to at least tell Percy that she was all right, but she understood Gerard's insistence that they be cautious. They could not bring jeopardy to those who'd shown them kindness. And her time was too near to indulge in possible danger.

She become a familiar sight around the LaValois properties, walking at a brisk pace until recent weeks when her stride settled to a slower lumbering. The island was a place of industry, and the LaValoises were wealthy planters. Marchand had a head for fair business and Nicole a heart for compassion, which made them popular with those they employed. But there were always a few dissenters who thrived on stirring up trouble to increase their own importance. One of these, Laure discovered, was one of the field foremen, Ezra McBain.

A large, intemperate, foul and angry man, from what little she'd seen of him when he'd come to the house, he managed his team of workers through intimidation. And his favorite form of threat was the nature of the LaValoises.

Laure came upon him quite by accident while on a late day walk. He had cornered several field hands and was frightening them with insinuations about their masters. If they didn't work harder, longer, more productively, they could turn up missing as a guest on the dining table in the big house, where the main course was blood. Shocked, Laure tried to avoid being seen, but one of the workers caught sight of her and that brought the bullying McBain's attention about.

It was none of her affair. But the LaValoises had been so kind to take her and Gerard in, she felt she owed them more loyalty than McBain displayed. She continued her walk, feeling McBain's squinty eyes upon her until she rounded a bend in the path. Only then did she breathe easier. And that night, when Marchand and Nicole greeted her, she felt it only right to tell them of the fear and rumor McBain was spreading. She knew too well what that kind of talk could breed.

When she heard McBain had been fired from his position, she wasn't sorry. She was concerned. And she said so to Gerard as they shared the time, if not the evening meal, together. The hour or two spent in each other's company was the highlight of Laure's day. Though Gerard never touched her, never was more than polite in his own cynical fashion, she lived for their moments alone. she'd grown accustomed to the nighttime rhythms of the beings she called friends and never was ignored, but often the loneliness was her worst enemy. The loneliness and the uncertainty breeding a constant fear of what was to come.

Gerard never spoke of the child. Though she could see his attention focus on the rounding of her belly, he never asked about the babe's parentage nor offered the protection of his own name. He also never brought up the reason for their exile. He never spoke of his trip to the past, or of her failure to keep her promises to him. But her knowledge of his disappointment grew heavier by the day. Though the LaValoises never complained of their company, she knew the time was coming when they would have to leave the island paradise for a future of their own. She could sense the restlessness in Gerard, but he didn't bring the matter up to her. He was waiting, she knew, for the baby to be born. What would happen then was the source of her greatest fear.

As she picked over her evening meal, Gerard seemed in a distracted mood. He waved off her worries over McBain with a haughty gesture.

"Men like that are no threat to us. Let him bluster. He can do no harm."

His arrogant words sparked the memory of a similar conversation between her father and mother on the eve of his death. Hearing them elicited a foreboding chill.

"You, of all people, should understand how dangerous rumor can be. I have seen—" She broke off, not wanting to bring back the circumstances.

"What have you seen?" Gerard demanded with his typical disdain for human suffering.

She met his bored gaze, her own direct and unswerving, as was her oration. "I have seen an unfounded rumor turn trusted servants into a howling mob. I have seen that mob turn on those who had cared for them like family. I've seen them drag the man who fed, clothed and gave them self-respect out into the night to hang him from a tree until he was dead, then dismember the body and burn it, denying him a peaceful rest. I've seen a home go up in flames and the remaining family forced into hiding to save themselves from one ugly whisper. A suggestion that a child died as a sacrifice to dark gods and that my mother, a witch, was responsible. My father, of course, denied it. He denied it even as his last breath strangled from him."

"Laure," Gerard began, his tone tempered with the softening of regret.

"That was the last time I felt safe. That was the last time I had a home. When my mother married Percy's father, I had hoped the rumors had died away. She was so happy and, for a time, I dared believe misfortune wouldn't follow. Then Simon Cristobel died of mysterious causes. Talk of witchcraft, of my mother marrying him to inherit his wealth after murdering him, drove her to her death soon after. No one knows exactly what happened to her, other than she disappeared from our home one night, and her body was found the next morning." Her voice failed for a moment, and she was forced to blink tears away before continuing. "They say she took her own life, but I have never believed it.

"My future could have been cut equally short if not for Percy. He took a stand for me. He took me into his home and fought off all rumors that I might somehow be involved. So you see, even though I know what kind of man he is, that he's a schemer with few compunctions, he saved me, and I owe him for that. He made me believe that I deserved good things."

"You do," Gerard agreed quietly. He glanced away as if made uncomfortable by her woeful tale. Did he fear she was playing upon his sympathy to worm her way back into his heart? Never that.

"I will make my own good fortune," she declared. "For myself and my child." She didn't include Gerard in that bold claim because she wasn't sure he'd want to be there. She didn't know if he wished to be a part of her future. Suddenly, she had to know. "Gerard, we must talk about what will happen when the baby comes."

A guarded blankness came over his features. His eyes were a clouded opaque. "Must we?" he drawled.

"My time is growing near, and I need to know what place we will have in your life, if any. We cannot remain here in hiding forever."

"No. We cannot. I have thought of returning home to Italy. I've not been there since...since I was mortal. I thought perhaps I could lay some ghosts to rest if I were to confront them where they lay."

A terrible tightness began to band within her chest. He hadn't mentioned her in his plan. An oversight, or a purposeful exclusion. "Am I to go with you, then?"

He didn't need to answer. She saw his intention in the way his gaze canted away. She couldn't draw a decent breath through the sudden wadding of anguish within her throat.

"I will see you lack for nothing."

Cold comfort offered at an equally chill temperature.

Lack for nothing.

Nothing except the man she loved. Nothing except the only dream she'd ever had—that of home and family. She sat perfectly still, battling the need to weep and cast herself upon him to beg for his forgiveness. She'd known, hadn't she, that he wasn't a man given to mercy. And there'd be none in his plans for her. Just a painfully civil separation, removing her from his life. She rose up from the table with all the dignity she could muster while big as a sugar barrel.

"I thank you for your offer of charity," she told him, her manner rigidly proper. "But it won't be necessary. I will be a burden to no man. Excuse me, please."

Her exit was graceless. She could hardly see where she set her feet, as if such a thing were still possible over her mammoth belly. Her eyes burning and blurred, Laure stumbled outside, seeking a way to cool the heat of her disappointment.

He was setting her aside.

For months, she'd resisted the possibility. She hadn't brought up the subject for fear of forcing this very point. She'd lied to him about the child, and now he wouldn't accept either of them. She'd offered him a chance at mortality and had failed to help him achieve it. She'd disrupted his life, thrown his finances into chaos, exposed him to the dangers of Eulalia LaClaire. All he wanted was a return to his quiet, shadowed life. How could she blame him for that?

How would she ever get over her desire to share it with him?

She made her ungainly way down the path to the beach, needing the soothing sound of the surf to ease her pain and panic. After the child was born, she'd contact Percy and make arrangements for her return to New Orleans. Alone. From there, she would disappear into obscurity, to make a life for the two of them. She'd take nothing from Gerard. The child would be her family, and she would find the means to survive. That was the legacy her mother had left her.

The sound of a footfall on the gravel trail behind her brought a leap of hope to Laure's heart. Perhaps Gerard had followed...But no. When had she ever heard her husband's approach. He stirred no sound in passing. So if not him—

Rough hands gripped her by the elbows, jerking them back and up behind her. Hot breath laced with liquor scorched the side of her face.

"Thought you could cost me my job and not suffer the consequences, eh? Well, guess again, little lady. Let's see how much those creatures will pay to get you back safe, but maybe not so sound."

Fighting not to panic, Laure gathered her strength to repel him with her inner powers, but before she could exert it, a tremendous pain ripped through her middle.

The child!

With a cry, she felt her knees go weak, but McBain yanked her back to her feet.

"None of that, missy. Walk or I'll drag you."

Panting too hard to protest his treatment or state the change in her condition, Laure staggered down the steep path. Even if she could break free, there was no way she could outrun her attacker. What chance was there that he'd see she got proper care when he discovered she was about to deliver? None. She had to think. She had to get help or face potential peril.

What had Nicole said about their psychic link? Shared blood, shared minds.

Help me!

She sent out the frantic call, focusing on Nicole, on Gerard, on Marchand, not knowing what to expect. Certainly not an abrupt freedom that spilled her face first into Gerard. While he gathered her up into his arms, a savage snarl from behind made her look then regret doing so.

Marchand LaValois dispensed justice with a shocking brutality.

"It's her time," she heard Nicole saying. "Get her back to the house, quickly."

That was the last Laure clearly remembered beyond cool cloths pressed to her brow, wrenching spasms, and Nicole's calm commands to push. Then a noisy wail that filled her heart with indescribable joy.

"You have a son," Nicole pronounced as she placed the squirming, red-faced infant in her beckoning arms.

"A son," Laure echoed. Through her tears of happiness and exhaustion, nothing had ever looked so beautiful to her.

Later, as Laure slumbered in exhaustion, Gerard stood at her bedside, cautiously admiring both mother and child.

"Be careful, lest you grow too attached to abandon them."

He turned to glare at Marchand. "I am not abandoning them, Frenchman. I will see they are well cared for."

"By strangers."

"It's better that way," Gerard stated. He looked back to the sleeping woman and child, trying to convince himself of it.

"Better for whom? You certainly."

"You know nothing of my reasonings."

"Enlighten me."

"She will be better off away from me, away from our kind, where she will be safe. She deserves that after all she's been through. Especially now with the babe to think of."

"Is that what you want as well? To be rid of them, so you can return to your prowling ways and ferocious lover?"

"No. It's not what I want. I want—I want what's best for them. What can I give them besides this skewed existence? We're here even now, hiding because of what I am. She was brought to labor prematurely because of what you are. I endanger her by my very nature."

"Is it her wish to go, to live safely, alone?"

"It doesn't matter what either of us wish. She wants a normal life, a regular family. She deserves to be loved."

"As Nicole and I love one another. As her father loved her mother and the woman to whom he's now married? Your arguments hold no water, Pasquale. You're a coward. You're afraid she *can* accept you as you are, so you'll have no reason to push her away. She's not the one who's afraid. You are."

Gerard refused to address that truth. "We are from two different worlds."

"They don't have to be so far apart. She's used to our pace. Perhaps she wouldn't be too resistant to living as one of us."

"Turn her? Make her live as one of the damned?"

Marchand winced, obviously disliking that summation of himself. "You overlook the fact that, for some unknown reason, the woman loves you and will be happy nowhere else but at your side, regardless of the risk. Isn't it time you put aside your petty excuses for doing wrong and do something right?"

"I am. By letting her go."

And as he left the room, Laure's lashes flickered, sending a single line of dampness to trace her cheek.

Percy scanned the news contained on the single sheet.

A son.

"Damn!"

Laure's sudden disappearance over four months before had caused no end to speculation and suspicion. He'd been able to cover easily at first. A honeymoon for the happy couple. But his excuses ran thin. One particularly annoying source of trouble, surprisingly, came from Edna Farris, Javier's old fiancé. He hadn't known the two women were acquainted, and that made for all sorts of uncomfortable suppositions. What were the two of them up to? Now he had the police sniffing around, and their presence was scaring away potential clients. He'd gone from Godchaux Golden Boy to the man on the receiving end of official questioning. With the police swarming around his books, he'd had to suspend his profitable 'borrowing' schemes, and his pocket was now feeling that pinch.

Worst of all, he needed Laure's signature in order to make the final transfer of Pasquale's funds into his own untouchable, untraceable account.

Where was she?

He stared at the message, trying to read between the lines for some clue, but Laure had left none.

His brooding was interrupted by a timid knock at the door.

"Mr. Cristobel, there's a Madame La Claire here to see you."

"Who?" he snapped irritably. Then he remembered. "Oh, yes! Send her right in, Mary Beth."

Eulalia La Claire, the voodoo witch.

Wiping the cold trickle of sweat from his palms, he reached out to take one of the old woman's hands for a genteel press. His senses recoiled against the touch, her skin feeling like the crackly paper in which they wrapped fish at the docks. He withdrew as soon as politely possible.

"Madame LaClaire, please have a seat. I understand you share my concern over my step-sister's disappearance."

The woman's bright black eyes fixed upon his, and it was like a steel rod piercing to his brain.

"You've heard from her."

"No. Yes. Well, just a telegram, actually, to say that I am an uncle."

"A girl or a boy?"

"A nephew."

"What else?"

"There was nothing else. Just a vague statement that she would be coming home. There was no posting to tell where the message originated."

The parchment hand extended. "Let me see the paper."

"As I said, there's nothing on it." But he surrendered the sheet to indulge her. He watched with growing uneasiness as she turned the paper over and over between her hands, her eyes closing, chanting in some foreign tongue.

"She, the child and the dark one are on an island."

"How do you—"

"Quiet!" Her ancient brow knit with concentration. "Martinique. They are on Martinique."

"They've left the country," Percy groaned. "They're out of my reach."

Eulalia's obsidian gaze bored into his. "But not out of mine. I can arrange for her to hurry home, but I need to know what your interest is, lawyer."

"Only in the boy."

"And your sister? You do not care what becomes of her?"

"She is not my sister." With that statement, his genial mask ripped away. Hatred gleamed in his usually placid face.

"So her death—"

"Would not disturb me at all."

They regarded one another across Percy's desk, reading a kindred purpose in each other's plans.

"I need the boy alive."

Eulalia smiled. "I will see you have him. The other two, I will take care of in my own way. They will not bother you again."

"Good." Then his eyes narrowed as he considered whom he was dealing with. "And why should I trust you?"

Eulalia's smile never faltered, nor did she betray a sense of insult. "This is not about trust. This is about necessity. Just as before, when you came to me to ask for Jeanette's death. You did not worry about trust when you arranged your step-mother's demise."

Percy looked uncomfortable with that reminder. "Yes, but you were well paid for that."

"And this I do for free, because we are both in a position to benefit from each others' intentions. It's as simple as that. If you do not interfere in my plans, I have no interest in yours. I don't ask that you trust me, but you had better fear me. I will have what I deserve and no one—not you, not my meddling niece nor her unnatural husband—will stand in my way."

That kind of sentiment he understood only too well.

"We are in agreement then."

A cold sense of satisfaction settled within him. Finally. Finally, he would see his father avenged by ending the threat of Laure, daughter of the witch who killed him. And, as justice would have it, he would be nicely rewarded for his patience. By raising the child, he could live in luxury off the trust arranged for Pasquale's 'heir.'

Until the child could be safely disposed of, too.

TWENTY

Mist akin to the thick threads rising off the Mississippi filled the room when Laure awoke.

Though she immediately recognized the familiar surroundings as her bedchamber at the LaValois estate, subtle differences had her instantly alert. From the peak of the ceiling hung a model boat swaying slightly in the evening breeze, the movement mesmerizing and menacing.

Who would have placed it there?

Who would know of its significance? That it was a symbol of the voodoo deity, Erzulie?

As she stared in fascinated horror, another awareness overtook her. Drumming. Soft and insidious at first, a heartbeat of sound, growing louder and more insistent. She couldn't mistake the discordant tempo.

She leapt from her bed, startled by the chill wrap of the fog about her bare legs. Beneath her feet weren't the smooth boards of her bedchamber floor but rather the marshy give of damp soil. She knew the dank smell. Louisiana swampland. It wasn't possible, of course. She was safe in her room at the LaValoises. Even though she could not see them through the dense blanketing mist, she knew she was standing upon heartpine planks, not unstable ground. Yet, when she took a step forward, she heard the slurpy sound of suction, of bayou muck reluctantly letting go.

She began to tremble.

The drumming was painfully sharp. Why hadn't it drawn the others? Surely with their acute senses they would have heard it too.

But the big house was eerily silent except for the hypnotic pulse.

Through the wispy veils of fog, she could just make out the shape of the baby's bassinet.

"Laurette LaClaire."

The voice was everywhere. Inside her head, echoing through the chill air. A hollow, inanimate female voice she didn't recognize. She looked about for the source of the sound but saw no one.

"Laurette LaClaire, you have called upon my power, and now you must pay my price."

Reason told her Erzulie was not in the room with her, but her body broke out in gooseflesh.

What price? What price would Erzulie exact for her inept call? What vengeance would she name to soothe her vanity and her annoyance at the interruption of her seduction of Gerard? It hadn't mattered to her at the time, but now she feared that consequence.

An icy wind cut through the mist, scattering it from around the bassinet, clearing her path to where her baby slept. Her heart began to pound faster, picking up the erratic cadence of the drums.

The baby.

No... No!

She ran toward the basket, her movements slow as the yielding earth pulled at her feet, dragging her down.

No!

She grasp the basket, bending over to see inside. Her gaze was momentarily distracted.

A tiny boat waved where it was suspended from the sheltering hood, dangling over the empty blankets that still bore the shape of where her son had been.

"No!"

"Laure."

"Where's my baby?"

"Laure, wake up. You're dreaming."

The sound of Gerard's voice pulled her back from the brink of madness. Her eyes flew open, her gaze focusing upon his familiar face. He was frowning slightly, concern puckering his brow. Her attention leapt past him to the infant's basket.

"The baby! Is the baby all right?"

"I'm sure—"

"Go look!"

Gerard went to the bassinet, glancing inside. "He's sleeping, though I don't know by what miracle with all the noise you've been making."

"I want to see him. Bring him to me."

He hesitated, uncomfortable with the idea of picking up the child. But with Laure extending her arms so needily, he had no choice but to scoop the warm, slack bundle up into his hands. So tiny. So light.

"Your son, madame."

She brought the babe eagerly to her breast, cuddling him there, all maternal possessiveness. Her relief was apparent.

"Just a dream," she murmured to herself as she kissed the crown of wispy fair hair.

Gerard remained at the bedside, features impassive as he watched mother and child together. Such a tender sight. Such unconditional love. How impossible for even the hardest heart not to be moved.

And his heart was hardly immune where his wife was concerned.

"You've not told me what name you've decided to give to your child."

Would it be after the father, he wondered with a sudden thrust of jealousy.

She looked up at him, emotion softening her gaze. He saw love there, and a deeper sentiment he could only identify as sorrow.

"I thought I would call him Gino after your friend, Nicole's father. Unless you feel my son unworthy of the honor."

For a moment, he couldn't speak through the swell of poignant feeling. He looked down at the peacefully sleeping babe.

Gino.

"Mille grazie." He studied the infant, with its chubby cheeks and

angelic wisps of hair. A wistful ache speared to his soul. "But shouldn't you honor the boy's father rather than your husband's friend, who means nothing to you?"

Laure's expression closed down tight, her eyes losing their warmth, her lips growing thin with suppressed fury. "Not if that man had no honor to begin with."

He'd told himself it didn't matter. He'd told himself he didn't need or want to know. The responsibility wasn't his. But suddenly it was imperative to discover who had given life to the boy.

"And what if this mortal decides he wants to claim the child?"

Her smile warped with bitter amusement. "You have already taken care of that problem."

For a moment, he didn't understand her words or her anger. What problem had he solved and how? He frowned, trying to think of how to ask her. And then it hit him. Hard.

Javier. The child had been fathered by Alain Javier. So the man had done more than just break her bones and bruise her spirit. He recalled the image of her the night of her party for her wretched brother. The fear and loathing etched into her face in the presence of her former...Gerard would not call him her lover. The man had put his hands upon his wife, had done worse before they were wed. Suddenly, he wished he had the chance to murder him all over again. Never once did he consider that Laure had been anything but the man's unwilling victim. Not after looking into her eyes and seeing the horror and hatred there.

And that changed everything.

The baby awoke with a fretful whimper, quieting when he heard his mother's tender voice. Instead of rooting instantly for his breakfast, he seemed to study Gerard with a somber interest that made the vampire smile.

"Gino," he mused. "Yes, he has that same look of fierce intensity, as if he must solve the puzzle of the universe. Gino Pasquale. A fine name."

"Pasquale?"

"You are my wife. This is my child and heir. What else would he be called?"

The sight of tears upon her cheek was almost his undoing. He brushed them away with gentle fingertips. When he spoke again, his voice was low and gruff.

"See to the child's needs, and I will see to mine."

She didn't say the words, but he could see them shining in her glistening stare. He could read them blatantly upon her heart and mind.

I love you, Gerard.

This time, he believed her.

The dreams came every night, each one progressively more disturbing. She tried not to worry her hosts or Gerard, but her edginess and increased pallor were hard to miss. Her attempt to wave it off as the weariness of a new mother fell short of the mark when it came to convincing Gerard in particular. She couldn't let him guess the cause of her anxiety. If it was Eulalia reaching across the ocean to her, she didn't want her touch to fall upon him, too.

But what if it was just her own anxiousness, her guilt for calling upon her ancient gods, despite her mother's warnings? Was it her worry over Erzulie's wrath that brought the nightmares in such vivid detail? Why alarm her friends and husband if that was the case?

Then there was another reason to cast her quasi-premonitions aside in favor of maintaining harmony. It was the way Gerard looked when holding baby Gino in his arms. His awkwardness in handling the tiny form was quick to disappear. He doted upon the babe and, when no other could quiet the noisy cries, Gerard never failed to charm him into a gurgling contentment. His Italian heritage, her husband claimed with unexpected modesty. Love of family and children was inbred in him. She began to hope it was love that gentled his gaze when he looked upon the child he now called his own.

And she began to wish that tender emotion would favor her as well.

Though he lingered in her company, it was mostly to play with

Gino, not to pursue any intimate intentions. As Gino grew stronger and her body healed itself, she began to chafe with restlessness, longing for some of her husband's lavishly shared attention. It was unworthy to be envious of a child, but Laure yearned to be on the receiving end of just one of those affectionate smiles.

Perhaps accepting the child as blameless and forgiving her for her failings were two very different things.

And so she kept her fears bottled inside where they fermented in juices of dread and solitude.

She moved through the thick mists.

The tiny boat rocked to and fro in a mocking prediction of what she would find when she gazed anxiously into the bassinet. But this time the blankets weren't flat and empty. A childish figure plumped them to earn her relieved laugh. She reached down to lift up her child, a cold terror beginning to well as her hands touched not warm infant skin but a cool, unnatural material. The blanket fell away as she looked into the white china doll face with its painted on mouth and blue marble eyes.

Her scream still echoed as she sat up in her bed.

"*Cara*, what is it?"

Her quaking hands brushed back damp hair from a sweat-dappled brow. She was trembling all over. Still, she managed a wavering smile. "Just a dream—"

"Do you think me stupid," he chided as he came to settle on the edge of her bed. The mattress never dipped beneath his weight. "These are more than dreams. They've troubled you since the babe was born. Tell me what is in them that puts you to such a fright."

"Silly things, nonsense really. I'd be embarrassed to speak of them aloud."

"I'm not leaving until you tell me."

Her chin tilted up a stubborn notch. "Then prepare to stay for a long while."

"All right, *innamorata*. I shall stay." He stretched out along the length of the bed, adjusting his lean form until he was comfortably reclined. "Now, you will return to your rest, and I will keep your dreams at bay."

She smiled at his bold assurance. And was still smiling when she lay down next to him.

"Close your eyes," he ordered with mock severity. When she complied, she felt a light caress upon her brow, whether his lips or his fingertips, she couldn't tell, but her tension was soothed away. Though she tried to hold onto awareness to appreciate his presence beside her, slumber slipped up over her, deep and undisturbed.

And as he promised, for the next few hours no dreams slipped past him.

For Gerard, though, hours were a dream. Listening to the waltz of her breathing, absorbing her warmth and unique mortal perfume, he lost himself in the study of the woman he'd wed. What a marvel she was. To endure the brutality of a man like Javier and yet still love the child he had forced upon her—such selfless emotion humbled him.

And when his life was threatened under the voodoo witch's knife, she'd straddled him like a beautiful Valkyrie intent on taking his soul to a hero's Valhalla rather than the hell Eulalia had planned for it. She risked her life, and the life inside her, for him. Without thought. Without hesitation. Being unable to understand or return that kind of passion had him wandering through an angry confusion these last months, feeling unworthy of her willing sacrifices and wary of emotion that powerful.

She loved him, and Marchand was right, it scared him to death.

Had he been able to make peace with his past, things would have been so different. Had he come back to her as a mortal, he'd have had no reservations. But how to justify what he was with what she made him wish to be? He was no hero deserving of a Valhalla welcome. But she made him think he ought to be, just to warrant her affection. He'd never met anyone's expectations before, and his own aspirations had fallen far short of their inception. Yet she made him want to reach for that ideal he'd set for himself when he and Gino were youths in Italy.

He'd seen in his friend everything that was admirable and had secretly envied his ease in attaining it. But now, after all these centuries, all those things were his to claim—wealth, social position, knowledge, family—and still he behaved like the greedy malcontent he was, needing more and never satisfied. Never believing he'd reached that same pinnacle of success. Never believing he was worthy of it. And now he had a wife who loved him, totally, freely, amazingly, who'd presented him with a child he adored. Why couldn't he accept his good fortune? Why was it so hard to embrace his dream?

Beside him, Laure made a soft sound as she stirred back to wakefulness. A forgotten emotion surged within him, something so big, so full, he couldn't identify it at first. To call it happiness was to give it little credit. To say it was the pride of possession barely scratched the surface. Naming it admiration or affection or any other weak second did both of them an injustice. So when her eyes opened, and he saw his future there in the soft dark depths, he could escape the truth no longer.

"I am in love with you, Laure Pasquale."

She blinked at his unexpected claim, her gaze going shimmery. When she would speak, he touched his hand to her lips to still the words until he addressed what she'd awakened in his heart.

"I did not plan to be. I did not want to be. I fought against it as if it were a fearsome enemy, only to find that surrender to it is so much sweeter than ever I could have imagined."

He felt her smile beneath his fingertips.

"You are laughing at me because you realized what I refused to weeks, no months, ago. You have watched me foolishly run in circles trying to escape that which I wished so desperately to have catch me. I thank you for your patience, *cara mi'amore*. No more running. I am where I wish to be."

His mouth replaced his fingertips upon her lips. There, he let his kiss express what moved him so miraculously with an eloquence he could not match in words. With a nibble at the soft underside, he voiced the wealth of his tender feelings. With the plunge of his tongue, he boldly stated the passion growling for release. The brush of his lips across her cheek, buffing the flutter of her eyelids, he declared his desire to explore all that she would offer. And on her tremulous sigh, she accepted all with one all-powerful word.

Yes.

While baby Gino slept blissfully unaware, Gerard stripped his wife of her sensible cotton gown and began showering her with the adoration she'd been denied for too long.

Beneath his seeking kisses, her supple skin burned. Beneath his roving palms, her body arched and ached for more. Beneath his conquering weight, she opened for him, drawing him inside with an ecstatic moan of greeting. And through it all, Gerard wondered wildly why he'd been withholding this spectacular pleasure when it was the expression of his unspoken passion for this unusual, exotic creature who whispered his name and made his heart whole again.

Entwined together in the peaceful aftermath of a hurricane's explosive power, Laure had never felt so content and secure. This was the man who would fulfill her fantasies and exceed the scope of her dreams. This unlikely, unnatural, arrogant, selfish being who had humbled himself completely with his admission of love for one so inferior to his near-godlike state.

If one such as he could reduce himself in humility, it was time for her to make her own abject apologies.

"I never told you how sorry I was that things did not work out as planned," she murmured against the yet cool contours of his chest.

"What things, *cara*?" he whispered back, spinning a web of gold as he threaded his fingers through her hair.

"It was unforgivably bold of me to make you promises I could not keep. I wanted so much to earn your admiration, I ended up risking both our lives. I should never have placed you in such danger, well knowing I was not in control."

"Say no more, Laure. You owe me no apologies. I'm done living off my regrets. You created a new future for us when you brought little Gino into this world. What is past, is gone. We will concentrate on what is to come. Are you agreeable, my love?"

My love. She held the phrase to her heart, where it sang unrestrained.

"I have no arguments, *caro mio*," she murmured into his kiss.

Laure came awake with a gasp. She sat up in her bed, her hand to her racing heart, feeling its frantic tempo through the damp cling of her gown.

A dream. Just a dream.

Her gaze leapt to the bassinet, knowing she couldn't quiet her panic until she had made sure all was well. The house was quiet but not unnaturally so. She could hear the birds outside the open terrace doors singing their twilight song. She could smell the tropical blooms upon the warm, early evening air. Everything seemed in order.

Thankfully, just a dream, but it was over now, and once she'd checked on Gino, she could go back to sleep. Soon Gerard would join her, and all would be well.

She smiled, holding to the thought of his tender passion the night before. Basking in the warmth of his words.

I am in love with you, Laure Pasquale.

The last glow of daylight slanted across the white wicker and glinted upon something she hadn't noticed there before. Something small hanging from the hood. Something terrifyingly familiar.

She drew a strangled breath.

No!

She hurled herself from the bed, casting off the covers that had tangled about her in the throes of her dream.

It had been a dream. It had been a dream.

"Gino?"

Sobs poured from her, each a wrenching agony as she came to the basket. One glimpse told her all.

It was no nightmare from which she would awaken.

Empty. The bed was empty.

Her anguished wail heralded the fall of night, the death of dreams.

*   *   *

Laure was inconsolable.

She sat curled against Gerard's side while Marchand questioned the servants and estate guards. No one had seen anyone or anything. Of course, they didn't. Laure knew the truth. One couldn't see the unseen. Her child had been stolen as payment for her vanity. Gino was the price of her demands upon gods she only served when it suited her. They would not be slighted or taken lightly.

She understood that now. Too late.

The next few days were a hellish blur of weeping recriminations. Gerard was her strength, her silent salvation. If she had told him the truth about her dreams, perhaps their child would still be with them. If she'd attached more weight to the possible danger, little Gino would even now be safely in his bed. But Gerard would hear none of her distraught confessions, refusing to attach any blame.

However calm he seemed in order to comfort her as she languished in his embrace, broken by the sense of loss, she was aware of the explosive tension within him just waiting for a definite focus.

If impending danger had a face and form, he wore it and wore it well.

Someone would pay dearly for what she suffered now.

On the third day, a message arrived from Percy. He'd received a ransom request for a princely amount but had no authorization to release the funds. What should he do?

"The money means nothing," Gerard told her tightly, earning her eternal gratitude. "I will go to New Orleans at once."

That pulled her from her sorrowful lethargy with a sudden, new purpose.

"I'm going with you."

"Laure, stay here where it is safe."

Her laugh rang with brittle truth. How safe could it be when their greatest treasure was stolen out from under them? She leaned into his shoulder, expecting tears to come, but her eyes stayed open, burning and dry. And a new emotion surfaced, one ripe with purpose.

Fury.

"I will not stay behind. I will have my child back."

"But there's danger for you in New Orleans."

"If they have my child, the danger will come from me."

She sat back to regard him, her gaze black as coal, ready to take flame.

Gerard gave no further protest. He sensed a new power in her, the fierceness of a female defending its young. A fierceness he understood, for it raged through him as well. He touched her taut cheek with adoring fingertips.

"Come with me, then. And together, we'll bring hell with us."

TWENTY-ONE

"Who has my son?"

Instead of answering Laure's frantic question, Percy crossed his office to embrace his distraught step-sister.

"Oh, my dear, I can't tell you how sorry I am that this has happened."

Laure pushed away. After days of sea travel, her nerves were raw, her temper frayed. She had no patience with platitudes.

"Percy, what do you know?"

"Unfortunately, nothing more than I already told you in my note."

"Let me see the letter!"

He went to his desk and withdrew a single sheet. His expression was carefully composed in lines of concern. Laure took the ransom demand, her hand quivering slightly. She forced it to steady. This was no a time for weakness. She read the few boldly printed words, trying to divorce her heart from her mind, to see not Gino in terrible danger but a criminal bent on greedy profit. She ran her hands across the cheap paper, letting her senses explore beyond what her eyes could see. There was no trace of Eulalia. She hadn't written the note.

"What now?" Gerard asked from his neutral spot near the doorway. His gaze alternated between his wife and Percy. Laure was by far the calmer of the two.

"I have the papers here for you to sign. They will allow me to liquidate several of your investments for ready funds."

"Not yet."

Gerard's statement took them both by surprise.

"But the note said—"

He cut off Percy's sputtering with a wave of his hand. "We wait until we are contacted."

Percy cast an anxious entreaty at his sister. "Laure, he is toying with the life of your child!"

But Laure met Gerard's steady gaze, a gaze that bid her to trust him, and Percy's panic passed her by. "We will be at home, Percy, should you hear anything more."

"Laure," he cried out frantically, "you are making a mistake by listening to him."

She took her husband's arm and smiled. "No, Percy. I am listening to my heart."

Once the house was opened to clear away the stagnant scent of disuse, it was like they'd never left. As if Gino had never been a part of their lives. There was nothing of him in the large rooms. No memories to cling to. No belongings to cherish. That unsettled Laure more than the fruitless encounter with her brother.

Rubbing her forearms to instill some warmth inside where she had been cold for days, Laure paced the front rooms.

"How long before they contact us?"

Gerard tracked her movement through impassive eyes. "I do not know. Do you still believe it is your aunt?"

"She didn't write the ransom letter."

"It could be the work of more than one, *cara*."

There was a gentle caution in his tone. What was he trying to prepare her for? What could be worse than what they already knew?

Their child was missing.

"We are in danger as long as we are here," Gerard reminded her, adding, "from more quarters than either of us knows. When we have the boy, we must be ready to protect ourselves by moving fast and leaving no traces."

Once that news would have distressed her. Now it meant less

than nothing. Home was not here inside these rooms, in the furniture she'd lovingly arranged. It was where her husband and son were.

"I'll begin packing my things." She never thought to ask if he had a destination in mind. It didn't matter as long as the three of them were together.

As she started from the room, Gerard called to her.

"Laure?"

She paused, turning toward him.

"We will have him back."

Her smile was tremulous. "I know."

"I must go out for a time."

"I know."

His expression was a tender version of his earlier mocking self. "Do nothing foolish in my absence."

She crossed her heart in promise and, with a braver smile, bid him to go.

She would have all her family together again.

Determinedly, she continued up the stairs to begin to pack this portion of her life away.

"You wasted no time in returning."

Laure whirled from the bedside where she'd been folding her gowns into a hurried stack. She wasn't surprised to see Eulalia standing in the hall. For the first time, she felt no awe, no affection for the older woman, just the cold fury of a mother torn from her child.

"Did you think I wouldn't?"

"I knew you would. I know how strong a mother's instinct becomes when her own is threatened."

"Is that what you're doing? Threatening me?"

"I do not threaten, child. I demand."

"And what is it that you demand for the return of my child, providing you have him?"

Eulalia smiled. With her withered skin and lifeless eyes, she resembled one of the patient alligators waiting in putrid waters for the unwise. Laure no longer was naive enough to step without care.

"Who else could have taken him from you without a trace, without a sound? A beautiful child, much like you were. A fine, healthy child who misses his mama."

And from out of the folds of her tattered cloak she produced a small patchwork animal, a child's toy. Laure didn't need a closer look to recognize it. Nicole had given it to her. It had been Frederica's. Gino slept with it in his bed.

Laure bit down hard on the anguish swelling about her heart as she gathered the toy within her hands. "Return him to me, Eulalia."

"It's not my wish to keep you separated. I would insist that you give your solemn vow not to interfere in the *societe*'s affairs. When my reign is over, my blood will inherit, not your mother's."

"I have no interest there. That's your obsession, not mine." Laure shook her head in sudden pitying understanding. "Why didn't I see it before? How jealous you were of my mother and grandmother. Is that why you perceive me as such a threat?"

"You are no danger to me."

Laure chuckled softly, not believing her arrogant claim. "It's because *grandmere* showed me the magic and not you, isn't it?"

Eulalia's black eyes sparked with fury. "She had no business going outside the family. Your mother had walked away from her future, and I was there, begging to learn."

"Perhaps she knew you could not be trusted with the knowledge. Is that why you overcame her and placed her soul in the *govi*? Out of spite?"

"Out of necessity. Because she knew or guessed what I had done...But you need know no more than that. I will, however, tell you how much I enjoy her imprisonment at my command."

"My son," Laure demanded, returning their conversation to its important focus. "All I need do is wave my rights as heir, and you will give him back to me?"

"Partly."

"What else?" she demanded, eager to make whatever concessions necessary to restore her baby to her arms.

Eulalia frowned. "Your tone used to be more respectful, child."

"Perhaps because I felt respect for you then. Not now. Answer me."

"I'll return the child in exchange for the vampire; a life for a life, a soul for a soul."

That, Laure hadn't expected.

But she should have guessed.

She remembered that long ago dream. *A life for a life.* Only then she'd believed her husband to be the villain. How naive she'd been not to see the truth. Her aunt was mad for power and terrified of the knowledge that had escaped her grasp. Only by fortifying her strength through absorbing the *bon-ange* of a revenant could she claim an equal status in the eyes of her followers.

She wanted Gerard to complete her sacrifice.

"No."

"I thought you loved the child more than life itself. More than the half-life of the *baka* you married? No? Was I wrong then? *Bien.* I will make due with the child, if that is your wish."

"Do not hurt him. He is an innocent."

Hearing the faltering in the younger woman's voice, Eulalia smiled, tasting victory. "Not with the power of your family flowing through him. I would prefer the vampire, but I will accept the child if I must. Either will bring me the prestige I desire. Which one? That is your decision. Tell me now, for the time of bargaining is at an end."

How could she choose? The husband she loved or the child of her body? Both were an integral part of her heart and spirit. But Eulalia's demand had to be met or matters would be out of her hands. There was only one solution she could think of, one that would satisfy her unbending loyalty to those she loved.

Speaking the words that ripped her soul asunder, Laure said, "I will deliver a vampire for your sacrifice, and you will see my child is unharmed."

"Of course. Tomorrow night."

As the dark priestess turned to go, Laure thought of something else that perplexed her.

"*Tante,* what will you do with the money?"

She regarded her niece, puzzlement genuine. "Money? What money?"

"Never mind."

"Tomorrow, Laure. No tricks this time, or the child will fall under my sword."

That graphic image cost Laure the last of her strength. Her knees buckled, dropping her to the floor where she wept into her hands, face buried in the small toy that still held her baby's powdery scent.

Wept for all that she was losing.

She felt him in the room before he made himself known. A personal agony like none she'd ever experienced wrung her heart in a vise of regret. How she'd wanted her life with him to go on forever, at least to the limit of her human years. That chance was gone, gone like her child was gone, unfairly, unbearably missing.

Because she couldn't have him guessing her intent, Laure carefully arranged her expression before acknowledging him. He stood in the hall, in the exact spot where Eulalia had been less than a hour before. Her dark, sleek and sometimes sinister husband. He regarded her stoically, feeling her mood the way one would test the ground in the bayou.

She went to him without hesitation, because she couldn't endure another second of separation when their time was so short. Her arms banded his neck, her mouth sought out his own. His lips were cool, though undeniably responsive.

"You've not fed," she stated quietly, remaining in his embrace.

"I was worried about leaving you here alone."

"I'm glad you've returned. I need you near me."

She felt him tense at her husky claim. The need for caution undercut her pleasure in that tiny victory. He no longer had any defenses against her. That's what she must count on if her plan were to succeed.

He must not suspect within those clever, wary turns of his mind that there was any other motive for what she did. Not that her desire for him wasn't real. Not that her yearning to feel him close then closer still was a lie. Not that her love for him wasn't a total commitment of body and soul. All of those things were true, and were both help and hindrance for what she must do.

"Gerard?"

Her hands pushed beneath his coat, rubbing over the fine linen of his shirt, stirring the anticipated response. His hands opened wide at her shoulder blades to begin a sensuous kneading. His face nuzzled into the loosely held knot of her hair until it came undone, the way her resolve nearly came undone. She closed her eyes and summoned all her strength.

"Gerard," she broached again, "what will the future bring for us once we have Gino back?"

"What do you mean, *cara*?"

"The future for you and me."

Now he understood. She could tell by his infinitesimal stiffening. "What do you want it to be, my love?"

"Long and happy. Longer than my years will allow. I heard you talking with Marchand."

"Oh?" He'd gone very still.

"I want what he and Nicole have together."

"We have that."

"But for how long? Until I begin to grow old? Until those who don't know us confuse us for mother and son? Until I must surrender myself to my own mortality and you continue on alone? Is that what you want?"

"No." The sound growled from him, low and passionate. "But that is how it must be." He couldn't help picturing an ancient Arabella Radman, her radiant beauty smothered in the folds of old age as she suffered her eternally youthful husband catering to her fragile needs. And he could see again Gino's tragic face as his love was lowered into the cold ground. Was that what awaited him?

"That's how it is," he restated for both of them.

"Why?"

"I cannot change what I am. We had hoped it was possible, but t'would seem it is not."

"But I can change. I can become as you, and we can have eternity together."

He pushed away from her so suddenly she nearly fell. No. That was not an option he'd entertain. "You are just upset about the child. That's why you are talking this way. I will not listen."

"It has nothing to do with Gino. It has to do with me loving you so much I can't bear the thought of us not being together." She didn't have to summon convincing tears. They were there upon her cheeks, glistening testaments to her inner anguish. "I'm not afraid of what you are. I'm not afraid to be what you are. Marchand has shown me the nobility of your kind, and Nicole the generous compassion that can coexist between your nighttime world and mortal beings. It doesn't have to be an unholy thing. You had no choice. You had no chance to choose. I do and have. Gerard," she leaned into him as she spoke, "share the magnificence of what you are with me."

He caught her forearms, levering for a saving distance. "Why? Why do you make this choice now?"

She met his intense stare unblinkingly. "Because I have been touched by the fear of death. I have seen my own mortality and that of those I love. I have been weak and suffered for it, but now, I want to be strong, so strong no one will dare harm me or mine again."

He said nothing, delving into the depths of her expression. Seeing her determination there.

"Gerard, share your strength and your future with me. I promise you will never be alone or lack for love. Free me from this mortal frailty, so I can do what I must to preserve for all time what we have together. Unless, of course, you don't want me to share it with you."

His arms crushed her up against him as he took her with his kiss. She gave herself to him completely, withholding nothing as passions ran wild. His hands fisted in the fabric of her gown, tearing it from her frame, so that only the thin gauze of her undergarments lay between them. With a powerful move, his arm swept behind her knees, hoisting her into his embrace to carry her to bed.

His kisses fell everywhere—on her parted lips, in the valley between her breasts, at the sensitive inner hollow of her arms, at the hot tangle of her maidenhair. She welcomed them with soft moans of delight, her fingers clutched in his hair, her knees spreading wide to invite a deeper, more intimate kiss. She gasped as he feasted there, as he drove her to a shattering climax that had her crying out his name as if he were a god she worshipped.

And then he was naked, too, a glorious sight she would forever revere. Her hands would not be satisfied until they had traveled the length and breadth of him, to the limit of his patience with her inciting touch. He found her eager mouth once more, sharing her hard and heated breaths as he filled her with one swift stroke. Time stilled as they savored the beauty of that instant when they were one in body and soul. And then he began to move.

Sensation, fierce and primal, flamed at the friction made between them. The give and take of power, the surrender of pride to the most basic of emotions. Want. Need. Desire. Love, wild, unbridled, unstoppable love. Never had Laure believed such joy, such freedom possible. She clutched at the hard flex of his shoulders as her body mated with his in desperate need.

I love you, Gerard. I love you, Gerard.

The words were her *langage*, her chant of power, spoken in her heart and mind, and greedily received by his without being shared aloud. And as she reached her capacity for pleasure, he stopped his fierce fencing with her tongue, his mouth lifting so her expectant gasps filled the air. And as tremendous spasms ravaged her body, the sharp sting of his teeth at her throat became an erotic part of the cataclysmic event.

She'd been prepared for pain, for fear, for a last moment of reluctance, but he made the act into one of exhilarating passion. The want to give, to give more, had her clutching at the back of his head, holding him captive as he partook of her life's blood. Her senses spun, wildly at first, then with a dreamy delight. She drifted, enjoying the calm, the peace, the soft glow of her thoughts.

Then the contact to Gerard was broken, and panic settled along her limbs like a cold, creeping mist, numbing her mind, reaching inward to silence her heart forever.

No...

"Laure, you must not stray far. Come back to me, *cara*. You must be strong if you want to live. Live, my love and be with me always."

Something warm drizzled across her lips. With a taste, she knew what it was. Her blood mixed with Gerard's, hot, thick and rich upon her tongue. At first, she tried to turn her head, to refuse the elixir that led to eternity. But then she heard Gerard's persuasive voice, not aloud, but a silken whisper within her head.

"Drink, *cara*. Be one with me forever."

But their forever could never be.

She swallowed reluctantly, because she knew she must, then, as the heat hit her system, streaking through it like flames, she could not take him in fast enough to fill the empty void where life existed no more. She heard drumming, not the angry *vodun* tempo, but a low, enticing rhythm that grew stronger and more a part of her. Gerard's heartbeat. She called it closer and closer, embracing the cadence and making it her own.

"Enough, my love."

She moaned greedily as the feast was withdrawn because nothing had ever satisfied her so completely. Gerard's arms became a welcomed haven.

"Rest," he whispered against her smooth temple, "for when you awake you will see with new eyes but love with the same heart."

She relaxed then, letting the strange whorls of bright color and sound lave her senses. It was beautiful. Trusting Gerard to see to her care.

And when she did open her eyes, she saw before her a different world.

"How do you feel?" Gerard came up on his elbow to regard her judiciously.

Laure blinked and looked about in wonder. "I never imagined things would have such depth and amazing texture." She wanted to see it all, delighting in the subtle changes created by her heightened senses.

"We exist on a slightly different plane from mortal beings. We can alter time, can control our surroundings, even our very substance, if we choose to. I will teach you all these things."

"Yes." Then she placed a hand upon his finely chiseled cheek to quiet his enthusiasm. "But first I want to learn how it will be between you and me."

"I suspect it will be, how you say, *magnifico*. But you are yet a new creature and should take your time—"

"There is no time. What I mean is, there will be no better time than this. Kiss me, my husband." And she kissed him first, desperately because she knew they didn't have an eternity.

This was the last moment they would have together.

It was magnificent.

Excitement came alive inside her, sprinkling up her arms, tickling along her breasts, tightening into an unbelievably sensitive center. When his mouth fastened there, the pleasure was instantaneous, rolling through her in volcanic waves. Sensations so rich, so thick, so devastatingly strong. Their couplings always enthralled her, but never before had she felt such power, such control. She gripped his sleek flanks and rolled so that she came up astride him. There, from that vantage point, she could watch his glorious face, depict his pleasure as she eased down over him by slow, exquisite degrees. Pleasure and the torture of delay became one. She shuddered as he filled her completely. It was the sight of Gerard's expression, so sharply cut in ecstasy, that carved the perfect moment upon her soul.

How she loved him!

His eyes opened slowly, their silvery glitter against the pale moonlight of his skin and thick black lashes creating a startling dazzle.

"I have waited centuries for you."

He reached up to lace his fingers through the bright fire of her hair, drawing her down to him so their lips could meet. Their breaths merged and, as they moved together in an increasingly urgent purpose, their gasps and cries and sighs fed each other's passion to the point of fiercely shared bliss.

Magnifico.

And as dawn's approach ended their union, Gerard led his lover, his wife, up the spiraled stairs to the place of their daylight sleep. Only there, upon seeing his coffin, did she resist her fate. She pulled back in alarm, staring at that box as a symbol of what she'd surrendered.

"I can't, Gerard."

"But, *cara*, you must. It is part of what you are. We must keep to darkness to preserve our strength, to protect ourselves from the sun's angry touch. That cruelty you never want to feel. Trust me on that, love."

But she continued to regard the casket with wide-eyed horror. He couldn't bear the sight of fear swimming in her lovely dark eyes.

"Wait here a moment, my love."

She stood in the dusty, imprisoning darkness, aware for the first time of how greatly her existence had changed. Afraid. Alone. Until Gerard returned, dragging a feather ticking behind him. He spread it on the floor and reclined upon it. Looking up at her, his features beautiful with their small inviting smile, his palm smoothed the space beside him.

"Is this better?"

Her smile was poignant, twisting about his heart.

"Have we made a mistake, *cara*?" he inquired gently, fearing the hesitation, the strangeness of her mood. "Do you feel regrets?"

"No," she declared at last, her strength of will and purpose returning. She settled upon the bedding, into his open arms. Curling close in an intimate tangle of arms and legs, she nestled her head upon his shoulder as a heavy lethargy descended.

"I love you, Gerard. Never doubt that."

And when he opened his eyes at dusk to find she was no longer beside him, it wasn't doubt putting a cold spear of terror through his heart.

It was dread.

TWENTY-TWO

Muttering under his breath, Percy shut the door to the bedroom behind him and turned. Running squarely into Gerard Pasquale.

"Where is my wife?"

Percy took a step back, eyes rounded in his surprise at seeing him, not only in his home but alive. It was all he could do not to babble incoherently. "I don't... She—she's not here. Do you think she heard something from the kidnappers? She wouldn't act on her own, would she?"

"I don't know. But I do intend to find out." His icy glare burned down into the little lawyer's like flares of an eclipse.

"Normally, my Laure is the soul of good sense. She wouldn't think to take on such a dangerous task alone. However, she seems to be acting a bit irrationally," Percy confided.

"Your point, Cristobel, providing you have one other than to irritate me beyond reason?"

"If I were you, I would check with those odd relatives she has out in the swamps. I wouldn't be surprised to discover they had something to do with the boy's disappearance." When Gerard didn't react, he hurried on with his theory. "I seem to remember her telling me there was bad blood between her great aunt and her grandmother. Perhaps some kind of family feud has been resurrected. It's hard to say with their kind."

The bitterness just slipped out. He thought, he hoped, Pasquale had missed it but should have known better. Pasquale missed nothing.

"What kind is that?"

"Poor bayou people," he explained hurriedly. "Laure's mother was quite ashamed of them and their pagan practices. I don't know if Laure's ever had anything to do with them. She'd be crazy if she did. Pagan worship, witchcraft. Disgusting, evil ways." He shuddered for effect.

"Perhaps I shall go see."

"Do you know where to look?" Percy offered, wanting to appear helpful rather than anxious to send him on his way. Anything to get him out of his rooms.

"I will find them."

"Good luck then. Let me know what you discover. Laure's welfare means everything to me."

Perhaps he pushed too far, for Pasquale gave him a quelling glare. But whatever he might suspect about Percy's sincerity didn't keep him from going to his wife's rescue. He started to leave.

Percy had just begun to breathe a sigh of relief when Pasquale froze on his way to the door. He paused, his head tilted, all preternatural stillness. The hairs on Percy's neck quivered.

"What is it, Pasquale?"

Gerard turned slowly. "You tell me, Cristobel. I cannot see you as someone who would good heartedly offer to care for a neighbor's child."

"Child? What are you—"

Then he heard it, too, a soft whimpering from behind his bedroom door.

"Oh," he said, thinking fast and furiously, "that's my clerk's daughter. He is running an errand for me and—"

Gerard thrust him aside with rib-bruising force, and with one step had breeched the threshold.

The fretful baby lay in a padded box on the bed. It's whining stopped when Gerard bent near. Instead, a cooing gurgle sounded.

"There, there, Gino, *mi' amore di bambino.*"

A tiny fist grabbed hold of his finger as the other waved happily.

"I—I can explain—"

Keeping his voice low so as not to disturb the child, Gerard said, "You need explain nothing to me, parasite. Save your excuses for when your sister comes to claim the child. Were I you, I would be very careful to see that nothing happens to him before we return. Am I understood?"

"Y-yes."

Gerard tapped the baby's plump cheek with his forefinger, then straightened to confront the child's uncle. Meeting Gerard's gaze was like staring into a hell one would soon call home.

"I leave him in your capable hands, then."

Percy didn't move. He was afraid he was going to lose bodily control.

"If you run," Gerard added almost cheerfully, "be assured that I will hunt you down in minutes and dine on your entrails while you watch."

Percy believed him.

Drumming filled the night like an evil heartbeat, drawing believers together at the *mambo*'s command. Clad in her crimson robe, the ritual *asson* rattle in her hand as a sign of her office, Eulalia gloated to herself as the crowd of worshippers parted to allow passage to a figure in a white cloak. Her smug expression fell when she saw it was her niece.

"Why are you here, Laurette? This is not the bargain we made."

She folded back the white hood so all would recognize her by the gleam of her red-gold hair, her gift from her grandmother's Celtic past. "I did not lie. You were promised a vampire, and I brought one."

Eulalia looked behind her, perplexed, and then she looked, really looked, at the young woman before her. Looked and saw the translucent skin, the burning intensity of her gaze, the aura of power and unnatural strength humming about her.

"What have you done?"

"I have become your sacrifice out of love for my family. Did you think you could make me choose between them? How would I ever live with that choice? So I will be their martyr, and they will go on. The family you have tried for so many years to destroy will survive. I have been such a fool."

Eulalia's black eyes narrowed. "Are you here to challenge me, girl?"

"I am here to fulfill a promise. You may take my soul, you may absorb my power, but if you harm my family again, you will know all that Moira LaClaire taught me. Too bad you will not live to practice it."

"A threat?"

"I don't make threats, *tante*, I make demands. You'll have your life for a life, soul for a soul. Where is my child?"

"He is safely away from here. No harm will come to him, I promise."

"Your word by your sacred office."

"Yes. My word."

"Then let's proceed."

At Eulalia's sharp direction, LaPlace gripped Laure's forearm and escorted her into the circle toward the altar stone. Laure went willingly. If this would save her son, it was a sacrifice gladly met. She wouldn't think about not seeing him grow up and grown old. That was too great a pain to control. She would concentrate on the certainty that Gerard would see him well reared.

If he could ever forgive her.

She stopped at the altar, reaching out to touch the *govi* that held her grandmother's *ti-bon-ange*. Looking into the clay pot, she whispered, "I will be with you soon, *grandmere*."

It was then she saw the truth, sent to her in a stunning vision from the grandmother she had adored. A truth that shocked her from her resignation with the secrets it revealed.

She confronted Eulalia in a throbbing fury. "You. You *are* responsible for their deaths. I wasn't certain until this very minute. Why did none of us see in time to save ourselves?"

Eulalia smiled, her venomous hatred clear in her poison-laced words. "Because you were weakened by the idea of family, and you forgot that power knows no loyalty."

"You spread the rumors about my mother that led to my father's death."

"So simple, really," she had the arrogance to boast. "A slain child, a whisper in the right ear." Why keep her silence? After all, it was a secret she'd been dying to tell for almost a decade.

"And her husband, Simon Cristobel? That was you, too. Of course. But how did you manage?"

"Zombi poison," she confided, proudly. "A substance so deadly it only needs be absorbed through the skin. I made him a gift, some lovely calfskin gloves supposedly from your mother, only they'd been cured in my own special blend of bouga toad, millipedes, tree frogs, and seeds from my favorite poisonous plants. A substance strong enough to paralyze, to make him fall into a mysterious coma. Could be he was still alive for his own burial."

She smiled at Laure's horror.

"And my mother?"

"She was too powerful to be left alive. Even though she'd promised not to challenge the rights of succession after I—took care of my dear sister. I, myself, performed the *dessounin* on her, as I will upon you."

Laure closed her eyes, filled with fear now that she knew her fate. A fate she'd share with her mother. After her sacrifice, in order to separate the *gros-bon-ange* from her body, her nostrils and ears would be stuffed with cotton, and her knees and big toes tied together. Her mouth would be laced shut and her pockets turned inside out. Then Eulalia would spray raw rum to the four cardinal points then over her corpse to cleanse it. As the *asson* was shaken over her and candles lit, her name would be whispered in her ear as it had been in her mother's. Once the loa of the dead were drawn, Eulalia would be reborn with the divine essence of the recently dead. Her spirit would become a part of the priestess as it tried to pass through on its way to *Ginen*, the world of the dead. That was her fate, and the unfairness of it made her tremble with rage and grief. Her poor mother and the men she'd loved, falling prey to the madness of a single woman bent on unusurpable power.

It would not be borne.

From out of the folds of her robe, Laure produced a colorful *drapeaux* bearing Baron Samedi's *veve*. Upon that flag rested a calabash rattle. Eulalia gasped as she recognized the beading upon it.

"Where did you get that?"

"It was *grandmere*'s. She gave it to me in hopes that I would one day wield it to the good of the *societe*. I see now that will never happen."

"Give it to me." Eulalia had looked everywhere for it after she'd dealt with her sister, but it could not be found. With Moira LaClaire's symbol of authority in her hand, she could command the loa's service. She would be unstoppable. She snatched the rattle and held it high, flushed with the sense of her own power. At last, her right would be realized. "Tonight I will finally rule supreme."

Laure regarded her with a small smile. "Yes. This is your night, *Tante* Eulie. The night when your sins are upon you, and the names of my grandmother and mother are freed."

"What nonsense is this, girl?" Eulalia snapped at her. "They are dead, as you soon will be. And I did not need your scheming step-brother's money to pay the way as I did with your mother."

Laure stared, shocked to hear it spoken aloud, but not disbelieving. What reason would the old witch have to lie? "Percy? What did he have to do with my mother's death?"

Eulalia laughed. "You are a fool. Do you think I am the only one who hates enough to kill? Only he is a gentleman and does not dirty his own hands. Where did you think all the Cristobel money went? It came to me in the name of revenge to ask a life for a life. Only the stupid boy had an innocent pay for my guilt in the death of his father."

How perfectly the pieces fell together. Eulalia killing Percy's father, laying the blame on his new wife. Percy paying Eulalia to slay her mother in an act of misguided vengeance. Such irony. How he must have hated her while pasting on that caring smile. And how pleased he would be to learn of her death out here in the swamps.

If only there were some means of telling her husband of Percy's part in these schemes of greed and retribution. She hated the thought of him going free. But Gerard was no fool. In time, he would figure it out for himself, and Percy would pay. And pay dearly.

Eulalia made a motion. "Prepare her."

Laure didn't struggle as she was lifted atop the altar. The stone bit cold and hard into her shoulders, back and thighs. Above her, she saw the gleam of LaPlace's *ku-bha-sah* as he passed the sword to Eulalia. This was it. This was how she would meet her death. She would call upon the memory of her husband and child and hold their dear faces near to give her courage. They would know her last thoughts had been of them.

As she closed her eyes, she knew a savage satisfaction. Though she'd not been sure of the extreme nature of Eulalia's treachery, she'd come prepared for it. She might now be paying for her own naivete, but she would not go alone.

Suddenly, there was a break in the chanting, a hesitation in the drumbeats. A murmur rippled through the members of the *societe*. Laure heard the whispered name of a *mort*, Baron Cimetiere, loa of the graveyard, as Moira LaCLaire's *govi* vessel rose into the air, sweeping over the heads of the awed believers and out into the night.

"What is this?" Eulalia shrieked, staring through disbelieving eyes. "I called upon no loa of the dead. What tricks are these? Are you doing this?" she demanded of her neice.

Laure smiled to herself as she shook her head. It was not her doing. She knew of only one with such a grim sense of humor.

Gerard.

"*Baka! Baka!*"

The terrified cry rose up in a huge swell through the crowd. They ducked down as if some invisible creature flew overhead. A luminous trail marked the empty air, and the sharp odor of sulfur burned the nose. LaPlace was plucked off his feet. He uttered a fearful cry, his hands flailing at whatever unseen being held him by the shoulders as he was carried away.

"Tricks!" Eulalia shouted, trying to calm her panicked followers, but even she cast worried glances about the quiet sky. "There is no power here but mine."

Taking her cue upon the stage set by her husband, Laure sat up to exclaim, "There, you are wrong. I have called the *tonton macoute* to act on my command."

The name of the evil bogeymen woke a new wave of fear within the milling crowd.

"I have made an *anajan* pact with the *Petro* loa in my family's name. We are partners in this most vile and black of magic, and they serve me to one purpose. Revenge." She paused in her spontaneous oration and turned to her aunt, fixing her with a cold smile. "And you will be their sacrifice."

Eulalia cringed back. She stared down at the *asson* Laure had given her. Her body began to tremble and stiffen, and she dropped the rattle. But it was too late. The poison Laure had placed upon it was already coursing through Eulalia's system like a raging disease. Her last cognizant thought before unconsciousness overcame her was of how proud Moira would be of her daughter's little girl. She fell to the ground, rigid as a corpse.

Laure stepped down off the altar and gestured for devotees to put Eulalia in the place that had been prepared to receive her sacrifice. Now was not the time for squeamishness or hesitation. The souls of her family cried out to be avenged. She picked up the sacred sword, and steeling herself for what had to be done, made one quick motion to separate head from body. Then she gestured for the two parts of the corpse to be placed in the coffin Eulalia had readied for her. Into it, Laure sprinkled sesame seeds, so the evil woman's soul would never rise again at anyone's command.

"Bury it deep in the swamps," she ordered. Then to those who knelt in recognition of her new authority, she said, "Tear off those robes. You will never assemble to serve the *Cochon Gris* in summoning the *Petro* for evil purpose. No *bokor* priest or priestess will command you. Go to your homes and wait for the call to worship *Rada*. Until then, pray to your Christian God so that He might forgive your sins, because I cannot. Nor will I forget who chose to stand against my grandmother's good. Go home. Hide yourselves and pray that I do not send my minions to find you."

They scattered into the trees like hens with a fox in their midst. Soon, there was only silence.

Laure closed her eyes, saying her own prayer that Gino had not been harmed by her actions on this night. And before she could open them, Gerard's arms were wrapped strong and warm about her.

"Very nice drama, *cara*. Worthy of opera."

He kissed her neck, and she could scent LaPlace's blood upon his breath. She turned toward him within the protective circle of his embrace. Her gaze was wide with anguish, desperate in its search of his.

"Gino?"

Gerard smiled. He was so beautiful.

"Our son is safe and waiting for us to claim him."

Laure sagged upon his chest, letting him support her in her sudden weakness. His hand stroked her hair with a soothing repetition.

"You would have let them sacrifice you. Why?"

"To keep those I love safe from harm. Gino, and you."

"And you would have trusted me to raise your child." He sounded humbled by her tremendous faith. The gesture over-whelmed his self-indulgent heart.

"Our child," she corrected.

They stood together for a long moment, united by the knowledge of each other's love. Then Gerard eased back to show her what he held.

"What do you want done with this?"

She took the pot from him with reverent hands.

In the darkness, Laure stood at an empty crossroad. She raised the *govi* overhead then smashed it to the ground. Pieces scattered about her as a huge tenderness brought forth a serene smile.

"You have saved me, *grandmere*, through your wisdom, and I have seen you avenged as was my duty. Now I free your spirit to join my mother in the land of the dead. Tell her I love her and I will keep my promise."

She waited there for another long moment then wiped her eyes. She turned to her husband, who remained respectfully off to one side, and held out her hand.

"Come. Let's go collect our son."

Percy was frantically packing.

The money no longer mattered. He thought only to escape with his life. He had no confidence that the witch Eulalia would defeat the malevolent Gerard, and he planned to be far, far away before the demon returned for retribution.

In the bedroom, his step-sister's brat squalled incessantly, adding to the painful ache in his head.

"Shut up, you little—"

Before he finished his diatribe, the crying ceased.

He froze, his breath catching in dread. Heart pounding, he peered around the corner to see Laure with the babe to her breast. When she turned to look at him, he took a startled step back. Something was different. Something about her had changed, but he couldn't quite get a fix on it.

"Laure, are you all right?" he gushed. The need to survive overcame his panic. His cunning would not fail him now. "As you can see, the boy is fine. He was delivered to me just minutes ago by some stranger. I was so worried—"

"You should be," came the purr of Gerard's accented voice behind him. "Isn't it time you told your 'dear' sister the truth?"

Percy looked between the two of them, seeing all his schemes dissolve to a single hope for his salvation. He took it, shamelessly casting himself at Laure's feet to sob in pathetic earnest.

"Forgive me, Laure. I am a wretch to have believed the worst of you. I let my anger over my father's death cloud my judgement. I actually believed your mother was responsible, and I almost let that hatred destroy you."

"My mother loved him."

Percy glanced up at that, his hostility glittering briefly for her to clearly see. Then he was all groveling apology once more. "I know that now. I allowed my grief to mislead me into thinking you were somehow to blame. I was wrong, dear sister. I was so wrong."

"Yes," Gerard drawled out, "you were."

Percy's frightened gaze flashed to the dark vampire then back to where he scrambled to find mercy. "Don't let him kill me, Laure. I am a victim of this as much as you."

"It was for the money, wasn't it, Percy?"

He blinked at Laure's cold summation. "No! No! I did what I did to protect you."

"By trying to sell me to Alain Javier? By pushing me into a vampire's embrace in hopes that I would not survive it? Hoping that I would not live to see how horribly you had deceived me? Did you scheme with Javier for his men to murder us?"

"Not you, Laure. Him! The monster. I was trying to protect you. Once I found out what he was, I knew I had to keep you safe—"

"You knew you had to keep his money for yourself," she amended with a brutal insight. "And for that, you would gladly sacrifice me and my child, wouldn't you, Percy?"

"No!" he wailed. He hugged to her skirts. "I did it for you, Laure. You must believe me."

"And for what reason did you conspire to have my mother killed? Was that in my best interest, too?"

Percy simply stared up at her, expression blank, no slick answers forming that would save him from this final damning revelation. He glanced about in terror as Gerard advanced.

But Gerard merely reached over his head to take the cooing child from its mother's arms. Laure, he kissed with a simmering promise and bid her, "I'll take the babe home while you see to your brother in an appropriate fashion. I'm sure you'll display the compassion he deserves." Then, he smiled down at Percy, all sinister amusement.

"Little lawyer, you have been afraid of the wrong thing. You've been fearing retribution from a monster's hands, when you should have been dreading the vengeance of a mother's wrath. Of the two, I would have preferred to confront the demon any day." He chuckled wickedly.

"Good night, my love," he said to Laure. "I will wait up. Be mindful of the dawn."

It was then Percy realized what was so different about his step-sister. He'd been throwing himself upon her humanity to save him from Gerard.

A humanity she no longer possessed.

She smiled, seeing his awareness of his fate.

Her fangs gleamed.

With the prickle of dawn behind her, Laure paused in the doorway of a hastily constructed nursery to savor a moment of complete contentment. There she watched as her husband rocked her tiny son to sleep. But the mood didn't last. All was not settled yet. He glanced up when he felt her attention and smiled.

"There you are. I was beginning to worry." He reluctantly surrendered the child to a plump, matronly woman who was waiting near the babe's bassinet. "Laure, this is Mrs. Bradfield. She will take care of Gino while we are at rest. She comes with impeccable references."

When the woman bent to place the child in his blankets, Laure saw her husband's mark upon the woman's throat.

"Mrs. Bradfield is experienced with children, aren't you, Mrs. Bradfield?"

"Oh, yes sir. I loves the wee ones. That I do. 'Tis grateful I am for the position and for such a generous salary. 'Tis almost a shame for me to take it, such a pleasure it will be to care for one so bonny."

Gerard had eyes only for his wife as he answered, "You have our greatest treasure in your hands, *signora*. No fee is enough to express our thanks, isn't that right, *cara?*"

"Yes, my love."

"I've told Mrs. Bradfield that we may soon be leaving New

Orleans."

"Is that a problem, Mrs. Bradfield?"

The elderly woman smiled at Laure. "Oh, no ma'am. I have no family left, and he is such a lovely child."

"We trust him to you, then."

"Rest easy, ma'am. I will keep him safe."

Gerard extended his hand. "My love, it is time for us to retire."

She slipped her fingers across his smooth palm, reveling in his possessive grasp. "Lead the way."

They climbed the stairs together, and as they lay in one another's arms, Gerard asked with a mild curiosity, "Did you see to Percy properly?"

"Only the bayou and the alligators can answer that."

He chuckled in appreciation.

Laure didn't respond with like amusement. Her expression was grim but not regretful. "I could not let him live."

"I know, my love. You needn't apologize."

"He was a danger to us. We would never have been safe. He arranged my mother's death and tried to do the same for us. Thankfully, he was not successful. But he would have tried again. I know it."

"You did the right thing, *cara*. Justice has been well served."

Then he grew pensive and a trifle uneasy with his thoughts.

"What is it, Gerard?"

"Before I rest, I need to know the state of your heart."

"My heart? I don't understand."

"But I do, now. I wanted to believe the reasons you gave me, but I know now that you had another motive for choosing this half life. It was to save the child, a decision I applaud, one I would have made myself had you given me the choice to make it. You should have, Laure. You should have trusted me. You should have let me go. Then you would not be eternally cursed to share this life with me."

He wasn't angry with her for her deception. It was pain she saw in his luminous eyes, and that was far worse. She wouldn't have refused him the right to rant and rave over her excluding him from danger, but she would not allow him to hold the misconception he'd come to. She took his gloriously featured face between her palms, directing his gaze to hers so that he could not mistake her sincerity.

"I did what I did for our family. For Gino, for you. I would do it again without hesitation. But never, never will I regret my choice to spend an eternity with you. Never. It is no curse; it is a blessing. If you believe nothing else I've ever told you, believe that. Neither of us will ever be alone again and I would wish it no other way. I love you, Gerard, and I will live this life or any other with you, gladly, without doubts, without remorse."

He said nothing for a long moment, and she began to fear it was too late to convince him of this all-important truth. It wasn't a lack of trust, it was love that had dictated her choice. A love for him and the child they would raise together, if they could get beyond this point of contention.

"One other question, *cara*," he asked at last. "I was wondering if you meant to take over control of your clan now that the witch is dead. I do not mind sharing the night with you, and I truly enjoy sharing my bed, but I am jealous of those demons who would demand equal attention."

Laughing with relief, she tipped up his chin with her thumbs, letting him read the adoration in her tender gaze. "The only magic I care to practice is in holding your heart captive."

"That spell is complete, *cara*. I am eternally enchanted."

He kissed her then and held her close as daylight sealed their dreams in slumber.

A Special Preview
of
Nancy Gideon's

MIDNIGHT GAMBLE

Coming in
October, 2000

ONE

Dawn.

Its pristine scent sharpened on the air, and the night creature hurried on his way lest that first wash of deadly pastel light reach him in an unprotected state. He darted down the trash-littered alleyway, just a flickering shadow and stirring breeze to the derelicts slouching in uncaring doorways. In their drink-glazed ignorance of what moved, unseen, amongst them, they were blisfully unaware how closely death passed them by.

Feeling the pinching discomfort that came with the brightening horizon, the dark being halted outside the heavy steel door barring entrance to his daytime lair. He risked much in his hesitation, but he risked more if he wasn't cautious now. For the past few miles, he felt sure he'd been followed.

Of course, that was impossible. Nothing could keep pace with his preternatural speed. Yet the uneasiness lingered, the sense that he was not alone. With all his self-preservation instincts tingling, he could not afford to seek his rest. Not until he was sure.

He scanned the dim alley, alarmed now by the way shadows began to lift and lighten. No movement except from those unfortunates foraging for a meal in the huge garbage bins. No hint of threat. He looked up, squinting against the sky, now a dangerous degree paler. Above him, empty rooftops cut a harsh black line across that slated heaven. Nothing there except the softening hues of morning.

He tried to shake off his worry as he unlocked the door and slipped inside the cooler quiet of the building. He would not be safe, even in those dark halls, once daybreak peeled back the concealing cape of night. No more time for delay.

He swept down the narrow flight of stairs into the welcoming dankness of the cellar. There, cobwebs, broken beams and crumbling brick kept the curious away. With morning sparking at his heels, he seeped smoke-like through a keyhole-sized chink in the wall. Issuing a huge sigh of relief, he reached the single object in his decay-laced sanctuary—a plain wooden box meant to embrace a weary soul for an eternity. But in his case, it was only a temporary housing, one he rose from with the setting of the sun.

He threw up the lid, wasting no time as he climbed into the padded interior which fit to his form after nearly a century. He gloried in the scent of his victim's blood that came with him, entwined with faint traces of the woman's floral perfume. Her fatal struggles left lasting impressions upon him, and he would enjoy them as he sought his rest. He liked it when they fought him. It made the ultimate victory that much sweeter. He smiled as he sank back upon the faded satin, drowsiness overcoming him in a pleasurable wave.

He was still smiling when the startling truth hit home.

He was not alone. His dark bower had been breached.

With a ferocious snarl, he started up and was met solidly by the downward slam of the coffin's lid. As he lay dazed and helpless in the thrall of daybreak, he heard the sound of nails driving through hard wood, sealing him inside his daily tomb.

And above the sound, he heard a soft, mocking voice say, "Sweet dreams."

There was nothing unusual about the sight of a woman escorting her loved one to a final rest. Tragic perhaps, because the woman was so young, but not unusual. Those she passed bowed their heads out of respect, and some crossed themselves as they mouthed words of comfort for the deceased. The young mourner walked by, unmindful of them, apparently lost to grief.

A horse-drawn hearse waited at the edge of the platform, wreathed in smoke from the train. The woman stood to one side as the casket was carefully loaded. Her quiet words stirred the heavy black veil that obscured her features from the travelers hurrying by. "Quickly now. The sun will soon be setting."

As the wagon pulled away from the crowded station, the woman climbed into a waiting automobile. She sat upon the stiff back seat, rolled up her veil and inserted a slim cigarette holder between soft lips set in a solemn line.

"Any trouble, Miss Frederica?"

She met the driver's gaze in the rearview mirror and offered a reassuring smile. "No, Oscar. Everything went as planned."

"*He'll* be glad to hear it."

She made a non-committal sound and leaned forward to accept his offer of a match. For a moment, her face was hidden behind a blue haze. Then she exhaled and sat back with a sigh.

"Let's not keep him waiting then."

A long warehouse of riveted steel hunched down along the river front. The docks, always bustling during the day, were slowing into twilight's leisurely pace as two vehicles drew up to its fenced perimeter. Two men, whose heavy coats didn't conceal the fact they were heavily armed, approached the gate. After exchanging a few brief words, they unlocked the chains to open the way inside. A sign hung above the entrance, but the name had worn away with the weathering of time.

Several indistinguishable figures emerged from one of the buildings, waiting for the black carriage to come to a stop. Then they served as silent pallbearers, carrying the unadorned coffin upon their shoulders while the woman climbed from the car and followed close behind. If any thought it a strange setting for a final memorial, none expressed it.

The room, where the wooden crate was placed almost reverently upon a cement floor, was in complete darkness. The men faded back into shadow with only the woman remaining at the crate's side. A small circle of light flared as she fired the wick of the lantern she carried. She set it down on the floor and went to work with the other tool she'd brought with her. The hammer's claw wrenched the spikes from the coffin's lid, each giving with a shriek against the surrounding silence. When the last one pulled free, the woman stepped back.

"Carlos Vincente," she called out in a loud, clear voice. "Come forth to face your judges."

The lid flew off the box as if by an explosive force. Carlos Vincente, thought dead to his family and friends for over one hundred years, sprang from his prison, a raging demon. As his lurid eyes fixed upon her and his thin lips rolled back to expose fangs that glistened with deadly intent, the woman remained calm and unconcerned.

"Prepare to die, *puta*," he growled.

She smiled. "I don't think so."

Slowly, illumination spread throughout the room. It wasn't empty, as Vicente first believed, but contained tier upon tier of seats, perhaps three dozen of them. And in each seat sat a cloaked and hooded figure. Vincente forgot the woman as he considered this sudden, greater threat.

"Who are you? What do you want with me?" he demanded.

One figure separated from the others and pushed back his hood to reveal a swarthy man with eyes as dark and hard as onyx chips. "We are your *corps du jugement*. You were brought before us to answer for your crimes."

"Crimes? What crimes?" The slight tremor in Vicente's voice betrayed his bold stance.

"For the reckless murder of human beings."

"Murder?" Vincente laughed, dismissing the claim with a wave of his hand. "It is no crime for our kind to feed upon mortals."

"Not to feed; to kill. You have endangered all of us with your slaughter of innocents. You were warned, but you chose not to obey. Now you must face the consequence of your greed and foolish arrogance. Will you renounce the old ways and know acceptance within our fold? Will you be our brother once more?"

"I see no reason to change, not for the sake of those pathetic humans. Who are you to judge me?" he shouted, challenging them all with the sweep of his glare. And to a one, they could scent his fear.

"We are as you are, no more, no less," the stoic speaker continued in his heavily accented voice. "And as your peers, we reserve the right to name the penalty for your defiance of our laws. And that penalty is death. May God have mercy upon your soul for we shall have none."

As Vincente shrieked obscenities and fled for the door, the robed figures were still no longer. They swooped down from their seats of judgement like dark birds of prey, descending upon the hapless Spaniard who had as little chance of escape as his victim of the previous night.

As his screams filled the cavernous room, the speaker, saddened yet satisfied that his sentence was being carried out, left the violent debacle, aware that the woman followed.

Upon entering the rear rooms of the warehouse, one would think they'd stepped into an elegant apartment rather than the office of a outwardly dirty import-export firm. Thick walls muffled the sound of industry from the waterfront, just as they muted the frenzy they'd left behind. Marchand LaValois crossed to an ornately carved sideboard to pour himself a glass of rich red wine. He drank it down in a quick swallow, then wiped his mouth with an unsteady hand. The wine was a poor substitute for what he really thirsted for, but he prided himself on being civilized. And a civilized being didn't cave in to blood lust.

"Oscar said you had no trouble with Vincente." He cleared his throat, pretending it wasn't hunger that made his words so hoarse, then, he turned toward the black-garbed woman.

"Vincente was a fool, an easy mark. It's amazing no one had staked him out in the sun long before this."

Marchand frowned as the young woman removed her veiled hat and black outer garments. He disapproved of what he saw as well as what he heard. She was the image of her mother, but that timeless beauty had altered to fit a more modern time. A slender hand raked through a bob of tousled black hair, the gesture momentarily distracting Marchand from the scandalously short hemline of the young woman's dress...if one could call the straight slip of jade-colored crepe de Chine with its long loops of precocious pearls a decent dress.

"Don't dismiss him—and those like him—so easily, Frederica. They are a dangerous and unpredictable breed. Your confidence could be your downfall."

She regarded him through a steady, emerald stare. "I am never careless. That's why I'm so good at what I do."

He scowled, not impressed. "What you do is a service for your kind, who hopes to blend into this twentieth century without dangerous fanfare. It is not a point of vanity, so don't look so smug with your accomplishments. You have a unique talent, Rica, one that provides us with a decided upper hand in dealing with the undead. It is an inherited gift not to be squandered or boasted about."

Frederica's direct gaze lowered, giving her a properly chastised air. Marchand wasn't fooled. He sighed in fond exasperation.

"Rica, it's not my intention to scold you. It's my love for you that makes me decry these unnecessary risks you take. You are my only child. It would devastate me if you were to come to any harm because you failed to display proper caution. And your mother would never forgive me."

Her sparkling eyes canted up, her smile teasing him into relaxing his authoritative stance. When he opened his arms wide, she stepped forward to fill them, declaring, "I am careful, Father. I know the seriousness of what I do, and I would never fail you by taking my position lightly."

Hugging her close, Marchand breathed in the scent of her short hair, cherishing this independent child rare good fortune had given him. "And you know my position, Rica. It must be unbending if we are to bring any kind of rule to those who would follow the old ways and threaten our survival. We can no longer afford to be seen as vile creatures of the damned, feasting off the blood of mortals in an animalistic frenzy. The days of hiding behind superstition are through. We can no longer command the fear that assures our safety, not in this modern world that's gone to war with itself. After facing death in foreign trenches, what man will shrink at the thought of vampires in the night? If we are not careful, we will be hunted down like unwanted vermin until every last one of us is destroyed. That is not the future I want for myself and my family."

"Nor I, Father." She stepped back from his embrace, his reflection intense and serious once more. "That's why I do what I must with the skills that I have. And I insist that you not let your affection for me stand in the way of sending me out amongst those who would jeopardize us all."

Marchand touched her cheek, marveling at its natural warmth when his own was as cold as marble. Regret colored his expression as he turned away.

"And I must send you out again, Rica, though your mother has begged me to bring you home with me."

"Tell her I will return when I've accomplished what I must. And tell her I'm being careful. Where do I go this time?"

Hours later, Frederica LaValois tucked a train ticket into her pocket. Gone were the trappings of mourning as she crossed the freshly scrubbed warehouse floor. Her expression was one of sharp anticipation, an eager huntress on her father's business. Her walk betrayed a spring of strength and confidence and something more, something that set Frederica LaValois apart as decidedly unusual.

Her brightly colored shoes disturbed none of the water pooling upon the cement. They made no sound, no mark in passing, as if she walked above that natural surface with an unnatural air.

And then she did what her father and all his followers could not do. The one thing that set her apart from her kind.

She stepped out into the light of day.

ABOUT THE AUTHOR

With 40 sales to her credit since her first publication in 1987, Nancy Gideon's writing career is as versatile as the romance genre, itself.

Under Nancy Gideon, her own name, this Southwestern Michigan author is a Top Ten Waldenbooks' best seller for Silhouette, has written an award-winning vampire romance series for Pinnacle earning a "Best Historical Fantasy" nomination from Romantic Times, and will have her first two original horror screen plays made into motion pictures in a collaboration with local independent film company, Katharsys Pictures.

Writing western historical romance for Zebra as Dana Ransom, she received a "Career Achievement award for Historical Adventure" and is a K.I.S.S. Hero Award winner. Best known for her family saga series; the Prescott family set in the Dakotas and the Bass family in Texas, her books published overseas in Romanian, Italian, Russian, Portuguese, Danish, Dutch, German, Icelandic and Chinese.

As Rosalyn West for Avon Books, her novels have been nominated for "Best North American Historical Romance" and "Best Historical Book in a Series. Her "Men of Pride County" series earned an Ingram Paperback Buyer's Choice Selection, a Barnes & Noble Top Romance Pick and won a HOLT Medallion.

Gideon attributes her love of history, a gift for storytelling, a background in journalism for keeping her focused and the discipline of writing since her youngest was in diapers. She begins her day at 5 a.m. while the rest of the family is still sleeping. While the pace is often hectic, Gideon enjoys working on diverse projects—probably because she's a Gemini. One month, it's researching the gritty existence of 1880s Texas Rangers only to jump to 1990s themes of intrigue and child abuse. Then it's back to the shadowy netherworlds of vampires and movie serial killers. In between, she's the award-winning newsletter editor and former vice president of the Mid-Michigan chapter of Romance Writers of America and is widely published in industry trade magazines. A mother of pre-teen and teenage sons, she recently discovered the Internet and has her own webpages at: http://www.tlt.com/authors/ngideon.htm and http://www.theromanceclub.com/nancygideon.htm. She spends her 'spare time' taking care of a menagerie consisting of an ugly dog, a lazy cat, a tankful of pampered fish and three African clawed frogs (adopted after a Scouting badge!), plotting under the stars in her hot tub, cheering on her guys' hobbies of radio control airplanes and trucks, bowling and Explorer Scouting or indulging in her favorite vice—afternoon movies.

**DON'T MISS THESE
EXCITING BOOKS**

DREAMSINGER
by
J.A. Ferguson

A WORLD LOST. . .
First Daughter Nerienne, heir to the Tiria of Gayome, faces
the destruction of her world when her mother's enemies kill
the Tiria. Nerienne is left with just her magic and with
Bidge, a strange, shelled creature that speaks only to
Nerienne. She is rescued by Durgan Ketassian, leader of the
rebels in the northern woods, but can she trust this man
whom her mother condemned to die?
A DREAM FOUND. . .
Durgan knows he cannot trust Nerienne, for the Tiria has
been his enemy since she began slaying dreamsingers, those
skilled musicians who sing the future through one's dreams.
He has vowed to see his people free of the Tiria's
domination, never guessing the Tiria's daughter could
awaken parts of his heart which he shut away.
A SONG WITHOUT END. . .
To save Gayome, Nerienne and Durgan must work together
to defeat their common enemy, but to become allies opens
them to the greatest threat of all. . .falling in love.

SEE ORDER FORM IN BACK OF BOOK

A LOVE THROUGH ALL TIME
by
Jean Nash

When Andrea Morrow moves to Manhatten to pursue an acting career, she experiences baffling visions of New York City in an earlier era. Though disturbing, the strange visions don't keep her from pursuing her dream.

Unexpectedly, she wins the lead in a television miniseries about a fact-based love triangle and murder that happened almost a century ago. When filming begins, Andrea is thrown into daily contact with Justin Dinehart and Paul Salinger. Soon the three are involved in a dangerous love triangle of their own.

Tensions mount on the set. Justin, in a jealous rage, tries to kill Paul, which sends Andrea catapulting into a spontaneous past life regression. There she learns that she, Justin and Paul were involved in a tragedy that now threatens to ravage their present lives.

Will the tragedy be repeated, destroying them as it did before? Or will Andrea reverse the tide so that she and her soul mate can fulfill their destiny and share...A Love Through All Time?

SEE ORDER FORM IN BACK OF BOOK

UPCOMING RELEASES
From

February 2000

Cupid: The Bewildering Bequest
by J. M. Jeffries

Mad for Max
by Holly Fuhrmann

April 2000

Timeless Shadows
by J. A. Ferguson

June 2000

Etched in Stone
by Dimitri Eann

Hold Onto the Night
by Shauna Michaels

To reserve a copy of these books call us toll free at 877-625-3592 or visit our web site at http://www.imajinnbooks.com. You will not be charged for your reservation nor will you be obligated to buy the book.

ORDER FORM

Name:_____

Address_____

City_____ _ __

State_____ Zip_____Phone*_____

QTY	Book	Cost	Amount
	A Love Through All Time	$9.95	
	Cupid: The Amorous Arrow	$7.50	
	Dreamsinger	$8.50	
	Midnight Enchantment	$8.50	
	Time of the Wolf	$9.95	

Total Paid by:	SUBTOTAL	
☐Check or money order	SHIPPING	
☐ Credit Card (Circle one) Visa Mastercard Discover American Express	MI Residents add SalesTax	
_____ Card Number	TOTAL	

_____

Expiration Date

_____

Name on Card

Would you like your book(s) autographed? If so, please provide the name the author should use._____

*Phone number is required if you pay by Credit Card

Mail to: ImaJinn Books, PO Box 162, Hickory Corners, MI 49060-0162

Visit our web site at: http://www.imajinnbooks.com

Questions? Call us toll free: 877-625-3592